Let Love Heal

Book Three in The Love Series
Melanie's Story

MELISSA COLLINS

LET LOVE HEAL
Copyright © 2013 by Melissa Collins

ISBN-13: 978-0-9910542-0-6

Cover design and graphics by Sommer Stein with Perfect Pear Creative and Toski Covey

Interior Design by Angela McLaurin, Fictional Formats

Edited by Becky Johnson Hot Tree Editing

Table of Contents

*For those who need a reminder, every now and then,
that beautiful does not mean perfect.*

Part One

Broken

Prologue

September 30, 1995

Past

The I-beam swings haphazardly in the clouds. Teetering and tottering in the crystal-blue sky, it's the perfect juxtaposition of artificial and natural – steel illuminated by the sun. Over a ton of metal effortlessly cascades through the air on the whim of a crane. It almost looks like a graceful ballet dancer as it swirls and twists, dips and dives. It's mesmerizing, actually.

And then disaster strikes.

A deafening crack of a snapped chain sounds through the once peaceful air. The lively chatter of construction workers and architects instantly morphs into chaotic screams. Everyone runs, seeking cover from the impending doom.

As the massive beam plummets to the ground, people scramble, frantically grabbing others along the way to pull them to safety. It all happens so quickly. In the blink of an eye, it seems as if everyone will escape unscathed.

Until they don't.

The beam changes direction, up-ending itself. Head architect, James Crane, exits the shell of the building. Hardhat on and earplugs in, he's always one to follow procedure to make sure that his work site is safe. His eyes are pulled away from the clipboard of today's itinerary as the shadow of a passing figure flashes before him.

His eyes are drawn skyward. The sun blinds him; his sunglasses are tucked into his front pocket rather than perched across his nose. He doesn't have a second to process anything.

Crushed beneath the massive weight of the steel beam, the last thought that passes through the mind of Jimmy Crane, is of his wife, Lucy and his unborn daughter.

Lucy Crane is consumed with decorating the freshly painted nursery. If ever there was a woman more excited to meet her first child, well, Lucy's jubilance would put her to shame. Purple frills and pink lace don every surface of the room. It's a princess' heaven and a mom-to-be's dream come true.

Lucy sits on the floor, sorting through baby gifts from her shower last weekend. Holding a glittery onesie with an attached pink tutu up against her eight-and-a-half-month pregnant belly, she whispers quietly to her unborn daughter, "Maybe one day you'll be a ballerina ... Melody." She tucks a piece of hair behind her ear and taps a finger against her lip as she contemplates one of her husband's, James' top name choices. "Hmm, no that just doesn't sound right." Still going through baby names, Lucy and Jimmy haven't been able to find one upon which they both agree.

Last night, as they laid in bed, they settled on a short list of names that they each liked. Lucy was leaning toward more trendy names – Jessica, Ashley or Emily. James, on the other hand, wanted his daughter to have a less popular name; she was one of a kind, after all. Well, how could Lucy argue with that? From the moment she'd told her husband of less than a year that she was pregnant, he had absolutely radiated with love and joy. Conceding on his name preference was a small way that she could repay him for how he's taken care of her through the entire pregnancy.

They'd been high school sweethearts and in the seven years that they'd been together, they'd shared a lifetime's worth of love. When James would place his lips up against Lucy's swollen belly, and talk to their child, she could swear that her heart would burst at the overly full feeling of love.

On a mission to finish her sorting all of the baby clothes, Lucy snaps out of her happy musings of her husband and their baby. But when she comes across a purple sequined outfit, she can't help put place it across her belly and talk to her daughter once more. "This is going to look absolutely perfect on you … Melanie."

The name rolls off her tongue and sings to her heart. It was one of Jimmy's first suggestions, liking "M" names more than any other. Lucy had originally dismissed it, but now, sitting quietly in her soon-to-be-born daughter's room, the name seems to fit perfectly. Smiling broadly, she says the name once more, "Melanie." Rubbing her belly, Lucy talks to the kicking baby who is rolling around inside of her. "Do you like that name, little Miss Melanie." Another kick and roll. "Well then, we'll just have to ask Daddy what he thinks when he gets home." Another kick widens Lucy's bright smile. "Okay now, Melly Belly." Lucy chuckles softly at the ridiculous nickname she's just given her daughter. A smile spreads across her face because she knows that James will be pleased with her sudden turn around on his top name choice.

With numb and wobbly legs, Lucy stands to put the piles of clothes away when she hears a knock at the door. Checking her watch, she realizes that it's past four in the afternoon. She's been so lost in her baby daydreams that she didn't realize that she hadn't heard from James all day. Knowing that he is extremely busy trying to manage this massive project, she immediately dismisses her concerns. No phone calls during the day means that he is guaranteed to chew her ear off at dinner. The man loves his building, that's for sure.

Brushing her hands over her trendy and modern dark-blue maternity shirt, Lucy flattens out the wrinkles that set in as she was draping onesie after onesie across her belly.

As she peeks through the curtain that hangs across the top window of the door, she smiles cheerfully at her husband's best friend and co-owner of Crane Building Associates, Ray Richards.

"Hey, Ray. What's going on?" Lucy steps to the side allowing Ray to enter into the small foyer. Closing the door behind him, she continues talking. "Jimmy isn't home from work yet, but come on in. Can I get you a beer?" Lucy's bright voice does nothing to lighten the darkness that is cast over Ray's face.

Ray shakes his head, declining the beer. He looks into Lucy's bright blue eyes, and says, "We need to talk, Lucy." His voice is even and curt. Ignoring her stunned reaction to his cold demeanor, Ray walks past Lucy into the sunken den of his best friend's new home - a home to which he'll never return.

Ray sinks into the old, beat-up couch and memories flood his head and heart. This is the couch that they had in their first apartment. It was a rat-hole of a place, but somehow Ray and Jimmy managed to make it work. The couch is a hand-me-down from Jimmy's parents and has survived remarkably well through their college years.

Burying his head into his hands, Ray can no longer contain the sobs that have been threatening to swallow him whole since he pulled in the freshly-paved driveway.

Lucy waddles over to the couch and, not-so-gracefully, lowers herself onto the cushions. Tenderly wrapping her arm around his broad shoulders, she says, "What's wrong, Ray? I'm getting a little worried here."

It's not unusual for Ray to stop over, but usually Jimmy is there getting ready for a golf outing or a ball game. There's something about *this* particular visit that just feels … wrong.

Her concern only makes him cry more. He's crying for the loss of his best friend. He's crying for Lucy, who he's come to love as his own best friend through the years. He's crying for the baby that Jimmy will never get to meet – for the baby that Lucy will now have to raise on her own.

Twisting in his seat, he faces Lucy and wipes the tears from his eyes. Lucy's face pales as all of the blood rushes from it. She can tell that this is not a routine visit on Ray's part.

"Lucy …" Ray's words catch in his throat, stuck behind the ball of emotion that's been lodged there since he witnessed his best friend being crushed by tons of steel.

Lucy covers her mouth with her hands, but her gasp is still audible. "No, no, no, no …" It's the only syllable her brain can manage. She's shaking her head wildly as if it will keep away the horrific news that is so clearly etched across Ray's tanned and youthful face.

Ray wraps his arm around her slumped shoulders and pulls Lucy into a tight squeeze. "I'm sorry. I'm so sorry. There was an accident and … it's Jimmy. He's gone, Lucy."

With those words, her world changes instantly. No longer able to contain her anguish, her chest heaves in sobs as tears pour from her eyes.

How? Why? What? All of these questions swarm her brain, but the bottom line is that none of it matters. Bits of Ray's strained explanation filter into her consciousness, but she can't make any sense of it. Something about a beam, about being in the wrong place at the wrong time, about wanting to come here to tell her himself, about not wanting her to have to drive to the coroner's office alone, it's all a garbled mess, because none of it is important. The only meaningful piece of information is that Jimmy, her Jimmy, the love of her life, is gone.

Visions that she will never be able to erase start filling her mind. In a vain attempt to escape them, Lucy shoots up from the couch and begins frantically pacing the room. But she's too weak to stand for long. As pain, anguish and loss eat her alive, she crumples to the floor and wraps her arms around her round belly. Again, the only words she can form are, "No, no, no …"

Unable to let her suffer alone, Ray moves next to her on the floor and pulls her into his arms. Cooing softly to her, he tries to calm her. It's a vain attempt at peace that will never come.

It's always been Jimmy. He was her first friend, her first love, and now he's her first true loss.

Calling on an inner strength that she doesn't truly feel, Lucy tries to stand, but her body rejects the attempt. All she can do is let the sadness swallow her whole, and hope that when it spits her back out, she'll be alive and whole enough to take care of Melanie.

Chapter 1

Thursday, January 24, 2013

Present

A vast empire of evergreens flashes past my window. A light dusting of snow coats the road, leaving only two clearly defined, black tire tracks in the wake of the passing cars. The sunlight barely breaks through the hazy greyness of the clouds. There's a dull, lifelessness pervading not only the scenery, but my mood as well, and I know it's because so much has changed in my life in the last few months.

Chipper as ever, Mom's voice breaks my silent sadness. "Hey, sweetie pie. Are you awake over there?" She playfully nudges my shoulder to try and rouse me from my feigned sleep. I've been turned away from her, staring blankly out of the window for most of the short trip back to Ithaca.

Twisting in my seat to face her, I respond, much

more dully than her happy tone. "Yeah, I'm awake, just tired, I guess." My flat voice and lame shoulder shrug mirror the oppressive feel of the grey sky hanging above us.

She doesn't say anything more; she just offers up a half smile and then returns her attention to the road. Mom knows I'm in a funk. There's no way she can't know. It's creepy sometimes how she's so attuned to what I'm feeling or thinking. It's like she's in my brain or something. Kind of freaks me out a bit, but she's my mom and it's always been just us, so I guess it's understandable.

My dad died before I was born – some freak accident. I try not to think of it and most days I succeed on that front. I won't lie, though. The stress of being the only person of real importance in my mom's life has taken its toll on me. I hide it well, or at least I think I do.

Seeking more distraction from an inevitable line of questioning from Mom, I fidget with the radio and leave it on some current top 40 hit. Mom taps away on the steering wheel while she sings, off-key, to the music playing through the speakers. I just let it drown out the thoughts racing through my mind. Turning away from her again, I return to my post at the window and watch the world pass me by.

Alone. Empty. Sad. That's how I'm feeling.

Knowing that Maddy's not here and she's not going to be coming back, makes my eyes burn with unshed tears. Maddy and I have been best friends since middle school; I met her a few years after her parents died. Hell, we even ended up living together for a few months in our senior year when her aunt passed away suddenly. For the last five years, Maddy and I were inseparable. We even had to beg the housing department to let us dorm together when we started college last semester.

Her world shifted when she met Reid and they both fell head over heels in love with each other. After she found out she was pregnant, yeah, that was a shocker for everyone, she decided to withdraw from Ithaca and go to a school closer to home. I can't blame her for choosing to move in with Reid. She's got her own life now – one of which I'm no longer a part. Even though I'm happy for her, my heart still hurts that she's not going to be with me every day.

Cammie and Lia, my other two roommates, aren't here either. They won't be here until at least Saturday morning – great grandma's birthday party or something like that. Honestly, with everything that's been going on, I haven't paid much attention to everyone else's life. I mean, I couldn't be happier that Maddy and Reid are back together and that things worked out for them, but I can't help but focus, almost to the point of making myself sick, on what's going to happen with me and Bryan.

Our relationship, or lack thereof for the last month, has been a huge source of distress and emptiness. I have this feeling in the pit of my stomach that when he gets back to school, Bryan is going to break up with me. He's seeing Courtney again; I know it. Well, okay, I don't *know* it, but I have my suspicions. He barely called me over the entire winter break. Come to think of it, he hardly ever texted or emailed me either.

Except for that one text.

I mean, come on, Bryan is always on the computer. Being a computer science major should mean that you're permanently attached to the thing, right? Or that you're at least part robot or something like that. He couldn't get in touch with me once? We talked, don't get me wrong, but I was always the one who initiated it.

I was supposed to go visit him for New Year's Eve, but when I told him about my plans, he said it wouldn't be a good idea for me to come. Then I got *the text.* Bryan and Courtney lip-locked at some party. It was pretty clear at that point that he had moved on.

Thinking back over everything, I'm suddenly more pissed than sad. What kind of boyfriend pushes his girlfriend away to the point that she no longer feels wanted? And then to push me away just to have your biggest fears thrown in your face. I know it's not an excuse for what I did, but I won't deny that feeling hurt was definitely a huge reason behind the actions I took.

My brain is seriously scrambled over all of this. By telling me not to come visit him, was he breaking up with me? Or was he just trying to conceal his cheating? Then there's the part of me that refuses to believe that he actually cheated. From the moment I met her, Courtney hated me and did everything in her power to keep me and Bryan apart.

But then again, maybe he thought we were broken up while we were apart? Before winter break, our relationship was perfect, really, until he started pulling away from me right before he left. Was he just trying to create some distance so he could let me down easier? Oh, who the hell knows? We hadn't dropped the "L" bomb yet, but I know he had to feel it; I know I did. He is my first – my first boyfriend, my first love, my first, well, you know – my first, like ever. Now, I'm just so scared to lose him, but I'm more afraid of knowing that I'm going to hurt him. That much is unavoidable.

The inevitability of us being separated over break and his distance from me over said break was just too much for me to handle, I guess. I turned into *that girl*. You know the one who lets her insecurities get the best of her, yeah, *that* one. I was weak and foolish and talked myself into believing that Bryan, sweet, funny, amazingly perfect, Bryan, was cheating on me.

I let myself believe that he didn't want me.

He's openly admitted to hating Courtney. Told me time and time again that he was done with her, but I could never believe him. But by stopping me from visiting him, isn't that what he said essentially? That he doesn't want me and that we're over.

Even if he was cheating and didn't want me, it didn't give me a free pass to do what I did. Neither one of us had said the words to end things, but we never said the words to say that they weren't either.

Wow. I am really one screwed up chick over all of this.

And let's face it, even if there is some kind of logical explanation for the text I got, he'll still break up with me. *I cheated.* God, I can't believe how badly I've screwed up. A sinking feeling settles down low in my stomach – both at the idea of having to tell him about what happened and at the knowledge that after I tell him, he'll leave me for good.

I've been lost in my own little world of self-pity for most of the ride here, and I'm thankful that Mom has left me alone for the most part. I haven't had the heart, or the courage for that matter, to talk to her about Bryan. Letting Mom down, or anyone for that matter, has never been an option for me. Hell, I haven't told anyone – except Maddy, and I didn't even give her all of the details.

I've always been the perfectionist. The perfect daughter. The perfect best friend. The perfect student. It's a cover, though. If I can maintain an image of perfection in every other area of my life, no one will ever know how unhappy I really am. On some level, I know it's silly to be unhappy with my life just because I'm not the perfect size-two supermodel that everyone else seems to be. You see, if I get the perfect grades and act the perfect way, then no one will notice me for my too-wide hips and my softly rounded belly. No one will notice that there isn't a lot, if any, space between my thighs. No matter how healthily I eat, or no matter how much I exercise, I will always be a curvy size 16. To be honest, I still don't understand what Bryan sees in me, why he's even attracted to me in the first place.

Not that it matters any more anyway. My track record of perfection, feigned or not, is officially ruined now. There's no way in hell I could ever be considered the perfect girlfriend. Unless sleeping with some random guy at a party is a new requirement for girlfriend of the year, I can officially pull my name from that drawing. I don't even remember who the hell the guy was; that's the really shitty part. I was too drunk to remember much of anything. What kind of girlfriend cheats and can't even remember who the other person is?

"Hey, Melly Belly. We're almost there." Mom's sweet voice rouses me from my blank stare out of the window. The towers of Ithaca College start to rise above the horizon and I know that we're less than five minutes from campus.

A sense of emptiness engulfs me as we park the car in front of the dorm. Part of me is happy that I'll be on my own here for a few days. Maybe it'll help me clear my head a bit. Maybe I'll be able to figure out how to deal with this whole cheating situation? Maddy told me that I have to tell him – some line about wishing she had been honest with Reid. I know she's right, but the coward in me wants to bury it down so far that no one ever finds out about it.

How can I publicly admit to being such a failure? Not being perfect just isn't an option.

After Mom and I have unloaded the car and set up my room, we grab some takeout for dinner and veg-out to some random television show. I can tell she's dying to say something, but I also know that she can tell I'm avoiding talking to her.

After dinner, Mom cleans up. She's always taking care of me and I just wish she would stop worrying about me. I can't tell her that of course, but I just wish she would go on with her life. She doesn't mingle in mine – I can't complain about an overly-nosey parent like some people, but her not having her own life has made me feel incredibly guilty.

Glancing over to her at the sink, my heart warms. She's standing there, washing a few dishes, humming happily. I know most little girls are completely enamored with their mothers. But there isn't a word out there for the kind of love that I feel for my mom. She's beautiful, genuinely caring – not at all in that "I'm your mother so I *have* to care" way. And oh, God, is she funny. Yes, she's a complete dork sometimes and I will openly admit to rolling my eyes at her at least once daily, but there's no hiding it; she's my favorite person ever.

Feeling overly sentimental, I walk up behind her at the sink and wrap my arms around her still very narrow waist. She grabs the small dish towel from the counter and wipes her hands before turning around in my embrace and wrapping her arms around me.

"Hey, now. What's all this about?" Her words are muffled by the mass of bright red hair piled atop my head against which she places her lips as she kisses me.

Still completely unwilling to open up to her, I just shrug my shoulders – a non-committal gesture. "Nothing, really. I guess I just got used to being around you over break. I'm going to miss you now that I'm back here." I break the embrace and lean up against the pale blue kitchen counter – the one that she just wiped clean, repeatedly.

She's folding the dish towel and looping it through the handle on the small stove as she says, "Oh, sweetie, I'll miss you too." Mom leans up against the counter opposite me and a sad look creeps across her face. "When you girls started school last semester, it was the first time in … well, in forever that I was really on my own. With Maddy moving out and you back here, it's just me. It's kind of weird." She brushes a few stray strands of her hair out of her bright blue eyes, but I think it's just an excuse to rub away the tears that are starting to form.

This is what I'm talking about. Even if I did want to talk to her about my problems, how can I even begin to unload on her when she's dealing with her own world of crap?

"Oh, Mom. I wish …" She shushes me before I can even finish what I'm about to say, not that I really knew what I was going to say. I wish what? That I was still home with you? That Dad was still alive so you wouldn't have to be alone? That Maddy was still here with me? That Bryan will forgive me? Too much to wish for if you ask me.

Mom just holds out her arms and I walk into them willingly. "There's nothing to wish for, baby. Things are how they are, because that's how they're supposed to be. I'll be just fine. Just have to get used to being alone, that's all." She plants a soft kiss on the top of my head again and holds me at arm's length.

Brushing my unruly hair out of my face and cupping my cheeks, she stares at me through shimmering eyes and says, "I love you so much, Melanie. And I am so proud of you for the woman you've become. You're doing so well here." She glances around my empty suite, but I know she means off on my own at college when she says "here."

My heart swells with love for her. I want her to be proud of me, but how can she be? She wouldn't be if she knew everything.

A sinking nauseating feeling gathers in my stomach. I feel like I could vomit at the sound of her undeserved praise. Forcing down my own tears, the rising bile in my throat and the words I so desperately want to confess to her, I just smile brightly at her accolades and hug her tightly once more.

"Okay, so what else needs to get done around here?" Mom asks in a weak attempt to dismiss the current conversation. She's scanning the suite, but honestly, everything is taken care of.

"I think I'm good, Mom. My room's all set up and you just scrubbed every scrubbable surface in this place. Your job here is done." I may be mocking her a little, but my appreciation still shines through.

Wiping her hands on her jeans, which are not "mom jeans" by the way, she scans the room once more before adding, "Okay, then I think I'll hit the road now. Maddy and Reid are moving tomorrow and I don't want that girl lifting anything."

"Oh, please, Mom! Like Reid would let her anyway." Mom just laughs at my arched eyebrow and sarcastic tone, but she knows Reid won't let Maddy do a thing. It'll drive Maddy crazy, but there's no way on Earth that Reid's girl is going to lift a finger.

Mom just chuckles a small laugh. "Yeah, you're right, but I want to help them get settled too. You sure you're not mad that I'm not staying the night?" We've been over this more than a few times, so I can't help but sigh at her. I offered to stay home an extra day to help, but Maddy told me that I should come back to school a few days before everyone else and clear my head. And even though I may be beyond thrilled for Maddy and Reid, watching them move on with their lives just reminds me how twisted mine currently is.

"Yes, Mom." Annoyance punctuates each word. "I told you I'll be fine. The security desk is manned all night long and Cammie and Lia will be here Saturday. It'll actually be nice to have the place to myself for a little while. Besides, I've got my *Sex and the City* marathon all lined up. There's ice cream in the freezer and chips in the cabinet. What more could I want?"

I walk her toward the door as she slings her purse over her shoulder. Stopping in the doorway, she gives me one more hug and a sweet kiss on the cheek. "Alright, sweetie. Please call me if you need anything. I guess I'll see you in a few weeks then."

I nod in response, afraid to speak past the lump of emotion that's swelling in my throat. One last kiss on the cheek, and a "Bye-bye, baby," and she's walking down the hall toward the stairs.

I can see her pull away as I watch from the living room window. I wave out to her and she blows a kiss up to me.

Unwilling to address my sorrow and sadness, I pop in a DVD and hope that Samantha, Carrie, Miranda and Charlotte will help break me out of this funk. And hell, if they can't, I'm pretty sure the slew of hotties who chase after them will help lift my spirits. I drift off somewhere in the middle of a random encounter between Carrie and Mr. Big that alters the path of her life.

Chapter 2

Monday, August 27, 2012

Past

Coffee. Must. Have. Coffee. I'm practically dragging myself across campus to the little coffee shop inside of the student lounge after my eight a.m. Western Civilization class. Why on earth did I sign up for early classes? This will *not* be happening next semester.

After a few sips of my much-needed caffeine fix, I stand looking at the large corkboard that's plastered with advertisements – looking for a new roommate, trying to sell a car, searching for Jesus. The roommate, I've got; the car, I don't need. And Jesus? I'll just leave well enough alone on that one.

Just as I'm about to walk away, a hot pink flyer advertising an opening in the computer lab catches my attention. I need to get a job. I know Mom will send me money and take care of me and all that, but I don't want her to *have* to. I want to be somewhat self-sufficient and this job looks like the perfect way to do that. And a computer lab will be nice and quiet; I'll be able to get some work done and I bet no one will even notice me. I can sit behind a desk and bask in anonymity while everyone else becomes engrossed in their own work.

Checking my watch, I realize I have less than an hour before my next class. That's just enough time to walk over to the lab and introduce myself instead of calling the number on the flyer. Luckily, the lab is in the same building as my next class so I have to go that way anyway.

Perfect.

Since it's the first week of classes and it's only ten in the morning, the lab is completely empty. It's quiet; all I hear is the humming and buzzing of the rows of computers and monitors. I walk toward the front of the room where I see a small office. There has to be someone here. Stepping up to the door and tapping on it lightly, I notice that there is someone crouched underneath the desk straightening out some wires and cords.

"Hello." I call out timidly. I hear a thud, as what I assume is a head bumps into the underside of the desk. A male voice calls out "Crap" and I can't help but giggle that I've surprised whoever is under there. He then says, "I'll be right with you."

"Okay, take your time. Sorry for interrupting. I'll be waiting out in the lab." I make my way back out to the main room and wait patiently for "under the desk mystery man" to meet me. And when he does, oh my dear sweet Lord of all things hot. I was fully expecting suspenders, a pocket protector, glasses, and plaid pants pulled up to his chest. I was expecting someone more along the lines of Sheldon Cooper from *The Big Bang Theory*, but what I got was Bradley Cooper from *The Hangover*.

That's two very different Coopers.

My mouth goes dry and I'm suddenly struck dumb. As he walks to me, he wipes his hands on his faded and oh-so-soft looking jeans and then inspects them to make sure they're clean. Standing before me, he extends his hand, and by some miraculous force, I'm able to put together, "Hi. I'm here to apply for the job." My voice is squeaky as I wave the hot pink sign in between us. Shaking his hand causes sparks of electricity to course through my arm. "Wow. I just put that sign up this morning. I didn't expect anyone to apply for a few days." His voice is like velvet and it does funny things to my insides. When he releases my hand, it's still hot from his touch.

"Let me go get some paperwork for you to fill out …" His sentence hangs in the air between us and I realize that I haven't told him my name.

"Melanie. I'm Melanie Crane. It's nice to meet you …"

"Bryan Mahoney." And when he smiles at me as his name rolls off his tongue, I feel like a giddy school girl.

"Okay then, Melanie. Let me go get that paperwork and we'll get the ball rolling." He turns to walk away from me and my eyes are glued to his body. What the hell? A hot computer geek. You have got to be kidding me. This boy is seriously fine. Tall, lean and just plain beautiful. I should leave right now. I thought this would be a nice quiet job where I could go completely unnoticed, but there's no way in hell I can work with him. He's freaking hot and I'm, well, I'm not. I'll be a bumbling fool the entire time I'm around him.

Just as I'm about to walk out the door, Bryan calls out to me. "Hey, Melanie! Where are you going?" Call me crazy, but there is a hint of desperation in his voice. With my hand hovering above the door knob, I inhale deeply and figure what the hell. I might as well go for it. The truth is he probably won't even know I exist. Guys like him never notice girls like me anyway. I turn toward him and smile as I say, "No, I just have class in a few minutes. I wasn't expecting to actually do an interview or anything. I don't want to be late;

that's all."

I flat out lie and just hope he doesn't catch on.

His returning smile is blinding. Perfectly straight, white teeth flash before me, but what hits me in the gut is how his eyes smile along with his mouth. They crinkle in the corners and he shakes his head just a little. It looks like he's laughing at me, but not in an "I'm making fun of you way." Maybe he's caught on, after all.

"Okay, so can you come back after class, Melanie?" The way my name sounds coming from his full lips makes my pulse skitter. For the first time ever, I feel noticed. This hot piece of man-cake is actually talking to me and looking at me and saying my name. And, call me crazy, but he's not just being nice because I'm applying for this job. There's something playful and flirty going on in his eyes, in his voice, in his body language.

I'm a terrible flirt – never had much practice with it, but standing here talking with Bryan has me all sorts of soft and mushy.

Oh, what the hell. I'll give it a try. Isn't that what college is about? Trying out new things and all that.

I bat my long lashes and reach for the papers that he's brought out for me to complete. When my fingers graze over his, I leave them there for a second longer than I should. I could still be adjusting to the bright, fluorescent lighting, but I swear that his eyes just widened a bit at my touch.

"I'll bring these back to you after class, Bryan." I don't mean for it, but my voice is pitched a bit lower than usual and has a sultry, feminine sound to it. It's enough to make his eyes widen yet again.

Oh. My. God. It's working. I'm flirting with him and it's working. I actually have an effect on him.

He lets go of the papers and says, "Great. Then I'll meet you here later." Cue the smile and the sparkly eyes all over again. He's just plain gorgeous.

As promised, I returned the papers to Bryan after class. I was completely shocked when he called me just a few hours after that to tell me that I got the job. When Bryan told me to come in the next morning to go over a few things and set up my schedule, my belly did that crazy flip-flop thing again. See him again? Yes, please!

Stepping into the lab for the second time is more nerve-wracking than the first. I immediately see Bryan set up behind the main desk. Sporting a vintage Pac-Man t-shirt and drool-worthy jeans, he looks edible.

When he catches sight of me, he smiles brightly, illuminating the entire room. As he walks toward me, he trips on a loose computer cord, but he quickly recovers. I can't help but giggle.

"What's so funny?" he questions, feigning injury.

"Oh, nothing. Just noticing that you seem a bit clumsy, that's all." My mouth quirks at the corners and my eyes dance playfully across his laughing face.

Dismissing the current topic of conversation, Bryan tells me that he's got a computer all set up for me to work on.

I pull out the rolling chair from under the desk and he does the same with the one next to me. Since we only need one screen, Bryan rolls his chair right up next to me. His knee brushes up against mine a few times, and when he reaches across the desk to type something on the keyboard, a flash of heat rolls across my arm at his touch.

He feels it too and he looks down at my goose bump covered arm. Tripping over his words, he says, "I ... um ... sorry about that."

My tongue feels too big for my now dry mouth. Saying "It's okay." takes a ridiculous amount of effort.

After filling in the last lines of my user profile, he saves the document and checks his watch. "That should do it for today." I stand and drape my bag over my arm, suddenly desperate for any reason to stay and talk to him some more.

"So when should I come back? I mean, do you have my schedule ready?" I tuck a loose piece of hair behind my ear and look up at him shyly.

"Yeah, hold on. Let me go get it." As I watch him walk back into the office, I try to calm my erratic breathing.

When he hands me the paper, I scan through it and see that Thursday afternoon is my first shift. I also have to be here early on Friday to be trained in opening the lab, which works out well because my first class isn't until ten on Fridays. It doesn't say anything about who else will be on with me tomorrow, so with hope in my words I ask, "Will you be here for any of these shifts?"

His eyes light with humor and he grins at me. "I guess you'll just have to wait and see" is the only response I get as he escorts me to the door.

About halfway through my shift on Thursday, Bryan comes into the lab with a brown paper bag and two Styrofoam cups. He winks at me as he walks to the computer that I'm working on.

"Hey, Melanie. How's everything going?" God, his voice is sexy.

"Good, I think." The computer takes that opportunity to bleep and yell some kind of error message at me. So much for "good" I guess.

"Oh shit! What did I do?" Panicking, I start hitting random keys in the hopes that I'll be able to undo whatever I just did.

Placing the bag and drinks on a desk away from the computers, Bryan leans over my shoulders from behind and reaches his hands to the keyboard in front of me. His cologne is warm and woodsy – so masculine, so yummy. He's typing something, but all I can see is the corded muscles of his forearm strain under his tanned skin. With his face right next to mine, his warm breath tickles my neck. "See right here?" he points to something on the screen, and by some miracle, I'm able to open my eyes enough to look at what he's pointing at.

"Uh huh," I say dumbly.

He chuckles softly. "Well, if that ever happens again, all you have to do is type in this command before hitting save and you'll be fine."

"Great, thanks." I look up over his shoulder at the clock and realize that it's just about time for me to leave. The other employee, Derek, who will be closing up the lab tonight, got here about thirty minutes ago.

I shut down the computer and start to gather my things. "Thanks again, Bryan. I'm done here for the night. I guess I'll see you soon."

The warm and firm grasp of his hand around my forearm stops me in my tracks. "Have dinner with me?" he asks bluntly as he eyes the bag and drinks that he came in with.

Out of some crazy instinct, I look back up at the clock and try to decline. "No, it's okay. Really, I should get going." I try to walk past him again but he won't let me.

"Please. Come on. Sandwiches out on the quad and then I'll walk you home. Nothing big. I promise." My stomach chooses this moment to grumble and I know that any further protest is futile.

"Okay," I agree and we walk out into the warm fall air.

Bryan sets us up under the shade of a large oak tree and the meal passes in mostly mundane conversation about classes and roommates. When the conversation stops altogether, I gaze at the beautiful mountain scenery out in the distance. It's at this moment that I catch Bryan staring at me.

Immediately self-conscious, I move to cover my mouth. "Is there something in my teeth?" I'm sure that my face is some shade of red – being fair skinned makes any kind of blush plainly visible.

He gently coaxes my hand away from my mouth. Bryan leans forward, and runs his thumb long my bottom lip. "Nope. Nothing in your teeth. Just had some mustard right there." He cleans his hand on a napkin but my lip is seared by his touch.

I'm fairly quiet the rest of the meal, because after feeling his finger on my lip, I can't think of anything worthwhile to say.

When he walks me to my building, I don't know what to do. A handshake is dopey – we're not business partners or anything like that. A hug seems too close, too personal. Jumping up into his arms and making out with him, well, I guess I'll just reserve that for my fantasy. So when we get to the door, I just smile at him dumbly and say, "Thanks for dinner. I'll see you soon."

His lopsided and goofy smile precedes his words. "Yes, you definitely will."

And before he's even out of my sight, I can't wait to see him again.

I have survived my first week of college. Well, almost. I only have one class today, some last minute I-need-another-class-so-I-can-be-full-time-student class. Before class, I have to stop at the lab and be trained in opening procedures. The wink and smirk that accompanied Bryan's instructions to be there at eight a.m. suggested that there was more to this meeting than just training me in how to unlock a door and turn on a few computers.

Normally, I wouldn't pay too much attention to

my clothes, hair and make-up, especially since it's only one class. But, since I'm meeting with Bryan first, I actually picked out my clothes last night – a khaki skirt and black baby-doll polo shirt with cute pink wedge sandals. With my hair falling in waves past my shoulders and my eyes lightly made up, I spent much more than my usual ten minutes getting ready. I feel like a dork for having spent so much time primping this morning, but I also feel pretty.

None of the other girls have classes on Fridays. They were actually smart about setting up their schedules. Me? Apparently not so much. The suite is ridiculously quiet as I creep out the door at 7:45. When the door softly clicks behind me, and I turn to walk down the hall, I nearly scream when I hear a male voice say, "Mornin', beautiful."

"Oh my God! What the hell?" My bag crashes to the ground as the shrill noise of my scream echoes off the walls. When I regain a little bit of composure, I look up into Bryan's sparkling brown eyes. "What are you doing here?" My heart is still pounding against my chest, but watching his soft lips curl up into the sexiest smile I've ever seen, makes my pulse race out of something entirely different from fear.

Extending an extra-large coffee in front of him as some sort of peace offering, he chuckles lightly at me as I clutch my hand to my chest. "Sorry about that. I didn't mean to scare you. I just thought we could walk together."

I snatch the coffee out of his hands and take a sip, which helps to calm my nerves a little. Bryan hands me my bag and extends his hand out to the side to let me walk past him and down the stairs. I only live on the third floor, so by the time we get to the ground level, we haven't said anything. But once we step out into the early morning sun, something dawns on me.

Turning around abruptly, I place my hand on my hip and eye him suspiciously. "Hey, how did you know which room was mine?"

"I … umm … well … it was in your paperwork." His final answer seems to have been pulled out of thin air. So, I shoot him an "are you kidding me face" and he rolls his eyes at me.

"Come on, we're going to be late." Essentially dismissing the conversation, he gently nudges me forward by placing his hand on the small of my back. The feel of his warm palm, even through my shirt, sets my skin on fire. It's as if there's a pulse of energy moving between us.

It's a short walk to the lab, so we don't say much. I'm pretty useless without my caffeine anyway. I think Bryan was too embarrassed to say anything. That last thought makes me smile for some odd reason.

We arrive at the lab about five minutes later and

opening it is just as easy as I assumed. Unlock the doors. Flip on the lights. Turn on the computers. You're good to go.

Bryan shows me a few other things before an awkward silence settles in. We're sitting next to each other at two computers checking our email before I have to leave for class. "So, um ... how was your first week?" His shyness is adorable.

So. Freaking. Adorable.

I turn my chair to face him and accidentally bump his knee just like he did to me last time we were sitting here. It throws me off balance and I grab onto his leg to keep myself from falling out of my chair. His eyes dart to my hand and he steadies me by grabbing my shoulder at the same time. "Geez, sorry. I'm such a klutz sometimes." I apologize though I'm feeling anything but sorry. I'd fall on my ass in front of a large crowd, if it meant that he would touch me again.

"Ehh, it's okay. I seem to be extra clumsy when you're around too." He squeezes my shoulder gently and brushes my hair to the side before letting go. My skin feels like it's on fire where he's just touched me and I realize that my hand is still on his leg. Pulling back quickly, I remember that he asked me something.

"My first week was good. Nothing too interesting. Yours?" I'm nervously twiddling my thumbs in my lap. He's too close for my brain or my mouth to function.

"It was great actually." The more than chipper tone of his words has me intrigued.

"Yeah? What happened?"

"I met you." A shy smile pulls at his lips, and if I'm not mistaken, a slight blush colors his cheeks.

Did he just say what I think he just said?

Thinking back over the course of my week, I have to admit that spending time with Bryan has been a huge highlight. Letting go of my self-doubt, I proceed more flirtatiously than I ever would have before meeting Bryan. There's just something about him that makes me feel comfortable and relaxed.

"Meeting you has definitely been the high point of my week too." We both smile somewhat sheepishly at one another before a few moments of tense silence stretch out between us.

I twist my chair back around and face my computer once again. Pretending to be engrossed in whatever random email I opened up, I'm trying not to pay attention to Bryan, but I can feel his stare. It's penetrating and puts me on edge. I glance at him out of the corner of my eye and he immediately looks away, busying himself with something on his screen.

He catches me staring a few times too and before long we're laughing goofily at one another with the dorkiest of grins on our faces. We don't say much of anything, but the light and flirty banter is all there. I can feel the energy pulsing between us and I know he can too.

We play this cat and mouse game of "I'm not really looking at you" until I glance at the clock.

"Oh, crap. I have to run." I slide my phone into my pocket and swing my bag over my shoulder. Bryan stands from his chair at the same time and we walk toward the door together.

When we're at the door, it seems as if neither of us knows what to say. "So, um, I guess I'll see you at work next week, right?" I nervously adjust the strap of my bag on my shoulder.

"Yeah. You definitely will." When he winks at me as he says those words, blood rushes to my head and to other places, and I know for certain that there is something going on between us. There's no way there couldn't be something going on if I feel this way from a simple wink and smile.

I turn to exit, but I'm so lost in my swoony thoughts and flirting that all sense of coordination escapes me. In some glorious combination of nervousness and discombobulated limbs, I pull the door open only to get it jammed up with my foot as I try to walk through it. My nose is squished by the force of me pulling the door opened while at the same time face planting into it.

I drop my bag and the papers fly everywhere as I

cup my hand over my nose. "Owww, stupid freaking door." I curse aloud. I pull my hand away and notice the smallest trickle of blood in my palm.

Bryan's at my side in an instant, tipping my head back and walking me over to a chair. "Are you okay? Here, take these." He hands me a wad of tissues that he's just pulled out from the box sitting at the desk. As he holds my head back, he sweeps a few locks of my hair out of my face and gently runs his fingers through my long red, wavy hair. It feels so good that I almost forget about my bloody nose.

After a minute or so, he tips my head forward slightly and kneels down in front of me. Gazing into his deep brown eyes, my insides go soft and I feel *it*. There's definitely something going on here.

He pulls my hand away from my nose. "Let me take a look." His words are so tender and concerned that I can't help but lean into his soft touch. When he's satisfied that the bleeding has stopped and that I'll be fine, he lightly kisses the tip of my nose and says, "There. All better."

In the past week, I can recall every single time that he's touched me – his thumb across my lip, his arms against mine, our legs bumping into one another. But now this - his lips on my skin, even if it was just an innocent peck on a banged up nose, is pure heaven.

"Thanks," I say as I grab one last tissue. As I try to

stand, my legs wobble a bit and I know that it has more to do with his proximity than the injury I've just sustained. Bryan wraps a strong arm around me to keep me from falling over. His fingers flex at the soft curve of my waist and I instantly feel self-conscious.

"Are you sure you're okay?" he asks, genuinely concerned about my well-being.

"Yeah, I'll be fine. Thanks for helping me." I try to move away from his touch, but he leaves his hand on me, gripping at my waist. "Let me walk you to your next class, please. I would hate myself if you left here and fainted on me or something like that." His eyes are pleading with me.

I decide to give in. I have to when he's looking at me like that. "Okay, but don't you have to stay here and work?" And, as if the Gods are listening in on us, Simon, our co-worker walks into the lab and plops down his stuff at the desk beside us.

"Hey, Bry. Hi, Melanie." Simon The Desk Plopper says as he starts unloading some books and an iPad from his bag.

"Hey, Simon. I'm off to class now. See you at noon?" Bryan says.

Simon tips his chin at us. "Sure thing. See you later."

Bryan returns his attention to me, though I have to admit, with his arm banded around my waist

41

through his short exchange with Simon, I felt like his attention was never off me. "See. We can go now." His tone is amused and his face beams with pride that he's just won himself a few more minutes of my time.

On the other hand, I don't know if I can take much more of being around him. My senses are in overdrive and my mind is scrambled a million different ways. Our little exchanges over this past week have me so confused. And then today, between picking me up and flirting all over again, I'm trying so hard to wrap my head around it all. He actually seems interested in me and I just don't get it.

Shaking away those thoughts of uncertainty, I bend to pick up my bag, but Bryan beats me to it. "So what's your next class?" he asks as he slides both my bag and his over his shoulder. He still refuses to break contact with me even as he holds the door open for me.

Rather than look at him as I respond, I stare blankly out on to the quad, which is visible through the wall of windows to our side. I'm afraid that if I look directly into his sparkling caramel-colored eyes, that I'll get lost there and never find my way out. "21st Century Technology. Room 235," I mutter. I didn't want to take this class, but being a freshman, my choices were limited and I figured it would come in useful somewhere along the line.

Bryan's deep chuckle is one of amusement. "You're kidding, right?" he asks as we make our way down the hallway, which is now starting to fill with students making their way to their next class.

Turning my attention from the quad back to his laughing face, I give him the side-eye. "And why would I do that?" I quip sarcastically.

"I'm the TA in that class. It looks like we're going to be spending lots of time together, Melanie." His words are laced with amusement, but there also seems to be a hint of a promise in them. My stomach drops, but excitement rushes through me. More time with Bryan? Yes, please.

"TA? Really? Are you a grad student or something?" I can't hide the shock in my voice. I guess when I saw him in the lab, I just assumed that he was a regular student like me. It never crossed my mind to ask him how old he was.

He shakes his head while softly laughing at my apparent misunderstanding. "No, Melanie. I am definitely not a grad student. I'm just a lowly senior." He smirks at me playfully.

My brows knit together in confusion. "Huh? Then how are you a TA?"

"I've just always had a knack for techie stuff, I guess." He shrugs his rugged shoulders. "I started at the computer lab when I was a freshman, and my boss

— I mean, our boss," he smiles down at me brightly. And, oh yeah, he still hasn't let go of his death grip around my waist. "Well, when Professor O'Neil saw how much I knew, he promoted me to shift manager. Then, in my sophomore year, he asked me to help out a little more. At the end of my junior year, he asked me if I wanted to be his TA this fall. It's a pretty sweet gig if you ask me." He winks at me and I'm pretty sure he's adding our recent encounters to the sweetness of his job history.

We stop outside of our classroom and he opens the door for me. Such a gentleman. I'm pretty sure that no one has ever held a door for me, ever. I slide past him, conscious of the heat radiating from his body, but cautious not to actually touch him. My ass gets in the way all the damn time and that's the last thing I need him to realize.

Bryan not only walks me to class, but he actually escorts me to a seat in the aisle. Before he walks away from me, he leans down and whispers in my ear. "Now, don't leave without me." His warm breath sends shivers down my spine and causes goose bumps to spread like wild fire across my neck. I can't form words, so I just smile and nod dumbly as he turns to walk toward the front of the room.

After the rest of the class settles in, the lecture begins. It doesn't take me long to figure why he put me in an aisle seat. Every time he walks past me, which seems to be fairly frequently, he brushes up against my arm with his. When he hands me a stack of papers to pass down to the rest of the row, his long fingers graze over mine and he winks at me while leaving his hand on mine for longer than he really needs to. He was openly flirting with me before and I just couldn't wrap my head around it. But now, it's clear. He's into me.

Well, color me surprised. In all my life, no one has ever been interested in me. I have always been the curvy wallflower of the group and I have hated every minute of it. His flirting makes me feel beautiful and important. And it's not just because he's gorgeous – though that doesn't hurt. It's more about the way that he talks to me, with passion and energy; it's in the way he touched my nose earlier, with kind tenderness; it's in the way he looks at me, as if he's actually seeing the real me.

As Professor O'Neil, drones on and on about binary code and HTMLs, I get lost thinking about what the hell Bryan sees in me. The only answer I can come up with is that he must have trouble with his vision. I mean, doesn't he see that I'm not perfect like the stick-thin Barbie girl sitting behind me? Back in the lab, he touched my hair so he had to notice that it was an unruly mess of red waves – not the perfectly, pin-straight blonde locks that all men seem to love and all women long to possess. Walking to class, he had his hand on my waist. He felt the soft give of my flesh — no skin and bones here. Yet, he is still actively making eye contact with me and smiling at me across the room.

Part of me can't help but wonder if this is some kind of cruel joke on the chubby chick. God knows that I've been there before. I wonder what his motives are. What's he getting at? Because no matter how much I feel that spark between us, I refuse to believe that he doesn't have an ulterior motive.

When class is over, Bryan eyes me amid the shuffle of the other students filtering into the aisles. Holding up one finger, he mouths "Give me one minute." And that smile, it's impossible not to smile back at him. So, of course, I do.

As I'm zipping up my backpack, I hear Barbie girl from behind me talking with her friend. "He's still so freaking hot," Blondie says. The tone of her voice has this quality to it that suggests she knows just how hot he really is – especially naked.

"Oh my God. You still want him, don't you, Courtney?" Blondie, who I now know is Courtney, gasps but then giggles at her friend's apparently accurate accusation. I twist in my seat just a bit to catch a glimpse of the two of them, but I don't want to look too obvious so I make it look like I'm bending down to adjust the strap on my sandal.

Courtney is more gorgeous than I originally thought. She's got legs that go on forever. They're long, lean and tanned, and most importantly, cellulite free. In other words, they are nothing like mine. Her super-cute denim shorts – you know, the kind that have more pocket than denim – are extremely short and don't leave much to the imagination. I laugh inwardly thinking that I have underwear that cover more skin than her shorts do.

She adjusts her already low-cut black halter top to expose even more of her perky breasts and I almost laugh out loud at her very obvious attempt to catch the attention of whomever it is that she clearly wants back. In all honesty, she looks like she's dressed to go to some night club instead of a technology class – well, any class for that matter, unless the college offers pole dancing classes.

Courtney shrugs her shoulders. "Are you kidding me, Tori? Um, hell yeah I do. Look at him. Wouldn't you want that back in your bed?" I follow the path that Courtney and Tori's eyes are traveling and feel absolutely sick when I realize that they are talking about Bryan, my Bryan.

Where the hell did that come from? My Bryan. Like hell he is. Especially when I'm up against a girl like Courtney.

I suddenly feel sick and foolish for letting myself believe that he would honestly be interested in me.

Shaking away thoughts of our earlier flirting, I stand from my seat only to be met with the disgusted faces of Courtney and Tori. Clearly, I'm obstructing the view of their eye-candy.

Courtney's glossy, full lips curl into a sexy smile and when I glance over my shoulder, I see that she is smiling at Bryan who is walking toward her.

I roll my eyes and sigh sarcastically at her overtly sexual posture. She's pushing her boobs out and pouting her lips. Do guys actually fall for this kind of stuff? I guess there was part of me that foolishly thought Bryan was different.

Talk about a naïve freshman!

I push past the girls and, as I'm walking to the exit, I hear Bryan call out, "Melanie, where are you going?" That magnetic pull I felt toward him earlier draws me back into the room. Instantly, I wish I hadn't turned around. The shocked and almost sickening looks on Courtney and Tori's faces make me feel less than insignificant.

Bryan is taking the steps two at a time, hurrying to catch me before I leave. He nearly stumbles when Courtney reaches out for him with her grubby little hand. I'm watching the whole scene as if it's playing out in slow motion.

"Hey, Bry baby." Courtney's words are laced heavily with seduction. When she reaches up to cup his cheek, jealousy and disgust swirl through my veins.

Keeping an eye on me, as I remain glued to my spot by the exit, Bryan wraps his hand around Courtney's and pulls it away from his face before she even makes contact. My heart sings when I hear him say, "I'm done with you, Courtney. Now, get out of my way."

Bryan is standing in front of me before I can even register what's going on, but one thing is clear – he just chose me over her.

Lacing his fingers with mine, he says "I don't know what she said to you, but don't believe any of it. She's a lying, shallow, heartless bitch." His words sound as pained and angry as his face looks and I just want to curl myself around him and comfort him. Yet at the same time, the need to protect myself from being humiliated and hurt takes over. I pull my hand from his, and adjust my bag over my shoulder.

I shake my head as I say, "She didn't say anything. But if looks could kill, well, I'd be dead by now."

He laughs, but it's a gruff and uneasy sound. "Yeah, well, that sounds like Courtney." He pulls my bag from my shoulder and once again effortlessly carries mine along with his as we leave the classroom and the shocked faces of Courtney and Tori behind us.

As we're walking back down the hallway, I remember that I left my student ID in the lab. I pulled it out to log onto the computer and forgot to put it away. "Shit. I have to run back to the lab. I'll see you around." I have to admit, this is a rather convenient mistake. Now I can get away from him and try to sort through my little pity party.

"It's okay. I'll go with you. I need to work on some stuff for this class anyway." So much for a little bit of distance.

When we get back to the lab, I find my card right where I left it. "Oh, here it is. That totally would have sucked." He smiles warmly at me as he hands over my bag. "Here you go, Melanie. I'm sorry about before."

Apologizing for something that is totally out of control just upped the adorable factor that he already had going for him. "It's okay, Bryan. It's no big deal." I adjust my bag on my shoulder, though it's more out of nervousness than anything. I need to get out of here. "Bye." I smile and walk past him, but he doesn't let me by. He surprises me when he gently grabs my wrist. "Wait," he pleads.

It's because he's touching me that I can't say anything. So I stand there mute waiting for him to speak.

Raking his other hand through his hair, nervousness sets in on his face. "What are you doing tonight? Can we go out?" His question completely throws me for a loop and all I can see is me in comparison to the last girl he dated.

Opting for self-preservation, I tell him, "No. I can't. I'm really busy tonight. Sorry." It's pathetic and about as solid of an excuse as a house of cards, but I'm sticking to it.

I smile lamely at Bryan before turning toward the door. He lets me get past him this time.

Just as I'm about to turn the knob, Bryan calls out, "Where are you going?" His voice takes on that desperate and longing tone again as he places his hand on my shoulder to try and turn me around.

I'm not sure if it's from exhaustion in general – early mornings never agreed with me – or if it's from the emotional rollercoaster that I've been on since he surprised me by picking me up for work, but my shoulders slump under his touch. Slowly turning to face him, I pinch the bridge of my nose, which is still sore from getting a little banged up this morning, and try to make some sense of what I want to say.

"I'm going back to my room. I figured we were done here." My words sound as exasperated as I feel. I just need to get away from him and sort my mind, but he just won't let me go.

His scans the room as if he's looking for something to keep me here. "Well, I mean, if you don't have class or anything, I could show you around … or maybe train you on some things …" He's clearly searching for excuses to keep me here.

Beyond frustrated with his subtle hints and more than a little curious about his motives to keep me here, I drop my bag to the floor and blurt out the question that has been on my mind since he first spoke to me. "What do you want with me, Bryan? I mean, all week you were flirting with me, or at least I thought it was flirting." The pause I take allows me to suck in an unsteady breath. "But after seeing your ex, I realize how stupid of me it was to think that you were flirting. There's no way on Earth you'd be interested in me if you have a chance of being with someone like her. So what the hell? Please enlighten me!" I tap my foot in front of me in frustration as I brush my unruly hair out my eyes.

Bryan takes a step toward me, and I swear, my heart stops beating. Standing before me, his eyes bore into mine and I realize that there are soft hazel and golden flecks in those deep chocolate irises. Another piece of my hair falls across my cheek, and Bryan tenderly sweeps it away. His eyes soften and dance with light as he says, "You need to know two things, Melanie."

He's so close to me that I can't say anything. The grey matter that used to be my brain will only allow me to nod dumbly at him.

"First of all, yes, Courtney and I dated last year.

But we broke up because she's superficial and shallow and we had nothing in common. She's not a nice person and I think you know that now. So please believe me when I tell you that I definitely do not want to be with her, anymore." He gives me a second to let his words sink in before he leans his forehead to mine.

Cupping the soft curve of my jaw tenderly, he moves his lips to my ear, making it completely impossible for anything intelligible to come out of my mouth. I can smell the cinnamon on his breath and I want so badly to lick his full lips.

Whispering softly, he tells me, "And yes, I am flirting."

My breath hitches in my throat as his soft lips graze the outer shell of my ear. The room spins and my knees wobble slightly. When the tiniest bit of my composure returns, I mumble, "I must be hallucinating then, because I *think* you just told me that you're flirting with *me*."

He pulls his lips away from my ear, but keeps his hand at my cheek. Lightly brushing the pad of this thumb across my freckled peaches-and-cream skin, he asks, "Why do you find that so hard to believe?" He's looks like he's searching my face for some kind of answer, but all he'll find there is disbelief.

I reach up and pull his hand away from my face. I can't concentrate when he's touching me. Shaking my head, I try to gather my thoughts. I'm pretty sure that if I tell him what I'm really thinking, he'll run away from me and my craziness. A few more seconds pass and I still can't come up with any kind of explanation that won't expose the insecure girl who I try my hardest to keep hidden. "Please, Melanie, talk to me. I thought we had a good morning. I thought things were off to a decent start this week." Bryan's words convey his confusion, and if I'm not mistaken, he also sounds a little hurt.

Sobered by the idea that I'm hurting him by rejecting his advances, I take a deep, cleansing breath and offer up the best explanation I can come up with. "No, you're right, we did have a good morning and I've really enjoyed spending time with you." Tucking a piece of hair behind my ear and averting contact with his searing eyes, I add, "And I was flirting too." I feel the embarrassment of admitting my flirtation spread across my neck and chest as it creeps toward my face.

"I knew it!" His eyes twinkle as his lips curl up into the most gorgeous lopsided grin I have ever seen. You know the kind you only read about in romance novels. Well, apparently, they exist in real life too.

I have no choice but to huff and roll my eyes at him and his goofy grin. "Fine, then. You flirted and I flirted, but that still leaves one very important question hanging in the air."

Bryan folds his arms across his chest and my eyes are immediately drawn to the way his t-shirt stretches under the strain of his muscles. He catches me staring and arches an eyebrow at me. "And that question would be?" he prompts and I have to peel my eyes away from his delicious body.

With my eyes cast downward, I barely squeak out the question that I've been dying to ask since seeing Courtney's perfect body. "Why me? When you can have her, why me?"

He immediately responds without missing a beat. "Because I don't want her." His words are curt and cold. But then his eyes rake over my body causing my face to go crimson again. "And, I like you. A lot."

He sees the look of surprise on my face and says, "Give me one good reason not to like you, Melanie. You answered the ad for the job less than ten minutes after I posted it, so I know you're ambitious. Based on the few questions you answered in class, I can tell that you're smart. We've shared plenty of laughs this week. And well …" His eyes rake over my curves one last time before he continues, "I think you're the most beautiful girl I've ever seen." He cups my chin to pull my eyes up to his again. Scanning my face, Bryan's eyes focus in on mine as he softly adds, "Why not you?"

I roll my eyes at his compliments. It's the only way I know how to react to them. But when my eyes return from their skyward journey, his are trained on my lips. Through a fog of lust that's just settled around us, I vaguely hear his words. "Just give me time and I'll prove it to you. You'll see just how beautiful I think you are. You'll understand just how much I like you."

When his soft lips oh-so-briefly brush against my cheek, I lose all sense of rational thought. As he struts away from me, without a backward glance, I can't help but wonder what he has in mind to wear me down.

Chapter 3

Friday, January 25, 2013

Present

It's early. Way too early for me to be up, but when the distinct sound of the door opening filters into my room, my drowsiness vanishes instantly. Bryan isn't back yet. Cammie and Lia aren't going to be here for another day. Who the hell?

I slip on my robe and flip-flops and tiptoe my way to the front door. That's when the fear takes over. I hear banging – almost as if someone is driving their shoulder into the door trying to open it.

My stomach drops and my heart thuds wildly in my chest. As my mind races through the endless and scary possibilities, I remember that Lia stowed an old baseball bat in the front closet for this exact reason. We all laughed at her craziness, but in this moment, I could hug the life out of her.

Hefting the weight of the old school, wooden Louisville Slugger up to my shoulder, I stand to the side of the door, nervously awaiting whoever is on the other side to make their way through.

The lock clicks, and as if everything is in slow motion, I watch the knob turn slowly. Bat cocked on my shoulder, I'm ready to attack, though I know I don't stand a chance against a potential attacker. My feeble arms can barely hold up the bat. Maybe I can at least shock him and sprint past him as the door opens.

A blinding light shines in my eyes as the door cracks open – sun shining in from the huge hallway windows that open out into the courtyard. Shoot, I can't see! Before I can do anything about it, I see legs stepping through the door.

Acting on pure instinct, I swing the bat wildly and it crashes against what I assume is a kneecap. A body falls to the floor and I lift the heavy bat above my head to get in one more solid crack before I slip past the intruder.

Arms cross above the intruder's head, and rather than a harsh and brutish voice, a small and terrified one reaches through to my ears. "No! Please! I live here. Stop, please!" Her voice is petrified and laced with pain. "Please … don't hit me again." I drop the bat from my hands immediately as she eases her body back against the now closed door.

She's holding her hands up in front of her in a sign of surrender and she tries to catch her breath through the pain. The bat rolls up against her outstretched legs; she grabs at her knee and winces painfully.

My hand immediately goes to cover my mouth. "Oh my God! I'm so sorry. Are you okay?" Now that I know she isn't a he and that she isn't going to rape and kill me, I'm all apologies.

Through a veil of chestnut hair, she peeks up at me. Her brown eyes, which are covered by her hot-pink rimmed glasses, are shimmering with unshed tears. "Yeah, I think I'm okay. You just scared the crap out of me." She rolls up the leg of her pants to reveal the huge purple bruise that I just gave her. Gasping at the sight of it, I run to the freezer to get her some ice.

Kneeling down to her side, I say, "Here, use this." I press the half-eaten container of Ben and Jerry's Chunky Monkey to her enormously swollen kneecap.

She just cocks an eyebrow up at me and says, "Thanks."

"Sorry, it was all I had. I just got here yesterday." I slink down next to her and she smiles weakly at me. "Who are you anyway?" I don't mean to be rude, but I'm not concealing it well.

"Me? I'm Peyton. I guess I'm your new roommate." She holds out a small hand for me to shake and I just stare at it in disbelief. Why hadn't I thought of this? Of course, the college would fill Maddy's place. There's no reason to let a perfectly good room go unused. I guess I just would have liked some advanced notice or something like that.

Tentatively shaking her hand, I say, "Oh, well, hi then. Sorry for busting your kneecap. I didn't mean to go all Tonya Harding on you. I'm Melanie, by the way." Okay so we're not off to the best start but she seems nice enough, and if she can get over my attempted assault, I'm fairly certain she'll think I'm nice too. Hopefully.

I stand before her and hold my hand out to help her get up from the floor. "Come on. Let me help you over to the couch." Peyton wraps her arm around my shoulder as I wrap mine around her waist. Hobbling over the couch, she occasionally winces or gasps in pain. I guess I got her pretty good.

I put a pillow under her knee as she stretches out on the couch and get her a glass of water and some Advil from the bathroom medicine cabinet. "Here. These should help with the swelling."

Peyton looks down at the pills, like she's afraid to take them from me. Fine, we didn't get off to the best start, but I'm not going to drug her or anything. I shove the pills into her hand, feeling slightly pissed off that she would think that of me.

She inspects them. Yes, she actually reads the lettering on the pills, and when she's satisfied with the knowledge that they are, in fact, Advil and not some kind of whacky hallucinogen, she swallows them down with a gulp of water.

"Thanks, Melanie." She hands me back the glass and scans the room, inspecting it. "It's a nice place here. Anyone else live here besides you?" Peyton tips her chin in my direction.

Folding my legs underneath my body, I situate myself on the beat up, old arm chair across from her on the sofa. "Yeah, Cammie and Lia will be here tomorrow. They share the other room. They're cousins actually." And now that Peyton is here and knowing that Cammie and Lia will be back tomorrow, I'm happy that I won't be alone any longer. I think it'll be good for me to have my girls back.

"They nice?" She chances an investigative question.

Suddenly, I'm anxious for them to come back to the suite. I didn't realize until just now how much I've missed them. "They're the best, actually. Really sweet and funny." A slightly nervous chuckling escapes past my lips.

Unless you're a bitch to them. You know, like you're being to me right now.

"Cool. So I guess that means I'm rooming with

you." Again, her tone is cautious, on edge almost. "What happened to your old roommate? Did you bash her over the head or something? Scare her away?" She's trying to be comical with her question, but she's still guarded and on edge.

What the freak!? Doesn't she realize I thought she was going to attack me?

Just as I'm about to lay into her, she breaks out laughing. Through her giggling, she says, "Oh my God! The look on your face. Please tell me that you know I'm kidding!"

I can't hold it in any longer; laughter bubbles out of my mouth, and tears are streaming down both of our cheeks. In our fit of hysterics, I bump into her knee and she pulls back from me in pain.

"Oh no! I'm sorry." I feel horrible. I really didn't mean to hurt her.

"It's okay. It's okay. I'm fine. Calm down." Peyton squeezes my hand that I just placed on top of her bruised knee. "I'll live, Melanie. We all make mistakes. We don't usually bash our new roommates as a means of greeting them, but you know, it's all good." Her bright and cheery smile helps me feel a little better about my attack. The mood seems a little lighter and some of the guilt has lifted. I just don't like the idea of inflicting pain on anyone – accidental or not.

Of course my mind drifts to Bryan and how much

I know I'm going to hurt him. Peyton's voice breaks through my mist of self-pity.

"So what really happened to your old roommate? Homesickness? Couldn't take the cold?" Peyton shimmies back up against the couch and folds her arms across her chest as she awaits my response.

I don't even know where to begin. It could take me two novels to explain Maddy's story so I just opt for a simple version.

"Maddy is my best friend. She had to move home." I shrug my shoulders as I add, "Health reasons." I can see Peyton and I being friends, but I don't feel right divulging Maddy's past. It's not mine to tell.

A genuine look of concerns flashes across Peyton's very pretty face. "Oh no. I hope she's going to be okay." Her hand is clenched at her chest and I can tell that she means her words. There's no false pretense in her tone.

"Yeah, she's going to be just fine." I know Maddy will be more than just fine, but I can't help that I'm going to miss her terribly.

"So then it's you and me, huh?" she repeats her earlier question regarding who she'll be rooming with.

"It looks that way. Hey, listen. I'm really sorry about that." I eye her knee and then the door indicating my earlier attack. "I wasn't expecting you at all, so I thought someone was breaking in. I promise I'm not usually violent." My lips curl at the corners and I hope that my self-deprecation will help keep the mood light.

It does, marginally at least. Peyton smirks back at me and lowers her now ice-cream-covered leg to the floor. I move immediately to take the container away and bring her a damp cloth to clean the mess.

"Thanks. I think I'll survive." Peyton wipes up the sticky mess and a bit more of the tension fades away. "Are those yours?" She points to the boxed set of the entire *Sex and the City* series that is strewn about the coffee table.

"Yes. I love them." I can't help but gush over my girls. I love them all, and while most women identify with Carrie – she is the main character, after all – I feel very connected to Charlotte and her quest for perfection. I never share that with anyone. They just think I love the show for all the hunky men. They're not so bad either, but for me the real draw is Charlotte.

Peyton reaches out for the DVD case and reads the back of it. "Hmm, never seen it."

"What? You've never seen this show?" I try my best not to sound like Gary Coleman, with the 'whatchotalkinbout' but I'm completely shocked that she has never seen *Sex and the City*.

Peyton just shrugs her shoulders and places the box back on the coffee table. "No, sorry. Just not much of a television watcher, I guess. I'm kind of a book worm." She adjusts her hot-pink glasses as she says the last part. "My nose has been in a book since I knew that letters made up words. And I've spent the better part of the last three years working my ass off for the Whitman grant for grad students."

Huh? Did she just say grad school?

She registers the look of confusion on my face and my furrowed brow and continues her explanation. "I'm actually here starting grad school a semester early. I was awarded a huge grant and I wanted to start right away. They accepted me into the English Lit program and I got a job at the student tutoring center. I searched up and down for an apartment, but since it was mid-year, almost everything was taken or it involved moving into a filthy frat house."

I wonder if she looked at Reid's old room. Talk about coincidence.

"Luckily for me, this place opened up at the last minute," she adds quickly and smiles over at me.

Yeah, lucky for you.

She realizes the impact of her last words and back tracks a little. "Not that it's lucky for you, I mean. Crap, I'm sorry about your best friend. I was just trying to tell you a little about me." A furrowed brow and soft words convey her apology.

With a deep cleansing breath, I decide to let the

craziness that has been my morning - hell, that has been the last few weeks of my life, fade away.

It hasn't been a perfect start with Peyton, but considering that we'll be sharing a room for at least the next four months, I smile brightly at her and hold the DVD box up in between us. "Feel like telling me more about yourself while we watch this? I've seen them more than I care to admit, but I'll start from the beginning if you want."

An equally bright smile graces Peyton's pretty face as she says, "Sure. That would be really nice." She angles her head back to the door where her bags sit. "I can un-pack later."

I bounce out of my seat and pop a disc into the DVD player. As the bubbly notes of the opening theme song play out, I offer to make us some breakfast. Of course, Mom made sure that the fridge was stocked before she left. God, I love that woman. If it wasn't for her, Peyton and I would be eating melted ice cream and stale chips for breakfast.

As I hand her a plate of toast with jelly and some fresh fruit, Peyton says, "Thanks" and then her attention is immediately drawn to the sparkly pair of Manolo Blanik's that grace Carrie's feet. "Oh my goodness, those are the prettiest shoes I've ever seen." And then when some shirtless piece of man-pie walks across the screen, Peyton nearly chokes on her orange juice. "Why on Earth have I never seen this show?"

We share a loud laugh and spend the rest of the morning getting to know each other, all the while getting lost in the wonder that is *Sex and the City*.

It's good to focus my attention on something other than Bryan, but when Aiden confronts Carrie about going behind his back with Mr. Big, I'm thrown full force back into my own world of problems – texts of kisses and cheating girlfriends. Forcing my brain to think happier thoughts, I get lost in the memory of mine and Bryan's first date.

Chapter 4

Friday, September 14, 2012

Past

I've been working at the computer lab for just about three weeks now, and so far everything seems to be going really well. I get to spend lots of time with Bryan, who oddly works just about every shift that I work – a part of his master plan to wear me down as he promised, I'm sure.

His plan has been somewhat effective. He buys me coffee every morning that we have class together and caffeine is most definitely a quick way to my heart. He also plays the dorky card every now and then too. Just last week when he was passing out papers during class, he put a sticky note on top of mine. On it, he wrote, "Go out with me" with two little squares. Next to one was the word "yes" and the other "no". A bit adolescent? Sure, but sweet nonetheless.

The cornerstone of his plan is the one that's having the greatest effect – proximity. When we work together, he's always leaning over my shoulder, reaching in front of me to type something on my keyboard. The feel of his hard chest pressed up against my back makes me melt for him. He's winning in his little plan, that's for sure. I don't dare tell him as much, but I think he can tell.

Bryan's not working with me tonight, though. It's just me and Professor O'Neil right now. I really like Professor O'Neil and I can definitely tell why Bryan has enjoyed working for him these past three years. He's well into his sixties and he's the quintessential absent-minded professor. He's bald on top, but what hair he does have left is an unkempt mass of salt-and-pepper curls. I think my favorite thing about him, aside from his sweet personality, is that his tweed jacket – you know, the kind with the leather patches on the elbows – is always smattered with chalk dust across his back.

Since it's a Friday night, it's very quiet in the lab. No one really wants to do homework when there are parties to attend and drinks to consume. I get out of here at eight, so I could still go out, but I'm not much of a partier.

Professor O'Neil has been here for most of my shift, but by the looks of it, he's not making it until eight. He actually looks like he's going to fall asleep at his desk.

When I gently tap on his door, I startle him out of his light sleep. "Oh, hi, Melanie. Is something wrong out there? Do you need help?" he asks as he wipes the exhaustion from his eyes.

I step toward his desk and pick a few stray papers up from the floor. They must have fallen there when he passed out on top of the rather large stack that's still sitting on his desk. Shaking my head, I say, "No, everything's fine, Professor O'Neil. I just wanted to let you know that I've got this covered." I angle my head out to the main room, which is completely empty. "There's no one here, so why don't you go home and I'll lock up."

Looking down at his watch, he smiles. "You know what? That sounds perfect. I can get home just in time to watch *Jeopardy* with my wife." He starts packing up his briefcase with random papers and books. It surprises me that the man is even capable of remembering how to get home or around campus. He's such a scatterbrain.

As he walks past me, he claps me on the shoulder. "You've done a really great job here these past few weeks. It's nice having you on board." He drops the keys in my hand and walks out into the main hallway. I smile with pride and escort him out. Walking left first, he then turns around sharply when he realizes that he needs to go to the right instead. I have to chuckle at him; he's just so likeable and so dorky that it's impossible not to laugh.

Okay, even I can admit that I have a huge soft spot for the dorky type.

Laughing softly at Professor O'Neil's lack of direction, I check my watch as I saunter back toward my desk. I only have about an hour left of my shift. It's boring as hell, but at least I'll get my studying done. As I pull my biology textbook out of my bag, not surprisingly, I smack my head on the underside of the desk. Laughing at myself, I have to admit that I'm the clumsiest person ever, well after Professor O'Neil of course.

"What's so funny?" Bryan's warm and familiar voice filters in to my ears. He must have walked in while I was getting my books out.

Rubbing over the small bump that's already started to swell on my head, I smile at him. "I was just thinking that I'm the most accident-prone person ever, but now that you're here, I'm starting to think you might have something to do with it."

Bryan chuckles, deep and throaty, while smirking at me playfully. "And please tell me what role I play in your clumsiness?" He rubs his stubbled chin as he waits for me to speak up. But somehow, all I can manage to do is watch his fingers touch his face. I wonder what it would feel like to run my fingers through that stubble, to trace my tongue along it, to feel it scratch my face, and some other places as well.

"Well …" His softly spoken word disrupts my silent, but delicious thoughts. Quickly recovering my flirty wit, which always seems to be in place when Bryan is around, I let my lips curl up at the corners. "Well, it just seems that I get banged up pretty good when you're around."

The sound of his loud, almost uncontrollable laughter takes me by surprise. I cross my arms over my ample chest, and narrowing my eyes I at him, I snare, "What the hell's so funny?" I feel slightly put-off by him laughing at me.

After his laughter subsides, he places his palms on the desk and leans into me. He's so close that I can smell the cinnamon on his breath; I can feel the heat emanating from his muscled body. "Believe me, Melanie, if it was up to me, you would be *banged* very well whenever I'm around. I thought I told you that already."

Oh dear lord!

His eyes narrow in on mine and I know there's no way for me to conceal the shock that washes over my face. He sees it and laughs softly at me again. "Now, don't be so surprised. I told you that I like you, repeatedly in fact. It's not my fault that you don't believe me." He pauses a beat before adding, "Yet."

I roll my eyes. That's been my reaction to his fairly persistent advances. Since we met on the first day of classes, he has taken every opportunity to be flirtatious or do something sweet for me. Just the other morning, he greeted me outside of my eight a.m. class with an extra-large coffee. That gesture prompted a face-splitting smile rather than the usual eye roll. His plan might just be working.

As I desperately try to calm the swarm of butterflies that have suddenly taken flight in my belly, Bryan scans the empty lab. He quickly realizes that we're by ourselves. "You're all alone? Where's Professor O'Neil, or Simon." Flirty Bryan is gone and now concerned Bryan stands before me.

Dismissing his protectiveness, I swat my hand in front of me as if I'm shooing away a fly. "It's no big deal, Bryan. Simon wasn't feeling well so he left early and Professor O'Neil fell asleep at his desk so I told him to go home and I would close the lab up at eight."

"Yeah, but you still shouldn't be here alone." He's still scanning the room as if some masked killer from a slasher film is going to jump out at me.

"So then stay with me." My words catch him off guard. Hell, they even catch me off guard. Ever since my first encounter with Courtney a few weeks ago, his drop-dead-gorgeous ex-girlfriend, I've tried to put some distance between us by dismissing his advances, but tonight, honestly, I'd like to spend a little time with him. Especially after his comment about banging. Okay, okay. It may have been lame and even a bit crude, but I can no longer deny that being around him ignites sparks in me that I've never felt before. His tender touch and kind words make me feel special and beautiful.

Just as he's about to answer me, with something sexy I'm sure, I hear a shrill but all-too-familiar voice call out from the entry. Courtney. That bitch.

"I thought that was you, Bryan. What are you doing here? Aren't you going to Liam's tonight?" Liam and Bryan are co-captains of the soccer team. He's asked me to go to a few of his games, but knowing that Courtney will be there, I always come up with some feeble excuse.

She's twirling her long, shiny-blonde hair in between her acrylic-tipped and brightly polished nails. Ugh, she makes me want to gag. But, rather than lose my lunch all over the place, I busy myself with packing up my things as it's nearly time to close up the lab.

Bryan lets his gaze fall back on me one last time before walking toward Courtney. So much for thinking he really wanted to spend some time with me.

As I'm shoving my books into my bag, I can

vaguely overhear his venomous whisper. "What are you doing here? I told you the other morning that we're done." Bryan's hand is clamped around her upper arm as he drags her out of the room. There's part of me that wants to take in the scene before me at face value. I want to believe that he's really done with her, and the morning that he's talking about is the morning that he brushed her off while chasing after me, but that kind of stuff only happens in the movies, right?

I'm more aggravated at him than I should be, because, honestly, he hasn't done anything wrong. I huff at him as I brush past his rather animated ongoing conversation with Courtney. I hear bits of it stream into my consciousness and I try to dismiss my stupidity for even believing, if only for a minute, that he really wants me.

She's droning on about still loving him and him making the biggest mistake of his life for letting her go. He's all but seething at her, telling her that he was never hers to lose. When he catches sight of my fiery-red hair moving past him, I see his eyes widen and hear his tone harden.

"I'm done, Courtney. We're through." There's a finality there that even I can hear, but Courtney pays no mind to it. Instantly glued to the spot, I watch completely in awe of what I'm seeing.

Bryan's back is half-way to me, but Courtney has

full view of my shocked expression as she eyes me over Bryan's strongly muscled shoulders. Wrapping her arms around his neck, as a snake would constrict its prey, she makes eye contact with me. When her tongue slithers out of her peachy, plump lips, my gut twists in sickness.

"You can pretend all you want, Bryan. But, I know that you still want me." Her tongue licks the outer shell of his ear and I have to look away. I've envisioned licking the very same spot myself.

Utterly disgusted, I force my feet to peel away from the floor. Sprinting down the empty hallway, I find myself near tears.

I fell for it. I actually believed that he wanted me, when, in reality, I'm just a distraction. She obviously still wants him and she's not going to stop until she has him. She licked his ear for God's sake. I can't compete with her.

I've never even been in the same league as girls like her.

When I make it back to my suite, which is in a building not all that far from the computer lab, I'm glad to find that it's empty. I don't know where everyone else is, and honestly, I just don't care. I'm more than happy to drown my foolish sorrows in a pint of ice cream and a *Friends* rerun.

Slumping down into the comfy couch, I force back the tears that threaten. I mean just how stupid was

I to think that Bryan was interested in me. Sure, he made a comment about sleeping together, but what hunky and horny college guy would willingly pass up an opportunity to get some ass. Obviously not Bryan.

Just as my spoon hits the top layer of peanut butter and fudge swirled ice cream, I'm startled by the loud banging on my door. Rolling my eyes and huffing a more-than-pissed-off sigh, I walk toward the door, all but yelling, "What the hell do you want?" without even asking who it is.

Needless to say, I'm more than shocked when I hear Bryan's deep and very apologetic voice vibrate through the metal door. "It's me, Melanie. Please open the door. I need to talk to you."

The softly pleading tone of his words is all I need to turn the knob and let him enter my world.

When Bryan's eyes rake over my body, I realize what a disheveled mess I look like. I changed into sweats and an old, frumpy T-shirt as soon as I got back to my room. My hair is in a loosely knotted bun of wild and unruly curls and it makes me look like a hot mess. Well, after seeing Courtney lay claim to him right before my eyes, that's exactly how I feel – one jealousy ridden and riled up hot mess.

Arms crossed over my chest and toe tapping not so patiently in front of me, I huff out, "What do you want, Bryan?"

Leaning his shoulder up against the door frame, with his legs crossed at the heels, he kind of looks like James Dean – cool, unaffected and sexy as hell. "I already told you what I want, but you refuse to listen to me." Just for effect, he lets his eyes travel the length of my body once more before asking, "Can I come in or are you going to make me explain everything to you from the hallway?" There's a seriousness to his words that disarms me. We're not just talking about the scene that just played out at the lab.

Rolling my eyes and huffing like a little girl suddenly seems inappropriate. Stepping to the side and extending my arm, I look up at him and smile warmly. "Umm, yeah. Come on in."

Bryan walks over to the stools at the kitchen counter as I make my way to the fridge to get us a drink. After sliding a bottle of water in front of him, I twist the cap on my own and sit on the stool next to him. At almost the same time, we turn so that we face each other. We're so close that our knees are nearly touching. I stifle a smile as the memory of sitting like this at work replays in my mind.

Long moments of awkward silence stretch out between us as we both sip at our chilled water. He's bouncing his leg up and down so frantically that I'm afraid he's going to break the stool. Maddy and I put them together so I can personally attest to their shoddiness.

Timidly, I place my hand on his vibrating leg to try to and calm him. It's there – that *something* that's there every time we touch. It was there when he helped me with my bloody nose, when our fingers were laced together as we walked to class, when our eyes met time and time again.

I'm the one who has been denying it, been pushing it away. Maybe it's time to stop doing that and just see what happens.

Squeezing his knee gently stops the nervous shaking and forces his eyes to meet mine. "What is it that you need to explain, Bryan?"

When he places his hand on top of mine, my breath hitches. "Well, there's a lot to explain, believe me, but first I need *you* to explain something to *me*."

Suddenly nervous, I pull my hand out from under his and stare, wide-eyed and shocked at him. "What do you need me to explain? My ex wasn't just licking my ear!" I sound like a green-eyed monster, but in this moment, that's exactly how I feel.

"You see, that's what I don't get. You're clearly jealous of her." Bryan arches an eyebrow at me as I open my mouth to protest his accusation – an accusation to which I refuse to confess. "Oh would you stop it already, Melanie?" His less than playful words catch me off guard and I keep my mouth closed. I want to hear what else has got him all riled up.

When he sees that I'm going to allow him to speak without any interruptions, he grins knowingly at me. "I'm going to ask you something, and even though I think I already know the answer, I need you to be honest with me. Okay?" His eyes search my face as he waits for me to answer him. When he stares at my lips for a brief moment, I lose all train of thought and speech becomes impossible.

I try my best to ignore the nervousness that I feel, but I can't get any words to come out of my mouth. So instead of saying anything, I just nod at him. Running his fingers through his soft, medium-length, dark-brown hair, he pulls on the ends in what seems like a gesture of frustration. The act just makes his messy hair even messier.

And sexier, too.

Straightening his shoulders and grabbing mine in his strong hands, he forces me to look into his eyes. "Why are you fighting this?" He gestures between us and then reaches up to brush a strand of hair out of my eyes.

My mouth is dry. My pulse is racing. I can't believe that he's just called me out like this. When I don't say anything, he steps away from me and starts pacing. "I just don't get it, Melanie. I don't understand why you don't believe me. I've told you that I like you, that I want to get to know you better. I've done nothing but be patient with you and try to prove to you that I'm a decent guy. Hell, I've moved around my entire schedule, even changed a few classes that I didn't need so that I could be at work while you're there and you …"

"You did what?" My barely whispered question interrupts his more-than-a-little-upset ramblings.

He takes a deep breath and stops pacing. "What?" Shock settles in on his fine face as he realizes that he just shared something he intended to keep hidden.

"You changed your schedule so that you could spend more time with me? When? Why?" Now I'm really confused. You don't change your classes, especially as a senior, just to spend more time with a girl.

Unless you really like her.

God, I'm an idiot.

He walks me over to the couch and we sit facing one another. Pulling my hands into his, his eyes soften and he grins a silly smile. "It was right after that first week. When I saw your schedule at the lab, I realized that I would only get to see you for one shift. So I changed things around and begged Simon to switch with me. You kept refusing to see me outside of class, so I did the only thing I could think of to make you see me."

An involuntary chuckle passes my lips. "You have to admit you did come on pretty strong that first week, though." Now it's my turn to arch my eyebrow at him.

"Yeah, okay. I'll admit that showing up to your suite to pick you up for work when you hadn't even told me where you lived was a bit stalker-ish." As timid as his words may be, his mega-watt smile fully conveys just how proud he is at trying to prove to me that he's interested.

"Okay, so stalker-like tendencies aside, can you please explain to me what just happened with Courtney? I mean, if you don't want to be with her," he opens his mouth to start saying the same thing he's tried explaining time and time again when it comes to Courtney, but I just talk through it. "If you don't want to be with her, then what the hell was that ear-licking about?"

Frustration sets in hard on his face. "We've been over this so many times, Melanie. I do not want her!" His last few words are harshly emphasized as he glares at me. Clearly distraught by the turn in the conversation, Bryan rakes both of his hands through his hair and pulls hard on the ends. Lifting his face back to mine, I can tell he's still pissed.

Hell, I can be angry too. "Don't you dare look at me like that, Bryan! I've told you before, that I don't like her, yet you think her walking up to you and licking you is perfectly fine!? Come to think of it, whenever I'm around you, she's always there. What the hell! None of it makes sense. I still don't …"

"What? Let me guess, you don't know why I would want you when I could have 'a girl like her.'" His words mock the insecurities that I've shared with him. Damn him for using them against me, for throwing them in my face.

"You're being a dick! How dare you use that against me! Excuse me for being too stupid to understand why on Earth you want me when she's skinnier and prettier than I'll ever be." Tears burn the back of my eyes, but I refuse to let them fall. I may be pissed that he's using my own words against me, but I won't let him see me be weak.

I don't let anyone see *that* Melanie.

Frantically pacing the small living room, Bryan is practically pulling his hair out of his scalp. We don't say anything for a few minutes. It's "do or die" time. We've clearly reached an impasse and, honestly, I'm being too stubborn to move.

Just when I think he's going to storm off and leave me alone to wallow in my own sadness, Bryan's eyes lock with mine as he walks toward me. I can see that the fight has left his body and I'm sure that he's just going to say goodbye. No one, especially not me, is worth this kind of frustration.

Bracing myself for the inevitable blow of his goodbye, I wrap my arms around myself and blink back more tears. I'm more than surprised when, rather than pushing me away and saying goodbye, he's pulling me into a tight embrace and cooing into my ear. "Shh. It's okay, Melanie." The tender way that his fingers run through my hair calms me almost instantly. Pulling back from him and looking into his obviously concerned eyes, I decide that I finally need to expose my insecurities, at least some of them, especially if I ever have any hope of laying them to rest.

Breaking from his embrace and holding my arms to the side, I ask, almost sarcastically, "Are you sure this is what you want?" I drag my arms up and down my body, much like one of those supermodels on *The Price is Right* does when they're showcasing a prize. "I'm nothing like Courtney. I'm not a size two and I never will be. I have curves and lumps and bumps so, no, I really can't understand why you want me when you can have her. She's beautiful, and I'm … well, I'm just me." My last words are no more than a whisper. I've never voiced my own feelings of self-loathing aloud to anyone else.

Pulling me back into the safe circle of his arms,

Bryan smiles at me and kisses my cheek tenderly. "You don't get it, but I want you because you're nothing like her. For what it's worth, I think you're beautiful, inside and out. And, not for nothing, Melanie, but you're the one who is making this all about looks. Now, I'm not going to fall into the pit of insane girl logic, because I know that you'll just use whatever I say to defend myself against me. So rather than *tell* you why I want to be with you, I'm going to *show* you." His large hands gently cup my face as he strokes the pads of his thumbs across my freckled cheeks.

I try, but fail, miserably, to hide my shock. Show me? What the hell does that mean? All sorts of crazy visions from silly romantic comedies swarm in my head. Is he going to sweep me off my feet and make love to me?

Hmm. He might not have been too far off base talking about that insane girl logic.

He brings our entwined hands up to his lips and continues explaining himself while I'm still somewhat distracted by my smutty daydream. "I'm picking you up tomorrow at noon. You're spending the entire day with me and I am going to show you, beyond any measurable doubt, why I want to be with you."

He doesn't actually ask me, so I can't actually say no. All I can do is nod my agreement and bask in the feel of his lips pressing up against my cheek once again.

Bryan doesn't let go of my hand as he walks over to the door. Leaning up against the frame, he says, "So I'll pick you up tomorrow at noon. Be sure to wear sneakers." His instruction on what kind of shoes to wear catches me off guard. With what I'm sure is a rather stupefied and dumbfounded look plastered to my face, he smirks at me and winks before walking down the hallway and out of the building.

"I really can't believe you've never hiked the gorges before." Bryan playfully mocks my inexperience as he pulls out my chair at the restaurant. A two-hour hike was the reason he told me to wear sneakers and I'm glad I listened. We're on part two of our date, and if it's half as successful as part one, I'll be one happy girl.

We both went back to our dorms after our hike to wash away the grime and get ready for tonight. Maddy helped me pick out my outfit, and with a few finishing touches to my hair and make-up – which I kept soft and simple – I feel beautiful.

When I told her about what happened with Bryan, she told me to just go for it. Actually, she was beyond giddy that I finally decided to give him a chance.

Unfolding my napkin and placing it across the pleated navy-blue skirt of my Marilyn Monroe inspired dress, I stick my tongue out at him. "Cut me some slack, will you? I've only been here a few weeks. You've lived in Ithaca for years now."

Reaching for my hand across the cream-colored linen tablecloth, his eyes shine in the flickering candle light. "Did you have fun though?" he asks timidly.

I can't stop the face-splitting smile that pulls at the corners of my mouth. "I had a blast, Bryan. I had no idea that Hemlock Gorge was so beautiful. I can't wait to see the pictures that we took."

"We could go to another one next weekend if you'd like. Another gorge, I mean. There are hundreds of them, you know." Bryan's face lights up with pride as he takes a sip of his water.

"I'd really like that, Bryan," I say softly as I squeeze his hand before reaching for my water.

"So my plan worked then?" His question catches me off guard. I didn't realize that he had a plan.

"What do you mean? What plan?" I ask genuinely confused.

"Yesterday, I told you that I would *show* you why I want to be with 'someone like you' – whatever that's supposed to mean." In true dork fashion, he actually uses air quotes around the words "someone like you". He ignores my light laughter at his inherent dorkiness, and continues his little explanation. "There was something about you. I could tell, from the moment I met you, that you were different. That you saw beauty in things that other people might ignore. I can't tell you how many times I asked Courtney to go hiking with me. But she always said no. Too much mud, too many bugs – you name it and I've heard it as an excuse." He stares into my eyes. "After a while, I guess I just got tired of hearing excuses."

Just as I place my glass back on the table, an older, very grandmotherly-looking woman approaches the table. She's wearing a sauce-smeared apron and is glowing with pride as she approaches Bryan. When he sees her, whoever she is, walking toward us, he stands from his chair and wraps his arms around her.

"It's so good to see you, Bryan." The older woman's eyes sparkle with love and affection as she holds Bryan at arm's length. "We might need you to come in next week and repair that whatchamacallit thingy … that makes the computer or the internet … or whatever work." Her words are spoken through a heavy Italian accent and she's waving her arms all over the place in front of her as she talks, trying to explain something about which she obviously knows so little.

Bryan stifles a laugh and says, "Sure thing. I'll come by on Monday after classes to take a look at the server."

"Perfect." She clasps her hands in front of her chest and turns toward me as if she's just realizing that

Bryan is not alone. "Oh and who is this lovely lady, Bryan?" I stand to greet her but can't help the blush that colors my face at her compliment.

"Bella, I'd like you to meet Melanie." I extend my hand to hers and she pulls me in for a hug. Shaking his head at her outward show of affection, he continues, what now seems to be, an unnecessary introduction. "And Melanie, this is Bella." Finally making the connection between her appearance and her name, I piece together that she must be the owner.

"It's very nice to meet you, Bella. This place is beautiful." Scanning the quaint Italian bistro, I take in the quiet and romantic ambiance. And, if the smells coming out of the kitchen are any indication, the food must be excellent.

Her round and wrinkled face glows with pride. "Thank you, Melanie. *Bella Cucina's* has been my heart and soul for the last twenty-five years."

"You're going to love the food, Melanie. Bella here makes the world's best gnocchi," Bryan says as he takes his seat. I return to mine and Bella dismisses his compliment, but I see the smile curving her lips.

"Well, now. I can't refuse a house specialty, can I? Gnocchi it is," I say as I hand her my untouched menu.

"I'll have the same," Bryan says as he hands her his menu as well.

"Perfect. You will not be disappointed." Bella

takes our menus and proudly walks toward the kitchen to make us our dinner.

"She's really sweet. How long have you known her?" I angle my head in the direction of the kitchen.

"Yeah, she is. I've known her and Gus, her husband, since my freshman year. That's when I started updating their technology systems in here. They're very close friends with Professor O'Neil and his wife."

"So was it like a side-job? I mean setting up their computers? Or did O'Neil just want to test out your skills before he hired you?" I quirk an inquisitive, yet still playful eyebrow at him. It just seems unlikely that someone, a college freshman no less, would want to help someone else without any kind of retribution.

"There's always got to be a motive with you, huh." Bryan points an accusing finger at me and laughs. "No. It wasn't a job or a test or anything like that. They needed help. The restaurant was in danger of going under if it didn't update and branch out. Bella and Gus knew nothing about social media and advertising, so I brought them into this century, because-"

I cut him off before he can finish. I arch my eyebrows and say, "Because you wanted a place to bring all your dates to impress them, huh?" My words are meant to be light and flirty, but as soon as they're out of my mouth, I realize that he must have come here with Courtney, often.

Damn, I am such a fool, thinking I was special or something like that.

Bryan's eyes narrow on mine when he sees the disgust settle in. He grasps my hand across the table and through a clenched jaw, he says, "Stop it, now. I told you I would show you why I liked you and I am. By bringing you here, I am. Can I try and explain?"

"Please do," I quip.

That tone garners an eye roll. "First of all, I have *never* brought Courtney here. She always thought this place was, I don't know, not classy enough for her or something like that. So, for your information, you are the first date I've ever brought here. Okay?" His tone and grip on my hand have softened; his eyes have calmed. Bringing my hand up to his mouth, he plants a soft kiss on my knuckles.

Appeased, I decide to approach this in a less-guarded manner. Maybe it will make me look like less of an ass. "You said 'first of all.' Is there more?" Batting my eyelashes, I give him my best pouty face. He sees the apology there and laughs at my silliness.

"God, you're a trip, Melanie."

Needing to keep my hands occupied, I reach for a piece of bread from the basket that the waitress has just brought to us. After dunking it in the olive oil, I bring it to my lips and catch Bryan staring at me.

"That right there is another reason," he says; his

voice is all throaty and gruff.

"What? Bread is another reason you like me?" I arch an eyebrow at him.

"Not bread, specifically. It's just that, you're not picky. When I asked you out, you didn't even ask where we were going. You didn't argue with me about anything. You let me get you all sweaty and dirty hiking, and now you're letting me feed you carbs in a little Italian place that I've never been able to bring anyone else to. And you didn't think twice about hugging Bella, even though the woman was covered in sauce from head to toe." He pauses briefly as if he's trying to find the perfect words. "You're not like the other girls that you think every guy wants. You're a breath of fresh air."

Yep, those were perfect. He just told me all of the things that every girl only dreams about hearing.

All the things I never thought I would.

He looks thoroughly pleased with himself. I'll give him credit; he sidestepped what could have been a few landmines in that little speech.

Pitching my voice low, I say, "I like it when you get me all hot and sweaty."

"Well, then. We'll have to see what I can do about that later." The wink and smirk added to the end of that flirtatious comment have my insides going all sorts of crazy.

Bryan breaks the hold on my hand when Bella brings us our dinner. The meal passes in companionable silence as we both clear our plates. Spending all day in the warm, autumn air helped us build up a healthy appetite, and a huge plate of home-cooked yumminess is exactly what we needed to recharge our batteries.

After our waitress clears our plates and we order dessert, the conversation begins flowing again. "So tell me about your family?" I ask as I take a sip from my water.

"There's nothing really all that special. We're your stereotypical All-American family. Mom, Dad, me and my little sister, a dog and a white picket fence. You?"

"Umm, not so stereotypical, I guess. My dad died before I was born so it's always been just my mom and I." His eyes shine with concern and care when he hears about my dad.

"I'm so sorry, Melanie." He reaches for my hand again and gently grazes his thumb over my knuckles.

"It's okay. I mean, I never knew him. I miss him, or maybe just the idea of him, but I mostly hurt for my mom. She never got remarried. I always felt like it was my fault, like she was too worried about taking care of me to take care of herself. Who knows? Maybe now that I'm away at college, she'll finally start dating again." I shrug my shoulders and hope for the best. I really do want her to be happy, perhaps even more than I want my own happiness.

When the waitress brings out our tiramisu my mouth waters. I have such a sweet tooth. Yeah, I never met a cupcake I didn't fall in love with and then swiftly devour. Quickly scanning the table before she steps away, the waitress realizes that she only brought out one fork. "I'll be right back with another one. Sorry about that."

Bryan stops her before she fully turns away. "Don't worry about it. We're good."

When he winks at me, I think I may have to check the floor for my panties. Yeah, it was *that* sexy.

He sinks the fork into the layered goodness and my heart starts fluttering like crazy when he extends the bite to me. "Ladies first." His voice is seductive and sexy, just like the gesture.

As the rich chocolate hits my tongue, my eyes roll back. It's sinful and heavenly at the same time. I close my lips around the bite he's just fed me. As he pulls the fork out of my mouth, I lick my lips making sure to catch every last crumb. When I open my eyes, Bryan's face is frozen in a look of pleasure. He reaches across the table and swipes the pad of his thumb along the corner of my mouth. Locked in a heated stare, I wrap my hand around his and pull his chocolate covered thumb to my lips. As I lick the crumbs away, Bryan traces his lips with his own tongue before pulling the lower one in between his teeth. Watching him be so clearly affected, makes me even more turned on than I already was.

We take turns feeding each other dessert – eyes locked and pulses racing. Bite after bite, we've worked ourselves up into a frenzy. By the time we leave the restaurant, I'm more turned on than I ever have been.

It's a short drive back to my dorm. Of course, Bryan insists on walking me to my door. When he places his hand on my lower back as he walks me down the hallway, I know that I'm falling hard. There's a fire igniting between us, and now that he's *shown* rather than *explained* why he wants to be with me, I'm going to let that fire burn – brightly and beautifully.

With my back pressed to the door, Bryan leans into me and grazes his knuckles across my cheek softly. "I had an amazing time today and tonight, Melanie. Please tell me you did too." I want to jump up and down and sing a song about how much fun I had today, but his nearness makes speaking impossible and he knows it.

Pressing his forehead to mine, he stares directly into my eyes. My breath hitches and he smirks at me. "I'll take that as a yes, then." I nod softly because speaking is still not happening.

Bryan cups the back of my head and tangles his

fingers into my long, wavy hair. Chills course over my skin and my pulse beats wildly. With his thumb brushing my cheek once again, he says, "Does this mean you're ready to finally give me a chance?"

"Yes." But before the softly spoken word is even past my lips, his mouth is on mine. Slow, tender, erotic – those are the only words I can come up with to describe how this first kiss real feels. He kisses every inch of my lips, the soft bow of the upper one - the plump fullness of the lower one. When his tongue licks at the corner, seeking permission to enter, I can no longer deny that I want him.

Wrapping my arms around his neck, I pull him into my soft body. His arms band around the curves of my waist, and after the amazing day and night that we've spent together, I no longer feel self-conscious at his touch.

Completely out of breath and full of desire, I pull back from him when I hear giggling on the other side of the door. He hears it too and laughs lightly in response.

"My roommates," I explain, thumbing the door behind me.

"Hi, Bryan!" Maddy, Cammie and Lia's cheery sing-song voices carry through the door and essentially kill the mood.

"So, can I pick you up for class on Monday?" he

asks as he presses his lips to mine one last time.

"Yes," I respond, my voice laced with lust. I could seriously kill those girls for interrupting us. But watching Bryan's fine ass strut away down the hall is a pretty sweet consolation prize.

For the first time since elementary school, I'm excited about a Monday morning.

Chapter 5

Saturday, January 26, 2013

Present

Cammie and Lia are coming back today and I'm beyond thrilled to see them again. It's been a while since I've been this excited.

There's a knock on my bedroom door, and before I can say anything, it cracks open and Cammie's bright, smiling face peers in at me. "Hey, girl!" She bounces over to my bed and nearly tackles me as I try to sit upright. I can hardly breathe as she squeezes the life out of me.

Breaking the hug, and holding me at arm's length, she says, "I missed you so much. I feel like I haven't seen you in forever."

I can't help but squeeze her right back. "I missed you too. It's so good to be back. Did Lia come with you?"

"Of course she did. She'll be up in a minute. She's just parking the car." Cammie squeezes me one last time and then breaks the hug.

She moves over and leans her back up against the wall. I follow suit and we're both staring at the neatly made bed on the other side of the room. Peyton's bed.

Scanning the room, and then pointing at the light blue bedspread, Cammie says, "So I guess the new girl is here, huh?" She sounds nervous as a bit of trepidation colors her words.

A look of shock passes across my face as I twist to face Cammie. "You mean, you knew? Why didn't you tell me? I nearly took her out yesterday when she got here. I thought she was trying to break in so I cracked her on the leg with that stupid bat Lia insists we keep up front." Upon my admission of assaulting our new roommate, Cammie claps a hand over her mouth to try and hide her shock. It doesn't work.

"You did what?" Her voice sounds banshee-like.

Folding my arms across my chest, I huff at Cammie as her shock morphs into laughter. "I'm not proud of it, but I didn't know we were getting a new roommate. Why didn't you guys tell me? Or, hell, why didn't the school tell me?"

Okay, I'm being a little pouty about it. It shouldn't be a big deal that I have to live with someone new, but honestly, everything in my life is such a shit storm of craziness right now; this whole new roomie situation feels like it's going to be the straw that breaks my back.

Smoothing a piece of hair out of my eyes, Cammie smiles warmly as she tries to bite back the last of her laughter. "Oh, Mel, we did tell you. I texted you a few times about it, but you never got back to me. The school sent us all letters, but maybe with everything that was going on over break, it got lost in the shuffle."

She's probably right. I've never been one to pay attention to regular mail anyway. I shrug my shoulders at her because, at this point, it doesn't matter — Peyton's here and Maddy's not. It's just that simple.

"It's okay." Shaking my head and sighing, I feel ashamed for how disconnected I've been from everyone for the last month. "Sorry about not texting you back. I guess I was just distracted while I was home." It's a lame cover up for what was really going on. But telling Cammie, or anyone for that matter, about spending my vacation drinking and partying and my all-too-dark secret of cheating on Bryan, well, that's just not an option.

Cammie's nosiness gets the best of her as she launches herself up from my bed and starts picking through the items sitting atop Peyton's desk. There's nothing all that telling on display — a few family pictures, some of her favorite books, a few simple cosmetics.

"She's cute," Cammie says as she hold a picture of Peyton and her parents in her hands. "Is she nice?" she asks as she replaces the frame.

"Yeah, especially considering I caused her physical harm on her first day here. She's really nice, actually." At this point, I decide that I should get out of bed and quit wasting my day. It's nearly two in the afternoon, anyway. Depression is not a mood that suits me and I'd like to kick this funk before Bryan gets back tonight. You can't pretend to be perfect when you're moping around all day.

Pulling my hair into a loose knot on top of my head, I'm startled when I hear another voice chime in from the door. "Hey, roomies." Peyton slides past Cammie and extends her small hand.

I know better than that. Cammie will not stand for formality. If you live with her, you will hug her. That's final. And wouldn't you know it, that's exactly what she does. Eyeing Peyton's hand as if it is disease infested or something, Cammie wraps her arms around Peyton's shoulders and hugs her instead.

Peyton is facing me and all I can do is laugh at the caught-off-guard look that's plastered to her face. I can't think of anything to say, so I just shrug my shoulders and try my best to convey an "I told you so" face.

When Cammie finally releases her, Peyton says,

"So you must be Cammie. Melanie told me all about your predilection to hugging. Well, she warned me actually, but I didn't believe her." Peyton's lips quirk up into a dorky smile and she rolls her eyes at me.

We may not have gotten off to the best start, but after a marathon *Sex and the City* session and lots of laughs, I feel pretty confident that Peyton and I will be more than good friends. She'll never replace Maddy, but, hell, no one ever will. Still, I think we're going to have a blast this semester.

"Can I get some help out here?" Lia's words carry into our room from the front door. She's pissed about something.

When we get to the door, I can tell why she's pissed. She's carrying in what looks like a month's worth of groceries all by herself. Narrowing her eyes on Cammie, she says rather sarcastically, "So much for grabbing Mel and coming down to help me, huh?"

"Here, let me." Peyton rushes over to Lia, who looks as if she's being swallowed alive by the reusable canvas shopping bags.

"Damn these are heavy," Peyton grunts as she hefts the weight of three bags in her right arm. "Who the hell loaded them up like this?"

Cue the death stare and snarky words, yet again. "That one over there," Lia tips her chin at Cammie, "likes to fill them to the brim because she hates making too many trips from the car."

Cammie moves to help Lia, and as she does, she holds her hands up in surrender. "I'm sorry, Lia. I didn't mean to leave you hanging." Cammie takes a few bags from Lia. At least now it looks like Lia isn't going to be squished under the weight of the bags.

"Who is she?" Lia asks, rather abruptly. I guess Lia didn't pay too much attention to who was helping her. She eyes Peyton up and down, and as if she can feel Lia's intense stare penetrating her, Peyton turns around from the counter and braces herself for yet another introduction.

"I'm Peyton, your new roommate." Her words are cheerful, but superficially so. I feel bad for her, having to defend herself just because she's the new girl. Lia's nice and all, but she can be a bit bitchy when she wants to be. Apparently, right now, Lia The Bitch is in charge.

Lia looks Peyton up and down once more and says, "Great, then you owe forty bucks for your share in the food." Cammie slaps Lia on the arm, but Lia barely flinches.

"Would you cut the shit, Lia? Be nice. Just because you're pissed at me, doesn't mean you get to take it out on her." Cammie's chiding voice snaps through the room.

Turning to Peyton, Cammie tries to clear the air. "You'll have to excuse my cousin here. Lia can be a bit of a diva when she wants to be." Lia moves in interrupt Cammie, but I chime in before she can say a word.

"Before you even try to defend yourself, close your mouth. You are most definitely a diva and you know it. Now be nice to Peyton and go take a nap or do something that will help bring back the real Lia. We know she's in there somewhere." That earns me an eye roll and a "whatever", but I feel the need to stand up for Peyton, especially after what I did to her.

Lia huffs out an exasperated sigh as she stalks out of the room. "Wow, is she always like that?" Peyton asks cautiously.

"Nah, she's usually great, actually. I'm sure once she naps and showers, she'll be back to normal." I try to explain Lia's antics, but she's such a firecracker that you never know what to expect. I look to Cammie for some kind of help in explaining what the freak just happened, but all she can do is shrug her shoulders.

Peyton begins rifling through her pocket. "Okay, then about the food. I only have a twenty, and I won't get paid from the tutoring center for another week or so." Before she can finish explaining, Cammie is cramming Peyton's money back in to her hands.

"Don't worry about it. This week is on me." Seriously, is there anyone out there nicer than Cammie? Well, if there is, I haven't met her yet.

After Lia calms her sorry-ass down, she comes

back out to the living room where Cammie, Peyton and I are eating lunch and getting to know each other a bit more. Laughing and joking around with the girls is so easy. It helps me forget all of the confusion over Bryan – whether we're even together or not, what I'll tell him, if anything, about that text, about my cheating. I don't have to be perfect when I'm with them. The easy-going nature of being back at school, well, at least just being here with my friends, helps me to forget my need for perfection. I try to forget my real life for a while, so when Cammie suggests that we go to Jack's tonight for a welcome back party, I agree all too willingly to go. Hopefully Lia will be in better spirits and we can all actually enjoy ourselves later.

After we've all showered and dolled ourselves up, we're ready to head to Jack's at around nine. I just have to do one last thing before we leave. Bryan is supposed to be back on campus today, but of course, he hasn't gotten in touch with me. I text him, because even though it hurts that he seems to be ignoring me, I have to check in with him.

Me: *Haven't heard from you in a few days and I just wanted to see if you made it back okay.*

I've come not to expect an immediate response, so when my phone buzzes in my hand, it takes me by surprise.

I'm really shocked to see that he's calling and not texting. My hands are shaking as I slide the icon at the bottom of the screen to answer the call. Now, after a month of barely saying more than a few words to me, he wants to talk.

I clear my throat before saying, "Hey, Bry." I hate that my voice is shaking with emotion.

My words are met with a deep, yet calming sigh. "God, I missed your voice, Melanie." Bryan's words cause me to melt. I sink down onto my bed and begin twirling my loosely curled hair in between my fingers.

"I missed yours too. I feel like we haven't talked in so long." I work hard to push back the emotion I feel rising in my voice. I'm one sad, excited, anxious and uncertain ball of nerves.

I hear him huff in exasperation before saying, "I know and I'm sorry for that." I hear him shuffle some things around and sigh yet again. He clears his throat. "We need to talk. But I don't want to do this over the phone. Can I come over?"

All I can think of is some snippy remark along the lines, "Sure. Come on over and rip my heart out. No biggie." But I bite back my sarcasm, because he doesn't deserve it.

Instead, I say, "Yeah. The girls are actually heading over to Jack's for the night." I don't know if being here alone with him is a good idea or not, but I guess it's better to just get everything out in the open sooner rather than later.

"Okay, great. I'll be there in about an hour." Bryan's words are suddenly chipper. Now I'm really confused. He's excited to break up with me? I've already convinced myself that's what his plan is. The bastard.

I push back those thoughts as I make my way out to the living room where Peyton, Lia and Cammie are all not-so-patiently waiting for me.

"Oh, well, look who's ready to join us!" Lia chirps playfully as she swallows down the remainder of her pre-party drink. I just roll my eyes at her. Everyone thinks it's just a cute personality quirk that I am always late. The truth is that I change more times than I can count before I find an outfit that I feel comfortable in. Not being comfortable in your own skin is a woman's worst nightmare. Having to showcase that skin to a bunch of horny college guys is about as scary as that nightmare when you show up to class naked.

But, yet again, rather than divulging that part of me, I just flip her off playfully and say, "You girls should know by now that I'm never on time for anything. Like ever." Cool and unaffected, my words tumble out of my mouth keeping the insecure version of Melanie well hidden from their sights.

Cammie stands from the couch and adjusts her black mini-skirt. Jack's going to lose it when he sees her - in a good way, of course. "Let's go, then!" Cammie smiles cheerfully as she walks to the door. I can tell she's anxious to get to the party.

Glancing over at Peyton, she looks a little unsure about everything. She definitely doesn't look like the other girls who attend these parties. By that I mean that she isn't dressed like she works on a street corner. Her black skinny jeans don't leave much to the imagination and neither does her curve-hugging top, but she doesn't look like a whore. Hell, who knows, maybe now that Reid isn't there, the number of whorish partygoers will decrease dramatically and Peyton will fit right in.

Just as they're all grabbing their bags and heading for the door, I say, "I'm actually going to stay in tonight." Lia shoots daggers and Peyton actually looks scared.

Leave it to Cammie to actually be concerned. "Is everything okay?"

Nodding my head to dismiss her misplaced worry, I say, "Yeah, everything is fine. Bryan just got back and he's coming over. We haven't seen each other all month so ..." I leave that hanging out there, because honestly, I don't know what we're going to do tonight.

My stomach roils at the mere thought of the fight that I know will ensue.

"Someone's getting laid!" Lia sings out from the door as she wraps her arm around Peyton's shoulder. "Don't worry. You can sleep in my room since Cammie's going to be staying with Jack." Peyton elbows Lia in the ribs and they share a laugh.

I guess while I was talking to Bryan they made up from earlier. That makes me feel a little better for not going with Peyton tonight. I know I don't owe her anything, but I feel like I'm letting her down by not going.

Pulling their heavy winter jackets out from the front closet, Lia laughs at the bat tucked into the corner. "Not such a bad idea after all, huh, Mel." She sticks her tongue out at me and laughs once more.

"Very funny!" I quip back at her.

Checking her phone, Cammie begins pushing everyone out the door. "Come on. Jack is downstairs waiting, and I don't know about you ladies, but it is freaking cold as fuck out there and I'm not walking." She hugs me on her way out and adds in a flirty tone, "Have a good night, Mel." Before she closes the door, she winks at me and I can't stifle the laughter that escapes my past my lips.

After a few seconds, the genuine laughs morph

into ones of nervousness as I look at my watch and realize Bryan should be here any minute.

That sickening rolling I felt in my stomach yesterday when Mom was here returns, but this time, I can't swallow it back. A nervous, panicking anxiety pulsates in my chest as I realize that I'm going to have to tell him about the cheating. A cold sweat breaks out on my brow and I race to the bathroom to empty the contents of my stomach into the toilet.

I feel marginally lighter, purged in some way. In a moment of clarity – or deception, depending on how you look at it - I've decided that I'm not going to say anything about his text. If I don't confront him about what he did, then I won't have to confess to him about what I did. And, if I can just hold on to this feeling until Bryan leaves, maybe I won't have to tell him, after all.

Chapter 6

Saturday, October 13, 2012

Past

"Omigod omigod omigod!" I'm flapping my arms in front of my like a rabid chicken — that is if chickens even get rabies.

"Will you just calm down, Mel. Everything will be fine," Maddy dismisses my little panic attack.

Sure! Everything will be fine! No big deal!

It's every day that you go to your hot boyfriend's soccer game and then go to a party with all of his friends, who you've never met before.

Oh and did I mention that his parents would be there too? Yeah, like that's going to calm my anxiety.

I know it shouldn't be a big deal. I finally caved, and since we started dating, I've gone to a few of his games. It's just that most of them have been during the week so I haven't had to deal with the after party. And meeting his parents, yeah, that is definitely what has me all sorts of screwy right now.

Maddy holds a turquoise, off-the-shoulder peasant top in front of her. "Wear this one. It will make your hair and your eyes pop."

Standing in front of the mirror and draping the pretty shirt this-way and that-way across my body, I scrunch my face and then toss it on the bed.

"Okay." She stretches out the word to emphasize her frustration with helping me get ready. "What about this purple one? This one is my favorite."

Pulling the purple shirt over my head, I play with the hem to make sure that it sits in just the right spot – hiding the curve of my waist, while still flattering the rest of my shape. I flop down onto my bed as I slide my black ballet flats on my feet. Sliding one leg under my body, I turn toward Maddy and sigh rather dramatically.

"What if they hate me? I mean, I've never done this – met a guy's parents before. What if I make an ass out of myself?" My shaking voice reflects my nervousness.

"Well, then," Maddy says as she pulls me up from the bed, and hands me my sunglasses and black bomber jacket, "at least you'll look like a pretty ass." She laughs and I can't help but chuckle with her.

"But seriously, Mel. You've been with Bryan for

what, like a month now. He's obviously into you, otherwise you wouldn't be meeting his parents at all. I'm sure they'll like you." Maddy's words boost my confidence a little.

Standing in front of the mirror, I take stock of the girl reflected back to me. Usually I'm the one trying to convince Maddy to play Barbie. But today, my hands were shaking with such extreme anxiety that I couldn't even do my own make-up. Silently nodding my approval, I have to say that Maddy didn't do such a bad job. My hair looks wildly tame – a perfect combination of auburn curls, softly brushed and smoothed so I don't look like Annie. Normally, I go for soft pink or peach on my eyes, but Maddy opts for a pale-green eye shadow and an eggplant liner, which, even though it's something I never would have chosen, really do highlight my soft blue eyes.

Adjusting the hem of my deep-purple shirt once more, and skimming my hands down the top of my dark-wash jeans, I ask "Are you sure this looks okay?"

Holding my shoulders tightly in her hands and squeezing gently, she says, "Melanie, you look beautiful. But, more importantly, you *are* beautiful. Bryan is not going to care what clothes you wear. Hell, I've seen the way he looks at you. He'd rather you weren't wearing any clothes at all." Maddy giggles suggestively as she wiggles her eyebrows at me.

"Maddy!" I gasp and slap her playfully on the arm. "You really think that?" I add in a more curious tone.

"Think what, Mel?"

Instinctively, I reach for a strand of hair and twirl it around my finger. It's a nervous habit. "Do you really think he thinks I'm pretty, I mean?" My voice is suddenly shy and timid.

"Of course I do, Melanie." Her soft green eyes are wide, but serious. Smiling brightly at me, she adds, "And I also think that he likes you because you're funny and smart and kind and fun to be around. Now go to his game and have some fun. Are you sure you don't want me to go with you?"

"I would love for you to go, but since it's some kind of special Parent's Weekend or something like that, he was only given two tickets. He actually had to bum one off of his teammate to get me in." I shrug my shoulders trying to make it seem like no big deal that Maddy can't go with me, but the reality is that I wish I had some kind of support. But instead, I reassure Maddy. "I'll be okay. Like you said, they'll love me." I pucker my lips playfully and pop my hip in some kind of fashionista meets drag queen stance.

"Oh my God! Whatever you do, don't do that. Like ever again!" Maddy laughs hysterically at my antics before pulling me into a tight hug. "But seriously, Mel. You'll be great. Just be yourself. I mean, you're *my* favorite person, after all." She smiles and winks at me and it's impossible not to smile back at my best friend.

As I walk down the hallway, I hear Maddy say, "Have fun!" in a rather cheery, sing-song voice.

Uh huh, fun. Sure. Meeting my boyfriend's parents for the first time while he's all hot and sweaty playing in his final soccer game – sure, that sounds like a ton of fun.

The dorm is not all that far from the soccer field. But everything in Ithaca is uphill. You know that old saying about "when I was a kid, I walked to school uphill both ways?" Well, I'm pretty sure that originated in Ithaca.

As I approach the entrance, I hand the ticket collector my ticket and walk through the gate. Bryan told me to sit in section ten, and that his mom would be wearing his jersey with the number 17 on the front. While part of my brain actually considers sitting anywhere *but* section ten, the other part tells me to just put on my big-girl panties and do the right thing.

Big-girl panties, here we come!

It doesn't take me long to spot Bryan's parents. They're in the first row of the section, which is sparsely filled at this point. Taking a deep breath, I walk toward them and hope for the best. When I get to the end of the metal bleachers, Bryan's mom stands and extends her hand to mine.

"You must be Melanie." Her huge smile is so genuine that I instinctively think of my own mom and how much I miss her. I should definitely call her.

"Hi, Mrs. Mahoney. It's so nice to finally meet you." Shaking her hand, I smile happily and she returns the look. Unfortunately, I don't get the same reception from Mr. Mahoney.

He's all too busy to stop tapping away at his BlackBerry lost in what must be an important message. When Mrs. Mahoney nudges his arm, he looks up from his phone, assesses me and then returns to whatever he was just typing.

"You'll have to excuse him, Melanie. Dan has been working a huge business deal these last few months and," she cups her hand around the corner of her mouth as if doing so will keep him from hearing what she's saying, "well, he's just been a bit distracted, that's all."

"I am not distracted, Jane." Mr. Mahoney smiles, but there's something off-putting in his eyes. Whatever it is, he recovers quickly from it, and extends his hand in front of him. "It's a pleasure to meet you, Melanie." His lips quirk up into what I can only describe as an odd smile toward Mrs. Mahoney.

Okay, I'm not sure what to make of him, but it's

not like I can just come out and ask Bryan, "So, what's up with your dad?"

Besides, it's not like I have much experience with dads in the first place. Maybe they're all just that weird.

Ignoring the weird vibe I'm getting from him, I choose to focus on the soft kindness twinkling in Mrs. Mahoney's eyes. Setting my bag down next to my feet at the end of the aisle, I extend my hand to him, and say "It's more than a pleasure to finally meet both of you, Mr. and Mrs. Mahoney." I know I sound way too formal. But there's something in the way that initial introduction went down that just rubbed me the wrong way.

As if I wasn't nervous already.

"Oh, please, Melanie. None of that 'Mr. and Mrs.' call us Dan and Jane." She sits in her seat and pats the bench to her side. I slide in next to her and cross my legs to keep them from bouncing wildly in nervousness.

The rest of the game passes in casual conversation. Jane asks me the standard stuff: What's my major? Where do I live? What are my parents like?

My answers are standard as well. I'm still undecided and I live in the dorms. There isn't much to tell. And, rather than get into that my dad is dead and that my mom never remarried and how that makes me feel guilty as hell, I just tell her that "my parents are great." I know I can't be sure about that as far as my dad is concerned, but if the memory that my mom holds of him is any indication, "great" is actually selling him short.

Dan doesn't say much of anything throughout the game. Occasionally, he looks up from his phone to watch his son get pummeled into the ground. He never happens to see a hard-won goal, or brain-jarring head-butt.

By the end of the game, my throat is sore from the constant cheering and my hands are chapped from the non-stop clapping. Jane has been right alongside me the entire time. We've had a lot of fun talking and cheering for Bryan. I just wish I knew what the hell was up with his dad. I guess whatever business deal he's working on must be really important because he even had to leave the stands a few times to take a few calls. Jane doesn't seem to mind though, so I let it go.

Watching Bryan score the winning goal is the shining moment of the day. As he turns the corner of the field, he expectantly looks up to the bleachers. I only hope that pride I feel for him shines through on my face. I'm in awe of his talents. Besides, watching his muscles strain under the clingy soccer jersey hasn't been all too hard on my eyes for the last ninety minutes.

Nope. Not bad at all!

After the game is over, there's a brief trophy presentation and the team lines up for their last picture. Even though Ithaca is only a Division III school for sports, the athletic competition is still fierce. So is the bond that's created between teammates. All of the guys are smiling and clapping each other on the back – congratulating everyone on a great season.

All of the parents stand in a line, snapping their own photos as well. As usual, I stand in the background and try to go unnoticed.

When the crowd clears, I make my way over to Bryan and his parents. But, rather than cheery smiles and happy conversation, I walk into a tension-laden atmosphere filled with jilted words.

"Fine. Leave then." Bryan's curt words are laced with hurt.

"Oh, honey. We don't *want* to leave. It's just that your father ..." Jane's voice is tenderly apologetic. I can tell that she really is sorry that she can't stay for rest of the weekend.

Dan stalks back over to Bryan and Jane as he slides his phone back into the front pocket of his khaki pants. "Sorry, son. But I have to get back. This can't wait until Monday." Dan may be saying that he's sorry, but his face conveys anything but an apology.

"Let's go now, Jane. I was able to move the flight, but we have to be at the airport in an hour." Dan is pulling Jane off the field as Bryan and I stumble behind them.

"What happened, Bryan? I thought they were staying."

"Yeah, well, I guess other things are more important," he mutters as we approach his parents' car. When I lace my fingers with his, I can feel the tension radiating off his body. He squeezes my hand in return and looks down at me with sadness in his eyes.

When we get to the car, Bryan releases my hand and gently brushes his lips against my temple. Opening the door for his mother, Bryan helps her into the car. The sweet kiss that he plants on her cheek suggests that he's not mad at her. The glaring look he shoots at his father across the roof suggests that he's more than angry with him. His father says nothing and just slides in to his seat.

Leaning into the window, Bryan tells his mom, "Be sure to call me when you land. I'll talk to you later, I guess. Tell Emmie I love her and I'll talk to her soon."

Smiling brightly up at her son, of whom I know she is so proud, Jane says, "I will, Bryan. Love you. You played great today. We'll celebrate in a few weeks when you're home, okay? I know Emmie would love to be there too."

"Sure, Mom. That sounds good. I'll talk to you

later." He's trying to make his words seem cheerful, to make it sound like he's not affected by their departure, but I know different. Bryan has been so excited to have his parents finally come here for a visit. Since he lives down in North Carolina, they don't often get the chance to fly to upstate New York for a random weekend to visit their son. He won't admit it, but I know he's upset that they're leaving.

Bryan's parents pull out of the small parking lot next to the soccer field, and when they're nothing but a small dot in the distance, I reach down and lace my fingers with his. "I'm sorry, Babe. I know you were looking forward to them being here."

He pulls our joined hands up to his lips and kisses my knuckles sweetly. "Ehh, it's okay." He's trying to play it cool, but I can see through his little act. I'm not going to push it, though. He deserves to celebrate and enjoy the last day of his successful soccer career.

"Come on. We'll go have dinner at Bella's and you can chew my ear off about soccer all night." I look up at him with my big, blue eyes and hope that his mood shifts. "You know Bella would love to hear how your game went." At the mention of Bella's name, Bryan's face softens and he smiles at me.

"Sure. Sounds good." A soft kiss to my lips and we're walking off to the dorms and hopefully into a good night.

To say that Bella is excited to see us again is an understatement. She practically hangs on every word as Bryan tells her about his game and the end of his soccer career. His parents may not be here to celebrate with him, but Bella has more than made up for that.

After she seats us at a quiet table in the corner, she insists that she'll bring us something special, so she doesn't even give us the menus. As she gently places her hand on his shoulder, she says to Bryan, "It's so nice to see you here for more than computer repair." Her warm face lights up with appreciation as she walks away to the kitchen.

"So what do you think she'll bring us this time?" It's a pointless question, really. We've been here a few times in the month we've been dating and every time it's something different, something not on the menu, something just for us.

"Whatever it is, she better bring it out soon. I'm starving," he says before he bites off a huge chunk of bread.

"Yeah, well you ran your ass off during that game." I smile and then, pitching my voice a bit lower, add, "It's a mighty fine ass too." His eyes widen a little at my somewhat forward statement.

"You've got quite a fine ass too, Melanie," he says without missing a beat.

Rather than roll my eyes at his compliment, I opt for playfulness. "Yeah, I know, right? This guy I've been seeing keeps telling me that." I deadpan, but rather than lightening the mood, what was supposed to be a playful quip, forces Bryan's look to harden. The atmosphere suddenly feels chilly, his stare cold and hard.

"You're seeing someone else?" His disbelieving and hurt voice makes me instantly regret my words. "I thought …" The rest of his words trail off and he reaches for his water.

"Bryan, I was just kidding. I was playing around. You know, like we usually do. I didn't mean anything by it." I wish I could take my words back, swallow them down along with the embarrassment and stupidity I'm feeling.

The moments stretch out long and awkwardly before he can even look at me again. When his warm brown eyes meet my blue ones, it's like he's baring his soul. "I just thought that … well, I mean … We've been dating for a while and I guess I just thought that you were only seeing me."

"Oh my God, Bryan. Of course I'm only seeing you. There's no one else. Is there anyone else for you?" I hadn't even thought of that. What if he is seeing someone? What if it's Courtney? No matter how many times I try to keep my insecurities at bay, they always seem to resurface.

Reaching for my hand across the table, he squeezes tenderly as he says, "Look, I know we haven't been together all that long, but I don't want to see anyone else besides you. We may not have gotten off to the easiest of starts, but I really, really like you, and just the thought of you being with someone else … well, it bothers me, a lot."

Talk about turning the tables. I now realize how he feels every time I mention him wanting Courtney over me. I make a silent promise to myself to bury down my feelings where she is concerned. I don't like how this feels so I can imagine it hurts him just as much.

I squeeze his hand in return, wanting so badly to take back my joke. "It was a stupid thing to say, Bryan. I really didn't mean anything by it. Believe me. You have nothing to worry about. I'm all yours." With pleading eyes and a face contorted in concern, I hope that my soft apology is enough to erase my words.

"Good. Because I really don't want to share," he adds as he pops another bite of bread into his mouth. If I'm not mistaken, there's a hint of seduction in the way he licks the drop of olive oil from the corner of his mouth.

I don't want to ruin the evening any more than I already have, so rather than say something about Courtney – about worrying that she's going to come and take him away from me – I smile brightly, take a bite of bread, and say, "Good. So since we've got the 'no sharing' thing out of the way, why don't you tell me more about that goal you scored, which was amazing by the way."

When his face lights with pride at his accomplishment, I feel like the crisis has been averted. Who knew he would be so possessive. I mean honestly, I've got him, why on Earth would I look anywhere else.

As he's giving me the play-by-play run down of the final minutes of the game, Bella brings us over two huge plates of her world-famous lasagna. "Enjoy," she says before she walks away.

I thought it was lasagna, but I was wrong. It is heaven - pure heaven on a plate covered in cheese and sauce and goodness. Bryan must agree because he's done with more than half of his in no time flat.

"So, who's Emmie?" I ask around a forkful of sauce-covered yumminess. Bryan and his mom mentioned the name earlier and it wasn't one that I had heard before. Maybe it's his dog or something like that.

Bryan stiffens slightly and wipes his mouth. Suddenly, he looks uncomfortable, and for the second time tonight, I feel like I've stepped on a landmine.

"Emmie's my sister," he says quickly, but I can't help but wonder why his body language changed when I mentioned her name.

"Oh, that's right. I remember you telling me." When we came here for the first time, he told me he had a sister but then never brought her up again. "How come you never talk about her though?" My curiosity is piqued now. The only reason I can think of for him not talking about her is that they don't get along.

"It's complicated." He's being short and dismissive – so uncharacteristically Bryan.

I laugh a little because it's the only reaction I can come up with. "What do you mean 'complicated'? She's your sister."

He settles back in his chair and sighs. Seemingly sorting through his thoughts to find the right words, I wonder "how difficult can this really be?"

Bryan is lost in some kind of internal debate. Trying to calm whatever fears he apparently has, I say, "Bryan, talk to me. Please."

It's only his sister. It's not like he's confessing some kind of secret human-trafficking operation where he's the ringleader. Oh no, what if he runs a puppy mill or something horrible like that?

Geez, at least I hope not.

He's still not talking, so I try to back track a little. Starting with something small, I ask, "How old is she?"

Baby steps. Let's see if he can do baby steps.

Leaning forward on his elbows once again, he rests is chin on his folded hands. "She's twelve," he says rather quickly, but his eyes are still on mine.

"Does she play soccer too?" Seems like a logical question. What little sister doesn't idolize her super-star brother?

"No." His dismissiveness has changed to sadness. I see it in his eyes and hear it in his voice. I reach for his hand once again because he seems more at ease when there's that physical connection between us. It's been there from the start, and ever since I came around and let it progress, he always seems more at ease, more himself, when we're touching.

"What is it, Bryan? Whatever it is, you can talk to me. I only ask because I want to know you better. But, for whatever reason, if you don't want to share, I won't push you." I only hope he can hear the concern in my voice. I'm really not trying to pry; I just want him to open up.

At my softly spoken words, he relaxes and starts talking. "You're not pushing me, Melanie. I guess I'm just a little protective, that's all."

That last piece of information doesn't surprise me at all. It's one of the things I love about him.

Do I love him?

No. It's too soon.

At least I *think* it's too soon. I've never been *here* before. Maybe it is love.

Refocusing my attention back to Bryan, I say, "Well, then she's very lucky to have such an amazing big brother." I pause briefly to gently squeeze his hand once more as I wait for his response. "I don't have any siblings so I'd love to learn about yours. Tell me more about her, please."

His lips pull up at the corners and I catch a glimpse of his white teeth through his small smile. He obviously adores her, and suddenly, I am dying to know everything about this little girl who clearly has a very special spot in his heart.

"Her name is Emerson, but we call her Emmie. She's the happiest little girl I've ever known." His face is glowing with love for his little sister. It's cute, really. I've always wanted a sibling. Even though I'll always consider Maddy my sister, there's a part of me that really missed having someone else around when I was younger.

"So why didn't she come with your parents? Did she have an event for school or something like that and couldn't make the flight? I would have loved to meet her." Come to think of it, the handful of times I've been in his dorm, I didn't see a picture of her anywhere. Do guys even put up pictures of their family? Either way, it's weird that he obviously loves her very much, but there isn't a trace of her anywhere in his daily life. I try not to be upset that he hasn't said anything about her to me so far. I mean, we've only been together for a month so it's not like we know every single little detail about each other. Distracted by my own thoughts, I forget that I've even asked him a question. His words bring my attention, quite abruptly, back to the conversation.

"She has Downs Syndrome," he blurts out and I'm a bit surprised. Not that she has Downs, but because his words are very abrupt and out of the blue. But suddenly, I know why he's so protective, why he doesn't talk about her much. Though, judging by the way his eyes are shining and his voice is wobbling, I can tell that his not talking about her isn't out of shame. It's out of his need to keep her protected.

My brows furrow together in concern and disbelief. "Why do you think that will matter to me? There's no need to keep me from knowing that." I only hope that my words help him understand how I feel. Even if she wasn't his sister, she's just a little girl, but I know all too well, having been the 'heavy kid' growing up, just how hurtful kids can be.

"*She* cared," Bryan's barely whispered words break though my painful memories of being made fun of when I was younger.

"Who?"

He sighs and scrubs his hand over his face. "Courtney cared."

I feel like I've just been punched in the gut. I thought there was no way I could hate her even more than I already do, but I was definitely wrong.

"What ... I mean ... I don't get it. What did she say?" I know I sound like an idiot, but I can't wrap my head around how she could have made an issue about this.

Are people really that shallow?

The waitress chooses this moment to walk over and hand us our bill, essentially halting the conversation. And then just as soon as the waitress walks away, Bella comes to our table.

Ripping the bill in half, she says, "No paying tonight. It's a special night." She winks over at me on that last line and I adore her even more than I already did. Bryan needed some recognition tonight and I'm glad she, and hopefully I, was able to give it to him. "Besides," she adds almost shyly, "I might need you to come back this week. The webpage thingy that you set up for me is, ummm, how do you say ..."

Bryan chuckles at her silliness and finishes her sentence. "Is it crashing, Bella?"

"Yeah, that's it. Crashing. Can you come by this week to fix it?" she asks hopefully.

Bryan stands from his chair, kisses her on the

cheek and says, "Sure thing. I'll be back on Monday." Extending his hand to me, he helps me out of my chair and wraps his arm around my shoulder.

Bella walks us to the door and tells us to have a good night. When we get outside, the cool autumn air breezes around us and a shiver creeps across my skin. Draping his jacket over my shoulders, Bryan says, "I'll tell you all about Emmie and Courtney on the way to the party, okay?"

I nod, not because I have nothing to say, but because I have so much to say that I don't want to scare him away.

After he closes my door, I watch him walk to his side and slide into his seat. Playing around with the knobs on the heater and the radio, I can tell that he's just avoiding the conversation. So I place my hand on top of his, and cup his cheek with my other hand. I don't say anything, but when I lean forward and skim my lips across his, he knows what I'm trying to say.

Grazing his knuckles across my cheek, he looks into my eyes so deeply that I think he might see straight through me.

Part of me knows that he already does.

When his lips collide with mine, well, I think we might just melt together as one. I'm in a complete state of bliss. His hand in my hair, his lips tentatively skimming mine at first, his tongue dancing wildly in my mouth – it all makes my pulse skitter, my heart race, my body tingle. It's a kiss filled with need, and dare I say, love.

It's too soon for that. So, no, I don't say it, but I know that my kiss conveys it. His sure as hell does.

Breathless and wide-eyed, we pull away from each other. He looks like I feel, and it's nice to know that I have the same effect on him that he has on me. But, getting me all hot and bothered isn't going to get him out of having to talk.

After another minute of staring at me blankly, I prompt him to finally start talking. "You can kiss me like that again, but you're still going to have to talk. So why don't you talk now and we'll kiss all you want later." I wink and arch a playful eyebrow at him to which his only response is a loud chuckle. At least, he seems a bit more at ease now that he's kissed the life out of me.

Lord knows if we didn't have somewhere to be, there would have been a lot more than kissing going on!

Settling back in his seat, he turns down the radio and stares out into the dark evening sky spreading before us. "Courtney and I were together last year for a few months. I liked her enough to stay with her, but it wasn't love. Definitely not love. I didn't think she was horrible or anything, so I stayed with her to see how things would turn out," he huffs sarcastically at that thought. I move closer to him, well, as close as my seat will allow me, and hold his hand. He starts running his thumb over my knuckles as he continues talking.

He rolls his eyes. "I was so fucking wrong though. Courtney saw a picture of Emmie in my room and well, let's just say, her reaction showed her true colors. She tried to cover it up, but her face was all twisted in, what I call, her 'gross' face. Courtney never said anything to me about it, but I overheard her at some party trashing Emmie to her friend Tori, who is just as evil as Courtney by the way." He takes a deep breath and resumes tracing his fingers over my knuckles. When he manages to calm down, I can see his face relax and his eyes soften.

The heat in the car is overwhelming, suddenly. I feel like I can't breathe. Memories flood my brain of being taunted on the playground, of hearing the mean words follow me everywhere I went. I don't even know Emmie, but my heart hurts for her. I wish I could hug her and tell her the world isn't as mean as it seems.

But, then I would be lying.

"What did Courtney say, exactly?" I know it doesn't really matter – mean is mean – the actual words are inconsequential.

He lets a huff slide past his lips as he swipes his hand across his face. "She called Emmie a retard. And she wondered why my family even kept her in the first place. And Tori, her evil sidekick, was standing there laughing with her. Hearing Courtney talk about my little sister like she was some kind of lame, old dog that needed to be put to sleep helped me really see her for who she was. An evil, cruel-hearted bitch."

My chest constricts at what it must have been like for Bryan to hear those things about Emmie. In an instant, my insecurities about Bryan wanting Courtney over me are gone. Catching this glimpse of the person she truly is solidifies Bryan's words that he doesn't want her, ever again.

"When I confronted her about it, she tried to play it off like she was drunk and I was overreacting. I broke up with her on the spot. I'm pretty sure I humiliated her, but I didn't give a shit. I still don't give a shit. I wish she would get it through her fucking head that I don't ever want to be with her again, but she just won't leave me alone." He runs his hand through his hair in frustration and a few pieces slide in front of his warm, brown eyes.

Swiping the stray locks out his eyes, I let my fingers travel along his scruffy jawline. "Bryan, I am so sorry you heard those things. You know I would never …" His lips silence me.

"Of course I know you would never say those things, that you would never feel those things. It's one of the things I lo … That make me realize how special you are." His last words are rushed and he clears his throat.

Was he just about to say what I think he was just about to say?

"I guess I was just nervous letting you know about Emmie. It's stupid, I know, but I was still worried. And, like I said, I'm protective of her." His chest puffs with pride that he takes care of Emmie, but then deflates slightly when he says, "I'm sorry I didn't tell you about her sooner." His thumb is still tracing patterns over the back of my hand.

"So why didn't she come today?" I gently squeeze his hand reassuringly.

"She can't fly. I mean, she goes into this sensory overload state and she gets all freaked out. When I'm here, she uses FaceTime and that's really the only way I can see her. She loves being on the computer. It's like a coping mechanism for her." And with those words it's like I'm seeing him in an entirely new light – a light that makes me love him even more.

I might be able to admit it to myself, but I'm not ready to say it to him.

Not yet.

"Is that why you're majoring in Computer Science?" I ask softly, amazed by the poignancy of his choice.

He rubs his stubble-covered face. "Yeah, I mean,

when I was in high school, I was able to rig a few things for her, and with the help of her occupational therapist and my computer stuff, she made some real progress. She was happy." The bright smile that splits his face is a clear indication of how much he loves helping her.

The pieces are all falling into place now. "So that's why you help Bella. It has nothing to with O'Neill, does it?" I feel like some detective on CSI who has just solved a crime or something.

"Yes." He gives me a quick peck on the lips and smirks at me. "I actually did meet Bella and Gus through Professor O'Neill, but when I saw how frustrated they were, it reminded me of teaching Emmie how to use a computer. They shouldn't be denied something that can help them just because they don't understand it initially. So, I wanted to help them learn, and bring them up to speed with this century. Is that such a bad thing?" He asks playfully as one side of his mouth pulls up into the sexiest smirk I have ever seen.

I repay him the quick peck. "Nope, not at all. In fact, I think it's a pretty great thing." It's actually amazing, and kind, and sweet, and well, you get the idea. It makes me feel shallow and ashamed that I ever thought Bryan would only be interested in me, or anyone for that matter, for their looks alone. In my very limited experience with guys, I never thought to encounter someone with so much depth and passion. I never thought I would be this lucky.

Ready to move on from the rather heavy conversation, Bryan lets out a deep breath and turns to me once again. "Okay, so are you ready to go to this party now? Because after that, I could use a drink!"

"Absolutely. Let's go have some fun." I smile cheerfully at him. When he first mentioned going to this party, my thoughts immediately fell on Courtney. Will she be there? What will she say? How will she try to make me feel uncomfortable? What will she do to try and get Bryan back?

But after Bryan sharing this obviously important part of his life, I know, beyond any reasonable doubt, that, even if she is there, there is nothing she can say or do to get between us anymore.

I just won't let it happen. And now I know for sure that he won't either.

Walking through the door at Liam's house, I'm overwhelmed by the distinct stench of vomit. When I turn to my right and see some guy wearing a soccer jersey throwing up into a shoe, I realize where the odor is coming from. The shoe isn't big enough, or maybe it's that he's throwing up too much, but when the puke actually spurts out of the sides of the shoe and splats to the floor, I gag.

"You okay?" Bryan asks as concern pervades his face. He rubs slow circles on my back and it's calming to feel his touch.

"Yeah, sure. I think I'll pass on the drinking though." I don't think my stomach can take much after that little show.

And then, as if she can sense that he's walked into the house, Courtney is strutting toward us. "Hey, baby," she coos as she reaches her hot-pink fingertips out to touch Bryan's chest.

Does the bitch not see me standing right here? I know she does; she just doesn't care.

I wish I had a little spray bottle so I could squirt her and yell "Down." But, that seems immature even for me.

So instead of paying her any attention, I stretch up on my toes and whisper into Bryan's ear, "I think my suite is empty for the night. Wanna get out of here?" Before moving away from his ear, I trace the shell of it with my tongue and stop to nibble on the lobe a move very similar to what Courtney did to him that day he came chasing me down.

He drops his arm from my shoulders and grips my waist, pulling me close to his body. Gently pressing his lips to the top of my head, he says into my hair, "Absofuckinglutely. Let's go."

And with that, we walk out the door and head back to my room for our own little party.

By the time we reach the door to my suite, the sexual tension that has been between us since we first met is at a boiling point. We've been together a month, and we've done *stuff* but not *it.* But now, tonight, I want him and I'm pretty certain that he wants me. When I pull my key out of my bag and start unlocking the door, Bryan places his hands on either side of my head and leans into my body from behind.

Yep, he wants me.

Unless that's something else pressing into my back and I highly doubt there's a banana in his pocket.

In a sudden movement, his hands are gone from the door. One is in my hair and the other is snaking its way around my waist, pulling me even closer to him. Sweeping my hair to the side, he runs his nose up the length of my neck and stops at my pulse point, right behind my ear. When his tongue darts out to taste the skin there, my knees buckle and my insides tighten. He must feel my legs tremble because he pulls me closer to his body and laughs softly in my ear.

Kissing the same spot he's just licked, he whispers against my skin, "Did you like that, Melanie?"

I can't form words. So instead of speaking, I place my arm around his at my waist and tangle the other up into his silky hair. Forcing his lips down to the same spot that he just kissed, all I can muster is, "Hmmmm."

Even though it's not all that specific, he understands my request and kisses me once more. "I can do a lot more than kiss your neck. You just have to open that door." I feel his smile against my skin and it's like he's extending a challenge.

And oh what a delicious challenge it is. While he nips and kisses my neck, I fumble with the key and actually drop it to the ground. When I move to pick it up, he wraps his arm in a steel band around my waist once again, essentially telling me to stay in place.

When he moves from behind me, my body feels cold – bereft in the absence of his heat. It's not cold for long though. After snatching the key up from the ground, he grazes the length of my legs with his long fingers. When he arrives at the curve of my ass, he squeezes my flesh and I feel a twinge of embarrassment. I hate my ass. He apparently doesn't, though.

He slides one hand into a back pocket of my jeans and reaches in front of me with the other. Key in hand, he unlocks the door. The anxiety that I thought I would feel, evaporates when I turn around into the warm circle of his arms.

Squeezing him tightly, I rest my cheek against his solid chest and inhale the spicy scent of his cologne. His hand moves into my hair and he pulls gently, forcing my head up and our eyes to meet.

"You know we don't have to do anything. We've talked about this. When you're ready …" My lips get in the way of his words. Slowly, seductively, passionately, I let my tongue dance in his mouth. When I pull back from the kiss, I meet his eyes, which are now hooded and lust-filled.

"I know you said you would wait. And you have. I'm ready … unless you don't …" I don't want to say it, but that shy, self-hating version of myself is screaming, *He doesn't want you.*

That voice is put out of her misery when Bryan's lips press oh-so-gently up against mine. Speaking against my lips, he says, "No. I want you." His hand cups my ass again and he pulls my hips up to meet his. His desire is clearly evident once again and I decide to just let *this* happen.

Gone is shy and insecure Melanie – at least for now. Here, with Bryan, I want to be worthy of his desire. I want to be everything that he deserves – sweet, hot, passionate … loving.

Not wanting to break the physical contact of our

interlaced fingers or the searing stare of our glued-together eyes, I pull him down the short hallway to my room, walking backwards.

I reach behind me for the knob and twist. Stepping over the threshold makes my heart crash into the wall of my chest. My pulse accelerates and my breath hitches in my throat. Anxiety and nervousness morph into desire. And despite my deep-seeded insecurities, I know that I see that same desire etched into Bryan's face.

He leans his face into the crook of my neck and kisses the part of my collarbone that's exposed from behind the neckline of my shirt. Hot, wet lips trace the path of exposed flesh until he arrives at my shoulder. Gently nipping at my skin, and then kissing his little bite, Bryan says, "You have the most beautiful skin. I want to taste all of it."

Emboldened by his seductive words, I step back from him and reach for the hem of my shirt. I pull it up over my head and toss is to the floor. Even though I'm standing before him in my jeans and black lace bra, I feel naked and exposed. Crazy thoughts fly through my head, but I try my best to silence them. Bryan's widened eyes fix on my breasts and suddenly I don't feel so shy.

I feel beautiful.

Wanted.

Desired.

Sexy.

I reach for the hem of his shirt and he pulls it up over his head. His abs ripple under the movement. I have to touch him. When my fingers trace tentatively across his muscled stomach, I feel him shudder and hear a breath hiss from between his lips. With steadier fingers than those that tugged at his shirt, I pull on the button of his jeans and pop it open. He repays the favor and takes it a step further by pushing my jeans down over my hips.

Standing before him in nothing but my bra and panties is exhilarating. The look in his eyes tells me that I have nothing to worry about. The bulge in his unbuttoned jeans tells me that he wants me. The pulse beating visibly in his neck tells me that he's about to lose control.

He steps closer to me, but doesn't stop when his chest presses up against mine. Instead, he keeps walking and pushes me with him until my butt collides with my bed. I stare up into his eyes and get lost there for a minute. Usually, they're the color of liquid chocolate – dark and molten. But right now, I'm seeing amber flecks and golden shimmers.

Bryan effortlessly lifts me up onto the bed, and for the first time in my life, I feel dainty and feminine. Wrapped up in his muscled body, I feel tiny and pretty.

He slides my body against his and lowers me onto my back.

With one hand supporting his weight, he unhooks the front clasp of my bra and pulls the straps down my shoulders. Dropping the bra rather unceremoniously to the floor, he stares at my breasts with hunger in his eyes.

Licking his lips, he says, "My God, Melanie. Do you realize how perfect you are? You are so damned beautiful." I shake my head, to both deny his statement and to avoid having to look into his eyes. He cups my cheek softly, and turns my head back to him. He doesn't use words to convince me of his recent declaration. His lips do all of the work.

They move from my lips to my neck to my shoulder to the soft curve of the tops of my breasts. He rolls to my side and supports his weight on his bent arm. Using his other hand, he cups my breast and kneads it tenderly. When his thumb strums across my hardened nipple, a groan eases out of my mouth. He does it again, but this time, instead of just passing over it, he squeezes the pink tip gently and pulls slightly. My hips roll seeking some kind of release. "Ahhh, Bryan."

His lips are buried into my neck. "More?" he asks and I just nod in return. I don't want to think about what I should say. I just want to feel.

Traveling the same path they did earlier, his lips

descend past the top of my breast. When he softly kisses one nipple while rolling the other between his fingers, my hips gyrate wildly and my insides pulse with desire for more.

Bryan senses that *more* is exactly what I want, so he licks and sucks at my breast like his life depends on it. Ravenously, he moves over to the neglected breast and pays it the same attention. I'm not sure who is more satisfied by the action.

My fingers tangle into his brown hair as it tickles my chest. My flesh prickles and my nipples pucker even more. His kisses follow a path down my body and his tongue dips into my belly button. In the month or so that we've been together, we haven't done much more than making out and groping at each other above our clothes. This is the farthest we've gone and he must sense that we're on some kind of precipice - some kind of point of no return.

His lips stop at the top of my panties and he looks up at me through his dark lashes. I nod, giving him the answer to his unasked question, and he hooks his thumbs into the sides of my panties. My legs shake and my insides quiver as he pulls the black lace over my hips and down my legs.

I'm naked. Fully bared to him as he kneels in between my spread legs, forces a heated blush to race across my body. Bryan is staring down at me like he doesn't know where to start, doesn't know what to do. I would give anything to know what's going on in his head, but he doesn't say anything. Instead of talking, he runs his fingers up from my toes, to my calves, across my thighs and stops just inches from my sex. He's unsure so I arch my back and force my hips up into his touch.

"Please, Bryan. I'm ready. I want you. I want this. Please," I'm begging, but feeling his hands roam all over my body reduces me to a needy, wanton creature.

He wastes no time with words or explanations. When his fingers trace delicately over my folds, I feel the pressure begin to build inside of me. It's delicious and unfamiliar. I want relief from it, but I never want it to end.

With my eyes shut and my head rolling from side-to-side, I'm lost to the pleasure of his touch. When he gently slides a finger inside of me, my back arches and my nipples pebble. "You're so wet, Melanie. But I want to take this slow, so relax." On his last word, he reaches up to tweak my nipple with his other hand, causing another hot gush of wetness to coat his finger.

When he slides another finger deep inside of me, my insides burn at the stretching feeling. The burn quickly vanishes though as he works his fingers from side-to-side, massaging me, preparing me. That last thought causes my insides to flutter and clench.

"You're close, Melanie," he tells me.

"Yes … Bryan … Yes … please." My words are breathless and match the pattern of his fingers plunging in and out of me.

When he starts kissing the soft flesh of my inner thighs, I know where he's headed. I know what he's going to do. At the thought of his mouth on me, my legs squeeze together almost involuntarily. I'm just not sure if I'm ready for that.

Bryan feels the tension permeate my body, so he places his hand on my thigh and tenderly coaxes my legs back open. "Shh, Melanie. Let me do this, please. I've been dying to taste you. Since the moment I met you, I've wanted this, please." I can't say no to the begging tone of his words. I'd be lying if I said I didn't want it.

Letting my legs fall to the side, he lowers his mouth to my mound and kisses every inch of me. Soft, almost reverent lips float along the surface of my skin while his fingers return to their gentle motion. Pulling back my folds with his fingertips, he exposes my clit, and when his tongue traces along the hardened bud, I claw at the sheets with such intensity that I think I might actually rip them.

Unable to control my body, Bryan drapes his arm across my belly to hold me in place while he devours me. Licking, tasting sucking – my God, it's all too much. On one final plunge of his fingers and one long, broad stroke of his tongue over my clit, my orgasm rips through me and I shriek out his name.

My skin flames and then cools as the waves of pleasure rise and fall throughout my body. Bryan pulls a blanket up over us and he lies to my side. Brushing the hair that has swept across my face out of my eyes, he kisses my lips sweetly. "I really enjoyed doing that, Melanie." He smirks and looks thoroughly pleased with himself for having given me my first orgasm.

Dazed and relaxed, I mutter, "Hmmmm. I really enjoyed that too." I feel his chest rumble next to me as he chuckles at my response. Lying next to him in this unfocused and hazy post-orgasmic state of bliss, I wonder if this glowing and overwhelmingly warm feeling in my chest is love.

But, I promised myself not to think – to just feel, so feel I will.

Overcome by the desire to touch his skin, I trace my finger along the waistband of his boxer briefs. Peaking up through my long lashes, I meet his gaze. "Is it okay if I touch you now?" Instead of waiting for a response, I cup his erection and watch in amazement as his eyes roll back. The sound of him groaning my name makes my body crave him more – even though I've just had him.

My touches grow firmer, more daring, and when I

reach inside of his boxers to free his hardened length, I kiss and nip at his neck. "Melanie, I can't take much more. Your hands … oh God."

When he starts pushing his cock up into my small hand, I know what he wants. I want it too. So I push his boxers down over his hips and stroke him from root to tip a few more times before asking, "Do you have a condom?"

Please say yes. Please say yes.

He rolls over top of me and presses me into the mattress. Reaching down to the floor, he picks up his jeans and pulls a condom out of his back pocket.

Thank God!

Kneeling between my legs, he tears open the foil packet and I watch in awe as he rolls the condom down over his cock. My eyes travel up the rest of his body and I'm amazed by how beautiful he is. His defined abs are accentuated with that glorious V etched into his hips. His chest is nothing short of a work of art. Perfectly muscled and lightly dusted with hair, I can't resist the urge to reach up and run my fingers through it.

When I look up to his face, I realize that he is staring at me with the same reverence. Could it be that we see each other in the same beautiful light?

"Are you ready, Melanie?" His voice is soft and laced with gentle concern.

I reach up and wrap my arms around his neck and pull his lips down to mine. Kissing him with as much passion as I feel, I say, "I've never been more ready."

I feel his tip nudging at my entrance, and then I feel his fingers relaxing me as they rhythmically dance over my clit – softening me, preparing me.

Relaxed and oh-so-ready, he pushes into me again. "Ahhhh ... Bryan."

"Shhh ... it's okay. We'll take it slowly, nice and easy." He lowers his body to mine, careful to sink into me as slowly as possible. It's a weird combination of pleasure and pain. On one last push, he's fully inside of me and then pain is quickly gone and replaced by the most deliciously full feeling I have ever known.

His lips are on mine, hot and hard. I can tell he's holding back; he's letting me get used to him, but I need him to move. I need to feel him. "I'm good, Bryan ... please ... move ... please, I need more ..." My words are lost to the rhythm of our hips, to the beating of our hearts.

"Melanie ..." My name barely escapes past his clenched jaw and his pace becomes erratic. He hooks one leg up in a muscled arm, causing him to push into me at a different angle. With his other hand, he kneads my breast and tweaks my nipple. I arch my hips so that my back is almost completely off the bed and he moves his hand from my breast in search of my clit. Gently brushing against my sensitive skin, I feel the pressure building again. My insides tighten in ecstasy and he plunges into me harder and harder. "Ahhh … oh God … Melanie …" On one final thrust, he comes and collapses on top of me.

I revel in the feel of his body pressing into mine, of my arms wrapped around him. When his breathing returns to normal, he kisses me sweetly and stares wildly into my eyes like he's searching for something. "Wow … that was …" I think it's the most adorable thing in the world that he's lost for words.

"Yeah … it was … perfect." I run my fingers along his jawline and kiss him as he rolls to the side.

Pulling the sheet around my body, I get up to go to the bathroom. "I'll be right back," I say as I walk away from him. "You better," he says as he stands and takes care of the condom.

Standing in front of the mirror, it's like I'm looking at a different person. I'm not the Melanie I used to be – and I don't mean the whole 'not a virgin' anymore thing.

The Melanie staring back at me is more sure of herself, more confident, and most importantly, she's in love.

Chapter 7

Saturday, January 26, 2013

Present

I'm brushing my teeth after my little vomitus fit of anxiety and I feel like I can't even bear to look at myself in the mirror. Luckily the knocking on the door breaks me out of my little pity party for one. Bracing my hands on the counter, I rinse the remainder of the toothpaste from my mouth and hope for the best.

When I open the door and see Bryan on the other side, my pulse accelerates and my heart beats wildly in my chest. It's not just out of nervousness; it's out of love and lust too. He's hot, and no matter how many times I look at him, I'll never understand how I got lucky enough to have him as my own - even if that time is now running out. His body is perfectly muscled, and even through his heavyweight leather jacket, I can see the clear definition of his upper body. He's got the strongest arms I've ever felt – not that I've felt any other arms, but, well, let's just say they're pretty damn strong.

I refuse to let my brain think about *his* arms – the other guy's arms. I don't remember feeling them anyway.

"Hey, beautiful," he croons into my ear and I squeal as he wraps those strong arms around my waist, effortlessly lifting me off the ground. It's moments like these that I forget about my body issues. Whether I understand why he wants me or not, when I'm with Bryan, I feel feminine and pretty – I feel like every girl deserves to feel.

His arms banding around me also make me forget about everything else – scandalous texts from ex-girlfriends and cheating.

When my feet return to the ground, our eyes lock and I see a storm brewing in his. "What's wrong, Bry?" I ask quietly as I gently brush my fingertips over his light stubble. My heart swells and breaks a little as he leans into my touch.

He shakes his head in an effort to dismiss his emotions. "I told you on the phone. I just missed you," he whispers as he leans in to brush his lips gently against mine. I can't help but wonder if his sadness has anything to do with guilt like mine does.

Having been together a little over four months, this is obviously not our first kiss, but it feels new on so many levels.

It's the first kiss we've had since I've cheated on him. That's how I'll always remember it.

It starts out soft and innocent, but when he nips at my lower lip, I moan in pleasure. The slight opening that my moan offers up is all the invitation that Bryan needs to slip his tongue in to meet mine. He tastes like cinnamon and feels like heaven.

The kiss rises in intensity as he cups the back of my head to pull me closer to him. The other hand roams freely over my upper body, from waist to shoulders and back again until his hand grips at the soft flesh of my hip. Bryan's fingers tangle in the wavy mass of red hair that falls past my bra strap, as mine travel up the back of his neck causing the skin there to prickle in the wake of my touch.

When we break from our heated kiss, I stare back into his deep-brown eyes and get lost there for a minute. "I missed you too." My words sound shaky, breathless almost.

"Yeah, I can tell," he chuckles as he places a far-less searing kiss to my cheek. Brushing a piece of hair out of my eyes and behind my ear, he kisses my forehead and pulls me in the large circle of his arms for a tight embrace.

We just stand there, in the opened doorway of my dorm room while partygoers walk past us to the use the stairwell. We're both hanging onto each other as if we're on the edge of some dangerous cliff. There's a palpable pull between us, a magnetism keeping our arms locked around one another for fear of falling. I know, at least for my part, that I'm holding on because I know once we break our embrace and close the door behind us, I have to face reality. And I just don't want to do that.

When a group of extremely intoxicated and obnoxiously loud kids from the other end of the hall come stumbling toward the stairwell, I step out of Bryan's arms and move to close the door. "Come on in. You said you wanted to talk." I reach down and lace my fingers with his and he brings our joined hands up to his full lips for a sweet kiss.

He tosses his jacket over the back of one of the stools that stand at the small kitchen counter and my mouth goes dry at the sight of him in a simple black T-shirt and tight, but not too tight, faded blue jeans. I try to drink in the sight of him, memorize every bit of him, because as we walk into the living room, it's as if I can actually hear the minutes that we have left ticking away in my head.

We sit on the couch and twist to face each other. Usually there's plenty of room on here for two of us girls to sit comfortably, but Bryan's large frame and long legs swallow up the extra room between us. I put on my cheery face, one I've used all too often in my life, and just hope that what he has to tell me isn't going to crush me. I know it's selfish, but I can't help it.

He reaches his hand out and I willingly place mine in it. Brushing his thumb over my knuckles, he looks at me with the most sincere look of apology in his milk-chocolate eyes. Taking a deep breath, I know that he's trying to put together the words to say what his look was just trying to convey.

I think about mentioning the text that Courtney sent me – the one of the two of them making out, but I hold off on it when I see just how distraught Bryan is. Whatever he's struggling with, I'll let him choose the words. Guilt permeates my every cell and I swallow down the bile that's bubbling up one more time. Feeling like I don't have the right to bring up his indiscretions when mine are so much worse, I sit as calmly as possible and wait for him to say something.

It's torture to sit here and watch him struggle with his emotions, but the coward in me stifles my words. She's beating down the person inside who knows that confessing my cheating is the right thing to do.

He clears his throat, and finally speaks up while my inner coward hides behind a thick cloak of shame.

"I'm sorry about winter break, about telling you not to come to visit me. I … it's just that my family … I don't really know where to begin." Frustration consumes him as he releases my hand and runs his fingers through his silky-brown hair. He shifts and rests his elbows on his thighs. Hanging his head into his hands, he sighs but says nothing. He's clearly torn about something, and my issues aside, I want nothing more than to comfort him right now.

I pull his head up from his hands and turn his face to meet mine. "Hey, you can talk to me. Tell me what's going on. Is it something with Emmie?" I brush a few strands of hair out from his eyes and kiss his lips tenderly, trying my best to convey just how much I want to be here for him.

I feel his jaw tense under my hand as I'm cupping his cheek. "No. Emmie is fine. She's great, actually." He takes a deep breath and then blurts out, "My parents are getting a divorce." He's squeezing his hands together so tightly that his knuckles are turning white under the pressure. "They told me over break. My dad has been seeing some woman he met online and, well, now he's leaving my mom. Can you believe that shit? Twenty-five years of marriage thrown out because my dad couldn't keep it in his fucking pants!"

Holy fucking hell! Did he really just say that? Of all the things that could happen to turn his world upside down – it had to be cheating! The Karma Gods must be having a field day with this one. Visions of the first time I met his parents flit through my head. His father was distracted and constantly on the phone on an "important business call", but now I wonder if that's anywhere near the truth.

But I can't exactly bring that up right now.

And I most certainly cannot bring up the infamous Courtney text now. I can't tell him about me sleeping with some other guy. Those words will have to stay dead and buried.

I can't focus on the irony of the scene unfolding before me for too long, because at just the mere mention of his parents' divorce, Bryan's entire body tenses and anger radiates off of him. My instinct to take care of him kicks into high gear and I sink to the floor in front of him. I kneel before him and wrap my arms around his waist as he remains seated on the couch.

"Baby, look at me," I plead with him as he tries to avert eye contact. But when his eyes meet mine, I can tell why. Unshed tears shine and shimmer. He's trying to be strong, trying to hold it together, but he shouldn't have to. For some reason, it's easier for me to allow someone else to be weak. My own weakness, however, is a completely different story.

I nuzzle into his solid chest and squeeze him tighter, if that's even possible. When his hands wrap around my shoulders and his chin rests on the top of my head, I feel him exhale a shaky breath. "I just can't believe him. I mean, my mom takes care of Emmie full time. He's walking out on her and leaving her with nothing. He thinks paying for half of the medical bills and the mortgage is enough. Fucking prick." I don't know what to say, so I don't say anything. I let him pull comfort from my touch and trace lazy patterns across his back.

After a few minutes in uncomfortable silence, he says, "It's okay. I mean, I'm okay." His voice is uneven and it's apparent that he's pushing down his pain; he's clearly not okay. My voice has sounded the same all too often.

"Bryan, it's okay to be angry. You don't have to hide how you're feeling from me. Please talk to me."

Maybe I should learn how to follow my own advice.

I pull back from him and gaze into his eyes once more. There's so much pain and anger etched on his beautiful face. From the moment I met Bryan, that's what I thought of him – that he was beautiful. High cheekbones and a chiseled jawline provide a perfectly masculine structure to the rest of his face. But right now, his beauty is eclipsed by pain, and I want nothing more than to take it away from him.

As he runs his fingers through my hair, I feel some of the tension in his body ebb away. A few deep, cleansing breaths later and he begins opening up. "I'm sorry I didn't tell you over break. I didn't mean to put so much distance between us." He looks down at me and softly grazes his knuckles over my freckled cheek.

"I understand that now," I say as I capture his hand in mine and bring it to my lips. Kissing the pads of each of his fingertips, I hear his breath hitch in his throat. His eyes widen; his pupils dilate. "Let's forget about that for now. There's no distance tonight. I think I have something that will help us forget about all of that." I skim my teeth over the pad of his thumb and then lightly trace over it with my tongue, soothing my little love bite.

His full, soft lips curve into a lazy grin as he traces the pad of his just-bitten thumb over my plump bottom lip. "What exactly did you have in mind, Melanie?" He arches an eyebrow at me and I return the gesture.

"Well, there would be some of this," I say, as I run my hands up under his t-shirt. I can feel his abs tighten and flex under the light touch of my hands. Raising my hands up higher, over his finely sculpted pecs, I feel goose bumps begin to dot his flesh. Sure, we've been together before, but we've only had sex a handful of times. And having been away from each other this past month, it feels like I'm experiencing his body for the first time all over again.

"I think I'm liking this little plan of yours, Melanie. Care to show me the rest of it in your room?" The pain and anguish that were in his voice earlier are now replaced by lust and desire.

I stand before him as he unfolds himself from the couch. Bryan's not extremely tall – somewhere right around six feet, but he easily towers over my less-than-average five-foot-five frame.

He swats my butt as we walk toward my room. I leer over my shoulder and give him the "are you kidding me" face. Bryan just shrugs his shoulders and says, "What? I love your ass and I missed it."

I arch an eyebrow at him. "Missed it? Well, that's nearly impossible. My butt is way too big to ever miss."

He slaps it again and narrows his eyes. "Cut it out. You know I don't like when you talk like that." On one last swat, he adds, "Now get movin'." I just roll my eyes and drop the topic. He hates when I can't accept a compliment and I try my hardest to keep my self-deprecation to a minimum, but in moments of nervousness, like this, deflecting is the easiest way to keep my insecurities at bay.

And tonight isn't about me. It's about taking his mind off the shit-storm at home. It's about reconnecting with him, if even for only a few hours. If only for tonight, I'd like to enjoy his touch once last time. It's shitty of me, to want him without telling him the truth, but I can't add to his pain.

When we get into my room, he closes the door behind him and clicks the lock. "We wouldn't want Lia barging in here on us again, would we?"

"That might have been the most embarrassing moment of my life!" I laugh softly, but my body heats as I recall exactly what we were doing when Lia walked in on us.

"Yours? You were all covered up." He points at me as he begins walking closer. Tapping his finger on his bottom lip, he says, "If I recall correctly, she got a spectacular view of my ass."

A playful eyebrow arches up on my face. "Oh, but what a fine ass it is." He laughs softly, but his demeanor changes as he takes another step toward me. He's suddenly stalking me like a wolf hunts its prey. My blood runs like molten lava through my veins. My feet are glued to the spot, and it takes conscious effort to inhale an unsteady and lust filled breath.

When Bryan runs his fingertips down my arms, touching the miles of exposed flesh that my lacey camisole affords, I actually shudder with delight.

Dropping his lips down into the crook of my neck, his fingers continue on their lazy exploration up and down my arms and across the creamy flesh above my breasts. His hot breath bathes over me. "You have the most beautiful skin ever." He nips at my neck and then soothes it over with his tongue forcing me to shudder once again. All I can manage in response is a lazy "hmmm."

My chest rises and falls between us and he pulls down the straps of my tank top to reveal the upper curve of my breasts, which are threatening to spill out of my pink lacy bra. Bryan's finger dips into my cleavage and he then traces up around each curve. Instinctively, I move to cover myself, but all I actually do is force my chest up more.

Bryan lowers my arms back down to my sides and snickers at me. "Oh no you don't. It's been way too long since I've seen you." He presses his lips to mine and kisses me with more passion, more ferocity than ever before. It's like he's trying to climb inside of me. It's so intense that I have to pull back from him to catch my breath.

"Are you sure you're okay? We don't have to do this. We can just talk, you know." I have to admit that part of me is saying this out of genuine concern for him, but for the most part, I'm saying it out of guilt.

Lucky for me, he doesn't sense my guilt. Instead, he just laughs – a soft, sexy-as-sin chuckle. "Why on earth would I want to talk when the alternative is getting lost in my beautiful girlfriend's body for the next few hours?" His words are mumbled against my neck and they make my nipples tighten and pucker against my bra.

He makes a good point.

Two actually.

And tonight, I'd like to get lost as well. I don't want to think about the horrible thing I've done to him – hell, I don't even want to think about the horrible thing I'm doing to him now, by not telling him.

So rather than confess my secrets, and break his heart even more, I run my hands up the back of his shirt and drag my nails lightly across the valleys and curves of his long, lean muscles. Reaching for the hem of my shirt, he pulls it over my head and unsnaps my bra allowing my breasts to spill free.

When he steps back to drink in the sight of me, he reaches for the hem of his own shirt and pulls it up over his head from behind.

He guides me over to my bed and gently lowers me down on top of the crumpled mass of blankets and sheets.

His elbows rest on the sides of my head as his hands trace lightly through my hair. Our legs are entangled, and even though there's no light on in the room, the cool-white moonlight illuminates his face. Bryan smiles down at me. "I missed you."

I don't want to talk anymore. I'm afraid of what I might say. So I wrap my arms around his neck and pull his lips down to mine. When we kiss, I can feel his desire growing and hardening as he grinds his erection into my hip.

His lips leave mine, but only to kiss a heated path across my jaw and down my neck. Bryan shifts so that he's next to me on the bed. Reaching out with one hand, he begins kneading and massaging my right breast. My hips buck up at the feel of his fingers tweaking my nipple. A low groan echoes through the room, but I'm not sure if it belongs to me or him. When he leans forward to capture my other nipple in his mouth, I know the scream that I hear comes from me. Wasting no time, Bryan moves his talented tongue across to my right nipple and tortures that one with equal intensity. He nips and bites at my tender flesh increasing my need, and by the feel of it, his too.

I fumble with the button on his jeans, but my unsteady hands are useless. He leans back on his calves and shimmies out of his pants and boxers all at once. "You're beautiful, you know that?" My words are laced with both lust and amazement.

He just shakes his head and says, "No. I'm not the beautiful one. You are."

I'm inwardly scoffing at his comment about me being beautiful – are you kidding me? I want to say that I'm the one who got the better end of the deal in this relationship, but I don't want to ruin the moment.

So instead, I just roll my eyes and pull him down to me to kiss him once more. Before I know it, I'm lifting up my hips so that he can slide my jeans and panties off.

Watching his face melt in pleasure as I stroke him makes me want him even more. I still don't understand how I affect him so much. But it's clear that I do as he calls out my name in a garbled mixture of pleasure and need. Swatting my hands away, he snickers at my advances. He rolls to my side in a quick movement. Whispering in my ear he says, "I need to touch you first."

I whimper. Yes, actually whimper, because I need his touch.

His fingers trace lightly over my hips, and when he moves them across my slightly rounded belly, I shiver. He hooks his leg around mine, forcing me to open for him. Goosebumps spread across my thighs as he continues his torturous journey to my mound. When his finger plunges into me, my hips buck wildly. "You're so tight, baby, and so wet."

He moves his finger round and round, in and out, readying me, stoking the fire that he's already set there. I gasp when I feel him remove his finger, but sigh in relief when he replaces it with two. His thumb gently brushes over my clit and I'm lost in a wave of pleasure. "Oh God … Bryan …" My words are cut short as he pushes his tongue in between my lips.

He kisses me with the same rhythm that he's fucking me with his fingers. It's wildly erotic and almost more than I can take. When he moves his mouth to my breast once more, I lose it completely. Fingers driving in me, thumb rubbing my clit, tongue flicking my nipple. My back arches as my orgasm crashes into me.

He doesn't stop, though. His hands and mouth continue moving and teasing through the crest of pleasure. He only slows when my head stops thrashing from side-to-side and when he feels the inner muscles of my sex unclench around his strong fingers.

"Beautiful. Watching you come like that is absolutely beautiful" he whispers against my ear and then brings his fingers up to his mouth to lick them clean. Embarrassed and unable to watch him do that, and unable to take his compliment, I just nuzzle into his chest and breathe in his scent.

Lips pressed to his chest, I kiss every inch that I can reach. He arches his neck and groans in pleasure. Raking my nails down his back once more, I pull him so that he covers me completely. With his hips resting in between mine, he's nudging at my entrance.

"Is it my turn now?" I mumble my question in between our heated kisses, but I don't wait for a response.

I roll so that he's now underneath me and I'm straddling his hips. I let my lips dance across his smooth skin. Licking, tasting and indulging in the flavor that's uniquely his. My tentative licks show just how unsure I feel about my skills, but when Bryan looks down at me and groans, I decide to let go of those uncertainties.

I close my eyes and revel in the feel of his cock passing over my tongue. Bryan sweeps the red veil of my hair out of the way. "Fuck ... Melanie ... your mouth is amazing. Oh God!"

The rumbling groans of his appreciation give me the courage to continue. Wrapping my small hand around the base, I stroke him mimicking the motion of my mouth.

His stomach tightens as does his grip on my hair. "I'm close, baby ... so close."

Those words make me pull back and reach for a condom in my bedside table. Once he's covered, I lift my hips over his.

"Make love to me, please, Bryan," I beg and he obliges.

Pushing up into me, he calls out, "Ahhh, Melanie. My God, you feel amazing." In an instant and with what seems to be very little effort, he has me flipped over so that I'm underneath him.

I wrap my legs around his waist and grab at his

taut ass, pulling him closer to me. His pace is instantly frantic. Hard, fast thrusts follow one another. I feel my orgasm building, cresting, almost ready to burst, but then my mind takes over. My infidelity is like an ice-bath numbing any feelings of pleasure. In a matter of minutes, he calls out my name one last time as his climax washes over him and mine vanishes completely. He tumbles to my side and wraps his arm around me.

We lie next to each other while our breathing returns to normal. He kisses my temple as he says, "That was amazing." I just smile and nuzzle into his solid chest.

A few minutes later, he rolls over me, places a sweet kiss to my lips, gets out of the bed and walks into the adjoining bathroom.

Left alone with my thoughts for a moment while he takes care of whatever it is guys take care of after sex, I feel bile rising in my throat. What have I just done? I can tell myself that I didn't want to hurt him when he was already hurting all I want, but that's a load of crap. I didn't tell him because I was too afraid to tell him. Guilt courses through my veins and sits heavily on my chest.

When he comes back in the room and I catch sight of his beautiful and still-naked body, I can't take it any longer. Panic rises and I bolt out of bed. That horrible sickening feeling returns and the only way to get rid of it is to purge it away.

I sprint past him into the bathroom and slam the door shut behind me. He can't see me like this – no one can. I hear his concerned voice through my heaving and retching. "Melanie, what's going on? Are you okay?"

When the vomiting stops and the nausea recedes, I reply, "Yeah, I'm fine. Can you just hand me my clothes."

He cracks open the door and brings me in my sweats and tank top. "Here you go."

"Thanks, I'll be out in a minute." He nods and walks back out into my room.

I can't stand to be naked in front of him like this. It's like my cheating is written somewhere on my body and he'll see it if I expose myself for too long. So I get dressed in the bathroom and brush my teeth once again. When I look at myself in the mirror, I'm disgusted at my own reflection.

The last few days have beaten the shit out of me. Between leaving Mom all alone, returning to school without Maddy, attacking Peyton, debating about what to tell Bryan, hearing what he had to tell me and then making love to him – it's all too much. It had to go somewhere; I had to deal with it somehow. There was no keeping it down any longer.

But now, having thrown up, and gotten rid of

some of the pain, I feel like I can at least face him again. When I step out of the bathroom, he's sitting at my desk chair waiting for me with a bottle of water. "I thought you could use this." I walk toward him and he pulls me down on to his lap.

The cool water soothes my burning throat, but does nothing for my tortured soul.

Bryan wraps his arms around my waist and nuzzles into my body. "You okay?"

I nod and dismiss his concerns. "Yeah, I'm fine. I probably just ate something funky. I'll be okay." A pathetically weak smile follows my words.

"I don't have to leave if you're not feeling well. I could stay, if you'd like, I mean." He's half offering and half asking. Part of me wonders if he's offering to stay just because he doesn't want to spend the night alone. This is probably the first time he's had any kind of comfort since finding out about his parents. That thought alone, keeps me from pushing him away.

Because that's what I want to do. I want to push him and everyone else away and curl up in a ball and cry myself to sleep. But I can't. I won't push him away if he needs me. Part of me hopes that if I can work past these feelings of guilt on my own, if I can convince myself and him that I'm the perfect girlfriend, then I won't have to tell him just how far from perfect I really am.

That's when a plan solidifies in my head. I'm not going to tell him. Ever. I can keep it hidden and do everything in my power to never let it out.

Strangely emboldened by my new plan, I say, "Nothing would make me happier than if you stayed."

Falling asleep spooned in Bryan's arms, I vow to wake up and be the perfect girlfriend that Bryan deserves despite being the person who deserves him the least.

It won't be the first time that I've had to cover up the real me, to hide my true feelings, but it will be the most difficult by far.

Chapter 8

Saturday, October 27, 2012

Past

"I freaking hate Halloween," I grumble loudly as I stand in front of my full-length mirror.

Maddy pokes her head out of the bathroom door and laughs. "So then don't think of it as Halloween. Just think of tonight as any other party except everyone's playing dress-up."

"Sure, easy enough for you and your cute little Tinkerbell costume. What is Reid going as anyway? Because I swear to God, if you tell me Peter Pan, I'm going to lose my shit!" Just thinking about her boyfriend wearing green spandex makes me laugh out loud.

Maddy comes out of the bathroom and holds her wings out in front of her. I help her loop her arms through them. "Thanks. And no, he is most definitely not going as Peter Pan. I don't think he's wearing a costume at all. I think it's against some kind of guy code to get dressed up for Halloween." She adds a thin layer of lip gloss and then puckers her lips. "Is Bryan dressing up?"

"No. Like you said, it's against some kind of guy code, right? I'm just happy he decided to come. It's not like he really knows any of you or the guys for that matter." I know he'll fit in just fine – he's terrific and we're great, but he's only met Maddy once. I feel like tonight is a test of sorts, and of course, I have to go through this test while in some stupid costume of course.

Looking down at my outfit, I huff and say, "Yeah, but it's like a requirement for girls to slut it up as best they can, right?" I arch an eyebrow and Maddy turns to the side as she eyes her costume in the mirror.

"You think I look slutty?" She sounds affronted, but I quickly take back my words. "No. No you look great, really you do. I just hate that every costume out there is just a 'sexy' version of what should be a normal costume. Why can't I just go as a nurse? Why do I have to be a *sexy* nurse?"

"Melanie, I think you look adorable." Maddy scans my costume. I chose to go as a black cat. I'm wearing black leggings, a cute cheerleader style black pleated skirt, a black long-sleeved billowy top, a headband with kitten ears and painted on whiskers. She's right. It's adorable and not at all sexy.

I harrumph and flop on the bed. She doesn't let me stay there. "Come on, the girls are waiting. You look great, so quit your worrying."

When we walk out into the living room, Cammie and Lia are waiting for us – as usual. Cammie looks gorgeous dressed as a Greek Goddess. She might freeze her ass off, but she looks stunning. Lia, well I don't even know where to start with Lia. She is dressed to the nines in fishnet stockings, knee high boots, a ridiculously short mini skirt and a blue tube top. The short pixie length blond wig completes her costume, but I still don't get it right away. "What are you supposed to be? A hooker or something?" That's exactly what she looks like, standing there snapping her gum, hip jutted out to the side.

She jumps up and down and claps her hands. "Yes! You got it! Yeah, I'm Julia Roberts from *Pretty Woman*. I'm a hooker!" I've never seen someone so happy to be identified as a prostitute in all my life, but that's Lia for you.

My phone buzzes in my hand and it's a text from Bryan. "Come on ladies. Bryan is downstairs. Let's go." He offered to be the designated driver for the night, but I think he had ulterior motives. He wanted to win over my friends and my heart softens at the thought that he wants them to like him.

Of course when we get to the parking lot, he's holding the door open for the girls. They all slide into the backseat saying "Hi" to him as they pass his extended arm. He opens the passenger door for me and closes it after I sit down. When he walks around to his side, Lia wolf whistles at him and we all laugh. Thank goodness she doesn't have any time to say anything. I can only imagine what would come out of her mouth. I just hope she can behave for the ten-minute drive to the party.

Bryan gets into his seat and pulls the seat belt across his lap. When he places his hand on my knee a tingle travels up my body. He leans in and kisses my cheek and whispers, "You look great."

Without even waiting for me to respond, he looks over his shoulder into the back seat and chuckles. "Well, this is the first time I've had a Goddess, a fairy and a whore in my car at the same time."

Without missing a beat, Lia chimes in. "I am not a whore." She clutches her hand playfully to her chest. "I am a classy hooker. Now drive me to my party so I can get my drink on." She makes a motion with her hand for Bryan to start driving and everyone else breaks out into loud laughter. He looks over at me from his seat and mouths, "Wow," as he pulls out into traffic.

When we pull up in front of the party, the girls

climb out of the car and immediately race up the stairs. Cammie and Maddy go in search of Jack and Reid, and Lia, well, I'm pretty sure Lia is just searching for some booze.

Bryan takes my hand and we walk into the house together. We weave our way through the large crowd. When we get to the living room, we find Maddy, Reid, Cammie and Jack. Everyone smiles at Bryan as he introduces himself to the guys.

"Nice to meet you, man. You want a drink?" Jack asks as he shakes Bryan's hand.

"No thanks. I'm driving tonight." He shakes his head and returns his hand to mine.

"Reid, what the hell are you wearing? Maddy said you weren't dressing up." I ask as I stifle a laugh.

"What, don't you think it's true?" he asks as he looks down at the gift-wrapped box he's wearing. It has holes cut out of the top for his head and the sides for his arms.

"Well that depends. If you're going as A Dick in a Box, then hell yeah, you're spot on." That comment makes Maddy snort in laughter. He wasn't exactly nice to her before the two of them started dating. But, since then, he's been perfect. I can't deny that I have a huge soft spot for my best friend's boyfriend. The fact that he takes me out to lunch once a week just to keep on my good side is a nice touch as well.

He laughs at my snippy comment and smirks at me. "Read the tag. You'll get it," he says.

I eye the tag that's folded closed and choke on my laughter when I read,

To: Women

From: God

Jack chimes in through my giggling and eye rolling, "He wears it every fucking year."

"What? I am." Reid's voice is laced with humor. He kisses Maddy sweetly and she rolls her eyes at him.

"You sure are, Reid. But does that mean I get to unwrap you later on?" Maddy's playful words definitely have an effect on him. It's cute to see them together. They've both been under each other's skin from that first night they met, and ever since they got together officially, they've been the cutest couple ever. There's just something about them that tells me they'll make it.

"Come on. Let's go get you a drink," Reid says to Maddy as he walks her out of the living room and into the kitchen. Jack and Cammie follow behind them and just as Bryan and I move to follow them, Liam, Bryan's soccer teammate, walks up behind us and claps Bryan on the shoulder.

"Hey, Bryan. I didn't know you'd be here tonight," Liam says as he stands in front of us.

"Hey, Liam. Yeah, my girlfriend, Melanie, is friends with Jack and Cammie," Bryan explains as he points to Jack as he walks into the kitchen. Liam says hi to me and politely shakes my hand, but there's something fishy in the way he looks at me.

"I guess it's not such a small campus, after all, huh. I'm in the Physical Therapy program with Jack," Liam explains as he lets go of my hand, which I promptly return to Bryan's.

"I didn't see you at the party after the soccer game. What happened?" Liam asks as he takes a gulp of his beer.

Bryan laughs a little. "Yeah, well, when I saw you throwing up in a shoe, I figured I missed the party. So Melanie and I left and well ... we had our own party." A heated blush creeps up my neck and across my face.

"Bryan!" I gasp and swat him on the arm.

"What? We did." He kisses my forehead and wraps his arm around my shoulder, pulling me into his side.

I roll my eyes, but when he moves his hand from my shoulder to the base of my neck and starts playing with my hair, he's forgiven.

"I'll let you guys catch up. I'm going to go find the girls. I'll be back in a few minutes." I stretch up in my toes and kiss Bryan on his cheek, but out of the corner of my eye I see Liam give me an ugly stare. I don't really need to find the girls, but I just want to get away from Liam.

Before finding the rest of the group, I decide to stop in the bathroom and freshen up. Luckily, since it's still early, there's no line so I go right in. After I'm done washing my hands and reapplying my lip-gloss, I reach for the door. I nearly stumble through it as it's pulled open from the other end. Tripping over my own feet, I land into someone in a slutty nurse costume.

Straightening myself, and pulling my face out of her tits, I'm less than pleased to see that I've just motor-boated Courtney.

Just my freaking luck!

I adjust my headband of cat ears and move to walk past her without saying a word, because, honestly, she's the last person on Earth who I want to talk to.

Well, that plan goes to shit, when she grasps my wrist and pulls me into the bathroom with her. For a skinny bitch, she's pretty strong.

After she slams the door behind her, she eyes me up and down. "What do you want, Courtney?" I practically spit my words at her. I wish I had fewer manners, because spitting in her face actually sounds like a great idea.

"I want you to back the fuck off Bryan." Her words are dripping with venom and hate. Of course, they make me laugh.

"And why exactly would I do that?" I cross my arms over my chest and stare her down.

Courtney takes me by surprise when she steps into my personal space and pokes her bony finger into my arm. "Because it makes me look bad!" Her finger presses into my shoulder to accentuate each of her evil words.

A snarky and dismissive laugh escapes my lips. Unfolding my arms from my chest, I poke her back. "And, please tell me, how the hell does it make you look bad?" I huff and try to walk past her. But, once again, she grabs my wrist and digs her fingers tips into my skin.

Oh, it's on now, bitch!

I let out a deep, steadying breath and turn calmly toward her. Wriggling my wrist free from her grimy hands, I place both of my hands on my hips and just stand there waiting for her to answer. Her eyes skim over my body before she speaks and I have a feeling I know what words are going to come out of her mouth. I brace myself for the blow that I know is about to knock me over. Her lips curl up into an evil little smirk, and she says, "Because he picked a fat, little wiry-haired bitch over me." Courtney steps into my face again and pokes me in the shoulder one more time. "Now, if you don't leave him alone, I'm going to have to do something about it. Just you wait and see." Her words are a calm but evil whisper. Unwilling to let her get the best of me, I glare at her, showing her that her words mean nothing to me.

"Well, maybe if you weren't a," I tap my finger on my lip as I call up the perfect words. "Oh that's right – a shallow, cold, heartless, bitch you wouldn't have lost him in the first place. Besides what kind of person, if that's what you can even call yourself, actually insults a child. You fucking bitch." I'm practically vibrating in anger recalling what she said about Emmie.

Rolling her eyes skyward and huffing at me, she says, "Whatever. She's a fucking little retard and it doesn't even matter. It's not like I insulted Bryan. I don't even know why he cares."

Before I can even hold myself back, my palm stings sweetly against her cheek. "Don't you ever fucking call her that again! She is not a retard!" Gripping her chin in my hands, I force her eyes, which are now filled with a few tears from my slap, up to meet mine.

"Here's what's going to happen. You're going to leave Bryan and me alone, for good. He doesn't want you, and after this little insight into who you really are, I can totally tell why." I release her chin and push her back slightly before glaring at her one last time. "You're not even worth the air I wasted on this conversation. Now, get the fuck out!" I hold my head high as she walks past me and out of the bathroom.

I really hope that puts an end to her whole "I'm

going to get Bryan back" campaign.

When some of the adrenaline fades, reality sets in. What the freak? She's acting like they were engaged or something like that. Yet, as much as I don't want to let her words affect me, I can't deny that they do. They speak to every issue I've had to this point and force me to question what Bryan and I have shared. The freaking bitch!

Trying my best to seem unaffected, I splash some cold water on my face and touch up my make-up once more. A knock on the door startles me and I call out, "I'll be right out!"

Exiting the bathroom, I walk past a huge line that's snaking its way down the hall. People give me the evil-eye as they wait. Great, just what I needed – more people hating on me!

By the time I make it back into the living room, a crowd of people are dancing to some loud club mix. I see Bryan off to the side; his back is to me as he's engaged in a conversation with someone I can't see beyond his body. When my eyes land on his solid back, a warm feeling of comfort and security anchors me. Courtney can say whatever the hell she wants, but I know that she's not who he wants.

As I make my way toward him, I nearly stop in my tracks. My gut churns and anger boils hot and fierce in my veins. Of course, Courtney is standing right in front of him. But what's more shocking than that, is that she's wrapped around Liam like a vine. I don't know if she's trying to make Bryan jealous or what, but the only thought that crosses my mind is that she looks like a whore. A bitchy, whore dressed up like a slutty nurse.

Bracing myself for the worst, I pad over to Bryan's side and I'm more than a little hurt when he startles at my touch. He doesn't include me in the conversation or look at me warmly or anything like that. In fact, he doesn't say anything as he pulls me away from his little chat with Courtney and Liam.

Maybe it's because I'm bristled with anxiety from my exchange with Courtney, but my words come out harsh and accusatory. "What's up with that? What the hell were you guys talking about? Why did you pull me away like that?"

He doesn't have a chance to answer me. His phone must vibrate in his pocket because I don't hear it ring. When he looks at the screen to see who is calling him, his eyes looks a little scared. "I have to go outside to take this. I'll be right back." And then he walks away from me, leaving me all alone in the middle of a Halloween party that I didn't even want to go to in the first place.

Scanning the crowd, I don't see any familiar faces. Maddy, Cammie and Lia are nowhere to be found, and since Jack and Reid are never more than a step away from their girls, I don't see them either. All I see is Courtney and Liam staring at me from across the room. The air around them stinks of some kind of conspiracy, and I have a feeling that the ugly looks Liam was shooting at me before I left to go to the bathroom are part of Courtney's plan to come between me and Bryan.

No longer able to stand their harsh scrutiny, I step out onto the porch where Bryan has taken his call. When I see him holding his phone in front of his face, instead of pressing it up against his ear, I know immediately who has called him.

Emmie.

I stay to the side because I don't want her to see me on the screen. Bryan has told me that she has a difficult time adjusting to new people so I don't want to overwhelm her. But Bryan catches sight of me out of the corner of his eye and he smiles over at me. He holds one finger up to the side to let me know that he'll just be another minute. I nod and wrap my arms around my chest, trying to block out some of the chill in the late autumn air.

Through the loud, raucous intensity of inside, I can hear bits and pieces of the conversation.

"It'll be okay, Emmie. I promise," he coaxes her, but it's obviously not working when he adds, "They'll calm down. Just stay in your room. Tell me about your new book. Yeah, the one I downloaded for you. What do you think?"

Bryan's face lights up like a flash of lightning when she starts talking about whatever book he must have set up for her. I'm lost staring at him and daydreaming about how sweet he is, when I catch the tail end of his last sentence.

"… no I'm not alone. You don't have to worry, Emmie. I'm with my girlfriend, Melanie." Bryan's warm eyes look over to me and his face softens. I take a step closer to him, but still stay out of view. I'm close enough now that I can hear Emmie ask, "Can I see her?"

Bryan eyes me warily, unsure about how I'll react. Surely, he's thinking about how Courtney reacted, or maybe he's thinking that I don't want to talk to his sister. Keeping my voice low enough so that only he hears me, I say, "I can talk to her."

He reaches out his hand to mine and pulls me to his side. Holding the phone in front of us, he centers it between our face so that Emmie can see both of us.

She bounces in her seat and laughs with such giddiness that it's contagious. I chuckle and ask, "What's so funny, Emmie?" I smile and make a silly side-eyed face as I stare into the screen of Bryan's smartphone. I don't want to make her feel uncomfortable, but there was something so bright and alive in her laughter that I couldn't help but be playful in my question.

"You're a kitty cat, Melanie!" She laughs again as she points up at my headband. I reach up to touch the ears that are sticking up at the top of my head. I kind of forgot about them. She's still lost in her innocent laughter so I "meow" at her and she laughs even harder.

When her chuckles subside, she proudly holds up a pretty pink princess costume. Placing the sparkly crown on her head, I gasp and sigh. "Oh, Emmie, you are the prettiest princess ever."

"Really?" I can hear the disbelief in her voice and I just want to climb through the phone and hug her tightly.

"Of course, you are! You're a beautiful little princess and don't ever let anyone tell you any differently." Now, if only I could apply my own words to myself– that would be progress.

Emmie shrugs her shoulders and tucks her chin shyly into her chest. "I think you're beautiful too, Melanie." Her soft words force a ball of emotion to rise in my throat. It's the first time in my life that I truly believe a compliment for what it is. It's her innocence, her shyness and playfully attitude that help me see myself through different eyes.

Instinctively, I lace my fingers with Bryan's and

squeeze tightly. I lean into his shoulder and feel the heat rolling of his body. He lightly places his lips to the top of my head and whispers, "Thank you" so that only I can hear him.

Turning my attention back to Emmie, I let her know that I'm going to go now so that she can finish talking to Bryan. I stand to his side once again and I'm close enough to hear him say, "I know, Emmie. I think she's beautiful too." His eyes travel the length of my body and the air no longer feels chilly. "Yes, I like her too, *very much*." His soft lips break into an adorable lopsided smile on his last words and it makes my insides turn to goo.

Through my hazy visions of what those lips are capable of, I hear Bryan say, "Okay, Emmie. You go read your book now. Put Mom on the phone, please." He pushes a few buttons to change his phone out of video mode.

Placing the phone up next to his ear, I see his back straighten. He's bracing himself for something.

Keeping my voice low so that his mom can't hear me, I ask, "Do you want me to leave you alone?"

The question garners a "don't be ridiculous" glare and a tight squeeze of the hand. So I stay by his side and listen to him talk his mom about the fight she just had with his dad. While Bryan's calming her down about his dad having to leave abruptly for another surprise business trip, I consider saying something to him about the weird vibe I got from his dad while he was at the game. I consider it, but it just doesn't feel like the right time.

So what I do instead is decide to conceal my reservations. Besides, "I have my suspicions about your dad" doesn't exactly seem like it would have a calming effect on him right now. I don't mention anything to him about the weird looks from his dad at the game, or the fact that I'm pretty sure that he wasn't on the phone with a business partner at all. I don't say anything about Courtney and her snide remarks. I bite back my concerns about her and Liam plotting against us.

I keep all of those concerns buried deep inside and just nuzzle closer to him. I try to calm him, and when he's done on the phone, rather than going back into the party, I offer to take him back to my empty suite to distract him further.

I'd rather not go back in there anyway.

"Are you sure you want to do that? What about your friends? Weren't we supposed to be hanging out with them?" he questions, but I can tell that he really wants to get out of here as well. My heart swells more than a little at knowing that, even when he's dealing with some serious shit, he's still thinking about me and my friends.

"I'll text them on the way. I think they'll be just fine spending the night here." I arch my eyebrow and shoot him a knowing look. "Besides, we have plans tomorrow to go hiking with them. They'll understand."

He nods and mumbles, "Okay." Then he pulls me into his arms and kisses me with the sole purpose of forgetting. I'm not sure exactly what he's trying to forget, but I'm more than willing to help him get lost.

Sitting in Bryan's car on the short drive back to my suite, I dial Maddy. I'm not all that surprised that she picks up on the first ring.

"Mel? Where are you? I walked away for like a minute and you were gone!" Her voice is frantic. We kind of have this "no girl left behind" mantra.

I roll my eyes and look over at Bryan who has just heard Maddy yell at me over the phone. "Calm down, Maddy. I'm fine. I'm with Bryan … something … umm … came up."

She chuckles and I hear Reid in the background. "Sure." She draws out the word insinuating what any best friend would insinuate.

I clear my throat in the hope that it will stop her laughter. "Would you stop it? Listen, we're heading back to the suite. I know we were all supposed to hang out tonight, but something did really come up." Her laughter subsides and she sobers when she hears the seriousness in my voice.

"Is everything okay, Mel? Do you guys need anything?" Maddy's concern is evident and I even hear Reid chime in behind her making sure that I'm okay.

"Yes, Maddy. I promise everything is okay. I just wanted to call you and let you know. That's all." Bryan reaches across the console and squeezes my hand. "I know Bryan was supposed to drive, but will you girls be okay there for the night?"

"Don't worry about that at all." Maddy dismisses me. I'm pretty sure Reid won't kick her out of his bed.

"I'll call you in the morning. Maybe we'll get together for breakfast before we go hiking or something like that."

"Of course. And Mel, if you guys need anything, call us. We'll be right there. We'll see you guys in the morning."

"Thanks, Maddy."

"Oh one last thing, Mel."

"Yeah."

"Have fun." Again, she draws out the word.

I eye Bryan as he pulls into a parking spot noticing the way his bicep flexes as he shifts the car into park. "I definitely will." I end the call and lean over to Bryan and trace my finger down his right arm. He turns toward me and his face looks sad and distant.

"Are you okay?" I tangle my fingers into the soft hair that curls slightly at the nape of his neck.

He swipes a strand of hair out of my eyes and smiles a sad little smile. "I've just never heard my mom so upset before. I don't know what's really going on, though. It sounded like she was covering something up." I tenderly run my fingers across his cheek. His hand softly cups mine and he brings the pads of my fingers to his lips for a sweet kiss.

"And I hate hearing Emmie upset. She doesn't know how to cope, and being here, well, I just feel a little helpless. That's all." Shrugging his shoulders, he tries to dismiss the sadness I know he's feeling. But his eyes, they scream of his unease.

Pulling his face into mine, I trace my thumb across his bottom lip. He darts his tongue out to lick my thumb and it makes me shiver. I softly trace every line of his face in an attempt to ease some of his tension. Arriving at his tightly furrowed brow, I say, "Let's just relax tonight, Bry. We'll deal with it all tomorrow. Okay?" I let my hand fall to his cheek once more and he nuzzles into my touch. He doesn't say anything, but when he opens the door and walks around to mine to open it for me, I know that he likes my plan.

When we get into my suite, I take off my cat-ear headband and pull the elastic from my hair. Bryan steps behind me and sweeps my hair to one side. Exposing my neck to his warm breath sends thrill bumps racing across my skin. I relax my shoulders into the warmth of his solid chest and enjoy the feel of his lips as they dance across my neck. As he kisses the tender spot where my headband sat all night, a soft moan of pleasure escapes my lips.

I arch my neck and turn my head to the side to grant him more access. Bryan tenderly wraps his strong fingers around the front of my neck as he runs his nose from my shoulder up to my hairline. He coos softly into my ear, "I want you, Melanie."

I mentally lack the capacity to say what those words do to me. Honestly, I just never thought I would ever hear them. Wrapped in the strength of his warm embrace, I know I'll do everything within my power to hear them again and again and again.

As I push the curve of my ass into his groin, I tell him, "I want you too, so much." A grumble of pure male satisfaction vibrates against my back. It makes my heart melt, and my knees weaken for that matter, to know that I can share this part of me with him. To be honest, I've never felt more like myself than when I'm with Bryan. I'm not different or better or skinnier or anything like that. I don't have to be the perfect version of myself that I present to everyone else. I'm just me, and what's really crazy is that when I'm with him, I'm happy about who I am.

Without much grace, Bryan and I stumble over to the couch. His hands race across my body with need as his mouth devours mine with a hunger I've never felt before. He's not simply kissing me; he's trying to become a part of me. I wrap my hands around his neck and pull his mouth closer to mine, if it's even possible, and kiss him back with all of the need and emotion I can muster.

When his thumb traces over my hardened nipple over my shirt, my entire body shudders in delight. He feels it. He plays my body like an instrument, each stroke deliberate and beautiful. "Bryan ... I ... I ..." I don't know what it is that I want. I know I just want him. It's as if his name has become a part of my lips, of my heart.

"What, Melanie? Tell me what you want and I'll do it for you. You should know that by now." The words fall from his beautiful mouth and I can feel the truth behind them. I can see the sincerity in his eyes. He would do anything for me, but right now, it's going to be about what *I* want to do for *him*.

Bryan is taken by surprise when I push up from underneath him and switch positions. Straddling his hips, with his hands spanning my waist, I dispose of my top and bra. I push his shirt up to expose his chest and crush my body to his. Basking in the feel of his skin on mine, I torture his neck with soft, wet kisses. The feel of his body writhing beneath mine is sexy as hell, and if I'm being honest, it's a strange sense of empowerment too.

When he wraps his arms around my waist and sits up with me in his lap, I pull his shirt up and over his head. Gently, I push him back so that, once again, he's lying down. I continue on my mission of kissing his neck, across his collarbone, down the solid muscles of his chest, into the valleys and ridges of his sculpted abs. I shimmy down the rest of the way and settle in between his legs. I trace my pointer finger down the line of hair that descends beneath his jeans before unsnapping them. As I pull the zipper down, I can feel him bulge and pulse beneath my fingers and it makes me want him even more.

Bryan arches his hips and I take the opportunity to rid him of his pants and boxers entirely. Staring down at his beautiful and completely naked body sends a jolt of pleasure in between my thighs. Tentatively, I touch him, afraid somehow that I'll hurt him, or do it the wrong way. But, the second my shaking fingers wrap around him, he pushes his hips up and grinds himself into my hand. "Ahhh, fuck. Melanie …" His words trail off to the slow rhythm of my hand gliding over his heated skin.

Emboldened by the fact that I am so clearly

affecting him, I begin kissing his stomach, licking that sexy-as-sin V muscle as I caress him. An overwhelming urge to taste him, to give him the pleasure I know he's seeking, consumes me.

When I move my hand away from him, I hear a soft breath pass through his lips. My tongue darts out and softly licks a path from root to tip. His neck arches; his stomach flexes; his chest rises and falls rapidly with ragged breaths.

Licking the same path a few more times has him moaning my name and breathing heavily as if he can't get enough oxygen to his lungs. I wrap my lips around him and take as much of his length as I can into my throat. Bryan sweeps my hair to the side as he gently cups the back of my head. There's no force or anything like that. Just a loving reverence as he guides my mouth up and down. "Melanie ... your mouth ... so fucking perfect ..."

When I feel his motion get more frantic and less rhythmic, I give him one last lick and stand next to the couch. I've got something that I hope will be even more perfect than my mouth. I step out of the rest of my clothes and pull the condom out of the back pocket of his jeans.

As I tear the foil wrapper of the condom with my teeth, Bryan rolls to his side and supports his body on his elbow. With his other hand, he softly traces a line from between my breasts, down my stomach, which flexes under his touch. When he plunges two fingers into my core, his name falls from lips without warning. Rocking back and forth on his fingers drives me crazy. "Bryan, I need you to be inside of me now. Please, baby."

As he continues the beautifully relentless motion of his fingers, he grumbles, "And I want nothing more than to be buried inside of you." With those words, he stops his masterful torture and takes the condom from my hands. After he rolls it down, he grabs me by the waist and pulls me onto him, but only a little bit.

"Go slow, baby. I don't want to hurt you," he whispers as he helps guide me inch-by-inch. When my legs are shaking and I feel like I can't take it anymore, I slam my hips down onto his and take his entire length inside of me.

"Oh God, Bryan … you feel …," I don't know the word to end that sentence. I just know that I've never felt like this before – so full, so connected, so in love.

"I know, baby. You do too." And then his lips crash into mine as he pulls my face down to his. His arms wrap around my waist once again as he takes control of our motion – pushing up into me and pulling me down onto him.

His tongue plunges in my mouth as his fingers tangle in my hair. Our chests are pushed together and the friction of my nipples rubbing up against the light dusting of hair scattered across his chest sends a gush of wetness to my core. When he angles his hips forward, hitting that sweet spot deep within, I lose control.

Bliss. Pure unadulterated bliss races through my veins and my body moves on its own accord. It thrashes wildly, yet still remains in perfect sync with Bryan's motions. He reaches his hand in between our joined hips and begins rubbing my clit, matching the frenzied and frantic pace of his thrusts.

"Bryan … Bryan …" His name falls from my lips as I fall beautifully over the edge of bliss. "Melanie … I can feel you … oh God …" And on one final thrust deep inside of me, he calls out my name and shudders with our joined release.

When the adrenaline fades away and our lungs calm, I move to get off of him. Instead of letting me go, he just pulls me closer and begins combing his fingers lightly through my hair. "Can we just stay like this for a bit?" he asks quietly.

I place my hand over his heart and press my lips lightly to his chest. "Of course we can." He offers no response. Instead, he just squeezes me tightly and kisses the top of my head, which is tucked securely under his chin.

Somewhere in between being fully asleep and still

awake, I hear Bryan's voice filter into my consciousness. The velvet timbre of his rich voice lulls me to sleep further. Through my slumber-induced haze, I don't even realize that I'm no longer lying on top of him and that he's sliding his arms under my knees and shoulders. Instinctually, I wrap my arms around his neck for support and nuzzle into his chest. The last thing I feel before he places me on my bed and pulls me into his arms once again, are his lips tenderly pressing against my temple as he wishes me sweet dreams.

Chapter 9

Monday, February 4, 2013

Present

"Hey, baby. How are you feeling? Did you sleep well last night?" Bryan asks cheerfully as I greet him at my door.

"I'm better. I guess I just needed some rest," I answer lamely as I pull my heavy winter jacket on. Closing the door to my suite behind us, we walk out into the brisk air and make our way across the quad to class.

When we get into the science building, he leans down and kisses my forehead as if he's checking for a fever. He won't feel anything, though. I wasn't really sick this past weekend. I just needed a break from the guilt-ridden feelings. I told him I had some kind of flu and just hid out in my room all weekend. Of course, being the caring man that he is, he insisted on coming over to take care of me. After more than a few reassurances that I would be just fine, he relented and let me get my rest.

It helped that Peyton was rarely in the room. Between researching for her thesis and working in the writing lab, she was gone practically the entire weekend. Of course Cammie and Lia were concerned and brought me chicken noodle soup and ginger ale. That didn't do much to abate my guilt. It just transferred it.

As we make our way up to the third floor, in what feels to me like an uncomfortable silence, Bryan pulls me close to his side, and asks, "Are you sure you're okay? You seem a little off this past week."

I smile up at him brightly and say, "Yeah, I'm good. I promise." The alternative would be a lot less pretty and all too real. So, instead of being real, I plaster on a smile and walk the rest of the way to class.

When we arrive outside of my biology lab, Bryan stands in front of me and laces our fingers together, holding our hands in between us. "Are you sure you're okay?" he asks again and it's starting to piss me off. Him caring isn't the problem, though. The fact that he knows me well enough to know that something is bothering me is what's getting under my skin. It just makes me feel even worse about everything.

Biting back my anger and guilt, I wrap my puffy coat-covered arms around his waist and hug him as tightly as our bulky winter clothing will allow me to. Angling my head up so that I can look into his eyes, I try my best to reassure him. "Really, Bryan. I'm good. I guess I'm still just a little tired, but I'm fine. I promise."

Burying his nose into my hair, he sighs. He doesn't believe me; I know it. Luckily, a few other students come up to the doorway, and I know I only have a few minutes left before class starts.

He pulls us to the side of the door and takes a step back. Scanning my face for some hidden answer, one that I hope he won't find, he asks "So then can I see you tonight?"

The professor chooses this moment to walk past us and he makes a concerted effort to clear his throat as he does, clearly indicating that I need to get myself in the room as soon as possible. "Sure. I mean, let me see. I have two tests this week and a paper due on Wednesday. I'll call you later." I kiss him quickly and slide past him and into the classroom.

Sinking into my seat as the professor closes the door on Bryan's utterly confused face, I know that I can't avoid him forever. I just have to figure out a way to be with him without getting sick to my stomach.

I've managed to avoid Bryan all week. I don't know if

that's necessarily something I'm proud of, but it's something I've done nonetheless. The overwhelming need to talk to someone about all of this gets the best of me. Plopping down on my bed after a grueling test, I dial Maddy, hoping that she's not too busy for me.

Just when I'm about ready to hang up, she answers the call. "Hey, Mel. Give me one sec." Maddy's all out of breath and I hear her curse as her keys and phone clunk to the ground. My heart lightens a bit when I hear Maddy say, "Shit, shit, shit."

After a few more seconds of shuffling, I register the crinkling sounds of plastic shopping bags as Maddy's voice comes back on the line. "Sorry, Mel. I was just carrying some groceries in. Stupid phone slipped right out of my hands. What's up, girl?"

"Look at you being all domesticated. If you tell me that you're cooking, I'm going to have to suggest a mental health evaluation." I laugh softly at the image of Maddy trying to make anything more than cereal.

"Oh, just shush, would you? So how's everything going?" I can't tell she's trying to tip-toe around the question she really wants to ask. I've been avoiding talking to her, just like I've been avoiding talking to Bryan.

"Ehh. They're going. Classes are okay. Oh and get this. I got a new roomie," I start nervously, twisting my hair around my fingers.

"No shit! What's she like?" I hear a bag crinkle in the background as cupboards clap opened and closed.

And the distraction works for a few minutes as we get lost in meaningless conversation about biology tests and new roommates, but when a stilted silence stretches for a few seconds, I know that Maddy is just trying to carefully select her words to ask about Bryan.

In a rushed huff of words, I answer her unasked question. "I still haven't told Bryan." I flop back on the bed and cross my forearm over my head.

"Oh no, Mel. Why not? I thought you were going to tell him." Maddy's words ring through the line with concern and not an ounce of judgment.

"I know. I know. I just … ughhh. It's so complicated. Maddy, I just don't know what to do." Guilty emotion coats my throat as I try to get the words out.

"So why don't you try explaining it all to me. We didn't really get to talk about it too much over break, but I'm here for you and I want to help you figure everything out." She's told me this before, but I always feel like such a burden dumping my problems on her. I know I shouldn't, but I do.

"Maddy, we could be here for hours, though. Don't you have dinner to make or something like that?" I can't deny that part of me wants to talk and part of me wants to avoid this conversation for as long as I can.

Her loud almost bark-like chuckle bursts through the line and I actually have to pull the phone away from my ear. "Pfft. I can try to make dinner as much as I want. We'll still end up getting take-out. Besides, we haven't talked at all since you got back to school." The pleading tone in her voice forces my will to crack and my voice to falter.

Tally up one more reminder of my failures. Shitty best friend right here.

When I still don't say anything for a few more seconds, Maddy pushes one last time. "Please, Mel. I just want to understand and I want to help you. Please talk."

Beyond frustrated and more than ashamed of the situation, I huff into the line. "What is there to say? I was wrong. He told me not to visit him. He didn't call me. I got a text of him and his ex-girlfriend making out at a party and then I went and fucked up royally by cheating. That about sums it up," I snap at her even though none of this is her fault.

Maddy softly gasps. "I didn't know about any texts. Did you ask him about them?" Surprise laces through her words, but she also sounds a bit hurt that I never shared that with her.

I sigh as if it will release some of the shame I'm feeling. "No, I just figured I didn't have a right to ask him about them after what I did."

"Is that why you started hanging around with Lindsey and those girls over break?"

My stomach twists in knots as I recall just how un-Melanie-like I behaved over vacation. "I guess so. I'm not proud of that, though. You know I don't drink, but I was trying to dull everything, trying to make it all go away."

"How'd that work for you?" she quips, but it's not meant to hurt or jab at me.

"Fan-fucking-tastic, obviously!" I retort with a feigned snippiness. "Okay, fine. It was a shitty way of coping, but I was just so angry and upset. And then *it* happened and I felt so guilty. Feeling nothing but a drunken stupor was better than feeling all of that." I can't bring myself to share my biggest source of guilt, though. The fact that I was too drunk to remember who I was with or what I did with him is something that I'll conceal from everyone. Except I guess Bryan at some point.

"Mel, I wish I could make it better, but you know the only way to make the guilt go away is to talk to Bryan. I mean, could there have been a mix up with the text?" Her casual question causes anxiety to bloom in my chest.

"A mix up? What do you mean?" I wrap my arm around my stomach as I feel a sickening feeling start to grow.

"Did you get the text from him or from her?" Oh crap. There's no stopping Maddy once she goes into her Nancy Drew mode.

"It was from her." Timid words slip past my lips. I can see where she's going with this. Of course, when I initially got the text, I didn't even pay attention to the number that it came from. I saw the picture and reacted. I know there's a lesson here about hindsight being 20/20 and all that, but all I feel right now is overwhelming dread.

"And did he happen to mention why he didn't want you to come visit?" Maddy's fitting together the pieces of the puzzle.

"Yes, he did." I choose not to tell her the reasons just yet. My conscience can only handle so much right now.

"Then you have to talk to him about it. I seriously doubt he even knows about the text. You know what a bitch Courtney was to you last semester. And if he had legitimate reasons for being distant, then you have to give him the benefit of the doubt." Damn her and her level-headedness.

I shift and straighten my back up against the wall next to my bed. "I hate when you're right." I can just picture the smirk creep across her face at my admission.

"I know, but really, sweetie, I just want you to be happy. I don't care about who is right or wrong." My belly flips again just thinking about Maddy's kind, green eyes crinkling with concern as she speaks those words.

I release a shuddery breath and try, in vain, to dismiss the heavy conversation. "Okay, okay. Enough about me. Tell me how things are going with you guys? How's the baby doing? What's Reid's job like? How is it living with a boy?" Teasingly, I stretch out the word "boy" and she giggles at me in return. I ask all of that because I do genuinely want to know, but I also want to feel happy for a bit. And the only way I can think of being happy is by not dealing with my world of crap right now.

The rest of the conversation is filled with Maddy gushing over her pregnancy, glowing over Reid, and stressing about fitting classes in around her work schedule. Even though I hear the anxiety in her voice from time to time, I can tell that she's just fine. Everything worked out for them. I just hope it will work out for me.

Maddy hangs up with me when Reid gets in from work and I feel better having talked to her. Now, I just have to work up the courage to talk to Bryan.

After I get off the phone with Maddy, I take a shower in the hope that the hot water will scald away some of the guilt I'm feeling. As the rising steam curls through the air, I run through an imaginary conversation with Bryan. I try to envision how the conversation will go, and as I work my crimson hair into a furious lather, Bryan tells me he forgives and loves me. But then, as I rinse the soapy bubbles from my curvy body, he's cursing me out and telling me that he hates me.

Where's that damn crystal ball when you need it?

As I step out of the shower, I wrap a fluffy purple towel around my body. Swiping my hand across the mirror, I catch a glimpse of my contorted face. I've never been able to say that I'm confident or that I truly love who I am, but staring at the guilt-ridden image reflected back to me, I'm utterly disgusted. And it's not just about what I have to tell Bryan. It's about who I've become over the past month. This self-loathing, indecisive, evasive version of me is hideous. Desperately in search of the girl I want to be, I take a deep breath to cleanse my lungs and hopefully my soul.

After getting dressed, I pull my hair into a loose knot. I sit in my desk chair, feeling undeserving of the comfort that my bed affords me, and pull out my cell phone once again. But, just as I'm about to dial Bryan, Peyton comes in. And oh boy, she is pissed.

Chucking her canvas bag into the corner, she yells,

"That fucker!"

"What the hell, Peyton?" I screech as I dodge the book that she just tosses haphazardly across the room.

Collecting the book from the foot of my bed, she huffs and says, "Nothing. It's not important. Just some asshole I met at the writing lab."

"Do you want to talk about it?" I ask timidly because honestly, right now, she seems like she's ready for murder or something.

"No, I most certainly do *not* want to talk about it! Right now, I want to drink about it! What are you doing tonight?" The hopeful lilt to her voice makes her seem a bit more human through this very Incredible Hulk-like blow out that she's having.

I glance down at my phone in my hand and debate whether or not to chicken out on my call. Knowing that I can't keep dealing with my guilt, I make a decision that I think will help benefit me greatly. I walk over to Peyton's side of the room, you know, the one that's seething in anger, and wrap my arm around her shoulders. Pulling her close to my side, I say, "Give me five minutes to make a call and then I'm all yours."

I can feel her body relax against mine and I realize that in the last few weeks, I've probably been a shitty roommate and friend. She rests her head on my shoulder and sighs, letting go of the stress. "Thanks, Melanie. I could use some girl time." I can hear the homesickness in her words as they reach my ears and feel the loneliness in her body as it slumps against mine.

"Well, then, that's what you'll get." I say as I hold her at arm's length. "Just give me a few minutes to let Bryan know what's going on and I'll be right out."

"You're awesome, you know that?" She winks at me from the door and for the first time since she stormed in the room and threw a book at me, she looks a little happier.

When the door clicks behind her, I don't hesitate one minute in calling Bryan. I know that if I do, I'll end up finding some reason to postpone the inevitable. Quickly dialing his number, I hold my breath and wait for him to pick up.

But he doesn't.

So, I dial again. But, shockingly, he doesn't pick up again.

Not-so-old feelings of inadequacy start to creep into my chest. Those feelings begin constricting my heart like the vines of a weed strangle a beautiful flower. I'm thrown back to just a few months ago. Calling him non-stop. Waiting for him to answer. Questioning myself when he doesn't.

Resolve sets in and I decide to call him once more. If he doesn't pick up, then I'll just deal with him in the morning.

I dial and this time he answers. "Hey, Melanie. Sorry about that. I was on the phone with Emmie." His voice is flustered and I feel like an ass for letting my insecurities get the best of me when all he has ever done is make me feel worthy.

Worthy of his time, because he's always given it to me.

Worthy of his body, because he's always worshipped mine.

Worthy of his kindness, because he's never been anything but caring and sweet to me.

"It's okay. Is everything alright?" I ask.

"No. Not really." The naked reality of his words shocks me more than a little bit.

I slump back into my chair and let *my* worries fade away. It's the only way that I can take on his. "Do you want to talk about it?"

I can hear the tenuous shaking of his breath as it escapes through his lips - lips I suddenly long to kiss and comfort. "It's just that she's having a really hard time dealing with things at home. Apparently, my dad is moving out this week and Emmie doesn't understand it. I just spent the last hour trying to explain it to her, but it's just too big for her to wrap her head around."

"Oh, Bryan. I'm so sorry." I hate that there's pity in my words. I hate that I'm just going to cause him more pain.

I hear a hardened sigh fly out of his mouth as something crashes down in the background. "Fuck!" he yells, his emotions obviously getting the best of him.

"Calm down. It'll be okay. I don't know how, but it will be. You're a good brother being there for Emmie. You know that, right?" My fingers itch to touch his face, to feel his stubble beneath them.

"I don't feel like that right now. I feel so helpless. I just wish I could be there for her." A throaty growl echoes down the line and my heart breaks for both him and Emmie.

"I'm getting another call, Melanie. Hold on one second, okay?"

"Sure." The thirty seconds that he's on the other line stretch out painstakingly. Yet in that short span of time, I decide that what I have to tell him can't be said over the phone, especially after learning this. Breathing out a tortured breath, I wait for him to click back to me.

"Hey, I have to take the other call. It's my mom. Rain check on tonight?" His anger has morphed into vulnerability and I just want to wrap my arms around him. He deserves so much more than what he's being handed. Unfortunately, that includes me as well.

I hear him shuffle a few papers before he says, "I think we're both off from the lab on Wednesday night. Can we get together then?"

Without even thinking about it, I blurt, "Yes. Of course. I'll see you then. Bryan, I …" the words I want to say get stuck in my throat, so instead of telling him that I love him, I say, "I'm here for you. Call me if you need to."

"I know. I will. I gotta go. Talk to you later, babe." And then the line goes dead.

So does a piece of my heart.

Chapter 10

Wednesday, February 13, 2013

Present

The freezing rain cuts through the winter air. Even though I'm wearing rain boots and a rain jacket, I feel soaked to the bone. Chills race over my body and I feel like I will never warm up.

And that may very well be true.

It almost feels like tiny razor blades slicing at my freckled face. It's a welcome pain, though. I'll take the physical kind of pain over the emotional torture I've been putting myself through. I just wish I didn't have to put Bryan through it too. No matter how many times I wrack my brain over it, there's just no way around not telling him the truth. I even contemplated just breaking up with him – no explanation, no reason, no justification. But I know, that despite how much this confession is going to gut me, I owe Bryan this much. I owe him at least a reason.

After a short ten minute walk, I arrive at the on-campus senior apartment suites where Bryan lives. I bring my purple-with-cold hand up to his door and knock timidly. The vibrations from knocking course through my arm and a pins and needles sensation pulses across my skin. A sinking feeling crushes in my chest and a lump of emotion rises in my throat as I hear his footsteps get closer to the door.

The knob turns and I swear my heart stops beating. Nervousness engulfs me and makes my legs almost too weak to even hold my weight. Through the grey haze of the early evening, and the crackling sound of the rain pelting against the building, I see and hear the door creak open.

"Melanie, what the hell?" Bryan reaches to pull me into his door when he sees me standing there, soaked and shivering. He grabs a throw blanket from his small couch, which is right next to the front door and wraps it around my shoulders after he peels my raincoat from me.

Bryan starts rubbing my shoulders and upper arms as he pulls me close to his solid chest. "What are you doing here? I'm supposed to pick you up in like two hours." He takes a step back from our embrace and tips my chin up so that I can look in his face. When he stares into my eyes, I swear he can see everything.

Concern knits at his brow. "Is something wrong?"

I nod my head and move past him to sit on the couch. Pulling the blanket tighter around my shoulders, I feel that sickening feeling creep up in my belly. The couch sinks as Bryan settles in next to me. I try to garner as much strength as possible from the arm that he's just wrapped around my shoulder.

On a deep breath and a silent prayer, I steel myself for the inevitable outcome of this conversation.

"We need to talk, Bryan." My voice shakes with both fear and a chill that just will not leave my body. My teeth start to chatter and I'm pretty sure that my lips are blue. Sliding one leg under the other, I twist to face him on the couch and he does the same.

That concerned look hasn't left his face. "What do we need to talk about, Melanie?" he questions softly as he coaxes a strand of soaking wet hair that's plastered to my forehead behind my ear. When he softly traces my jawline and cheekbone before placing his hand on mine, I can actually feel my heart split in two.

Here goes nothing.

"I have something to tell you," I blurt out.

He softly chuckles at me. Tilting his head to the small window behind us, he says, "Well, I kind of figured as much since you walked here in this weather. What's the matter?"

I've run over this conversation a million times in

my head and I still can't figure out where to start. What feels like hours pass between us, and I still can't find the words.

With two fingers under my chin, Bryan angles my head up to his. "Hey, baby. Whatever it is, you can tell me. I'm here."

My God! Could he be any more perfect?

Just as I'm about to speak, he cuts me off. "I know I've been distracted lately with my parents. But I don't ever want you to think that I'm not here for you. I ... I've actually wanted to tell you something for a while." Cupping my face gently in his warm hands, the pads of his thumbs trace over my cheeks and his warm lips dance softly across mine. I melt into him knowing that it will be the last time I'll ever feel *this*.

When he pulls away from the kiss, he traces his knuckles lightly across my face. The action makes my eyes flutter open, and what I see before me is amazingly breathtaking. Bryan's warm eyes are wide and sincere. The soft crinkle in the corners that's always there seems softer now as his lips pull up gently at the corners.

He pulls both of my hands into his and brings them up to his lips. Returning our laced-together fingers to my lap, Bryan gazes at me one last time as the words, "I love you" tumble freely from his mouth.

Involuntarily, I gasp. My eyes widen and my heart

speeds up. Pulling one of my hands from his, I cover my mouth. Not knowing what I have to tell him, Bryan must confuse my reaction for excitement because he laughs at what he must perceive as crazy girl antics.

Without letting me say anything, he covers my mouth with his once again. He starts speaking against my lips, through our kiss. "I've never said it to anyone before, but I do. Melanie, I love you and I'm so sorry that I've been a crappy boyfriend lately."

With wide eyes and trembling hands, I inhale a shuddery breath and try to find the words that I know I need to say. But instead of words coming out of my mouth, tears stream down my face and my throat constricts.

"Shh, baby. Don't cry," he coos into my ear as he pulls me to his chest. Dancing lightly through the tangled mass of my wet hair, Bryan's fingers calm me a little.

"I'm so sorry, Bryan. I'm so sorry," I say I'm sorry over and over again, but he doesn't know what I'm sorry for.

Yet.

Looking at me once again, his eyes still soft and warm, he calmly says, "It's okay. You don't have to say it back. Just know that I love you." He kisses his lips gently to my temple and I lose it.

Wrapping my frail arms tightly around his waist, I

tell him the words I wanted to tell him so long ago. "Bryan, I love you too, so much," I whisper the words a few more times into his heather-grey T-shirt before pulling completely away from him. My body chills again without his warmth pressed up against me.

I wipe at the tears streaking my face and take a deep breath. Straightening my spine and squaring my shoulders, I swallow my guilt and let the words fall.

"I love you too. And no, I'm not just saying it because you said it. I do love you, but I have to tell you something else, and I know that after I tell you, you won't love me anymore." He gives me a "don't be crazy" look and moves to speak, but I cut him off.

"I slept with someone else."

I wish I could say that I feel lighter for finally having said those words, but I can't. All I feel now is crushing pressure as my heart begins to implode.

Bryan recoils from me and shoots up from the couch. There isn't much space in the small room, but he's frantically pacing the small patch of carpeting that's there. I can't imagine what's racing through his head. Hell, with everything going on with his dad cheating, I *don't* want to imagine it.

I notice that his hands start to shake so I stand up next to him and try to hold them to calm him. Not surprisingly, he doesn't let me touch him. Instead, he folds his arms across his chest and stands stoically in front of me. He scrubs his hand gruffly across his face and growls out a loud "fuck" which reverberates through the small living room.

I can feel his anger pulsating off him. The tension is so palpable that I just don't know what to say. Nothing matters now, anyway.

Roughly, he stuffs his hands into his pockets and stares at me harshly. "With who?" he grits out.

"I don't know." A mouse squeaks more loudly than I just spoke.

Seething now, he steps in front of me. "What did you just say?"

"I said, I don't know." My eyes are staring at the old, stained carpet – that sight more pleasant than the anguished filled look I'd surely see on Bryan's face.

"You don't fucking know? What the hell kind of answer is that? Tell me everything, Melanie." He yells and it forces more tears to spill past my lids. Still unable to speak, he yells at me again. "Fucking tell me!"

I fall back on the couch at the anger in his words. I hate myself for putting them there, for erasing the beauty that is usually etched onto his face.

Through my sobs, sobs to which I have no right, I choke out, "It was over Christmas break. I'm so sorry, Bryan. Please, I love you. I'm so sorry."

More pacing and more sobs. An awkward, painful silence. Our hearts are being torn in half, with the hope of ever being repaired off in the vast unsure distance before us.

After a few minutes, my tears stop enough for me to see that his anger has morphed somewhat into sadness. Bryan flops onto the couch and huffs a loud sigh.

I look over at him – his shoulders sag and his face sinks with pain. With his eyes searching the ceiling for some kind of escape, he whispers, "Why?"

His elbows fall to his knees and his head drops into his hands as he whispers "why" over and over again.

"I … I … don't know. I'm sorry." I stumble over my words unable to find any that will help to explain my motives.

"No!" he barks. "Tell me, now. Why? Was I not good enough?" The hurt that tramples across his face makes me cave and tell him everything.

"It was because of the text. And then you weren't calling me. I wanted to come visit you, but you told me not to. I thought you had moved on." I let the words race out of my mouth and hope to God that they make sense.

Huffing, he stares at me confusedly. "What text?"

"Courtney sent me a picture of you two kissing and I just figured you got back with her. And then you told me not to visit you and you were so distant … I just thought … well, I just thought you were done with me."

"Done with you?" he seethes quietly, but his flippant sarcasm shines through. "I thought I'd never be *done* with you," he adds sadly.

A beat later, his anger returns as he recalls the rest of my words. "Why the fuck would I get back with her? Especially after everything I told you about her! Hell, even if she wasn't a stuck-up bitch, the fact that I have told you over and over again that I don't want her … that I want you. I don't fucking understand why you never believe me."

"I don't either, Bryan. I hate that part of me … that part that questions everything. That can only see me as worthless. I …" Crying sounds emerge as my words trail off.

"You are not worthless," he says as he sits back down next to me. His words are a little softer than they were a few minutes ago, but he's still distant and cold. "And I told you not to visit because my parents were splitting up. None of that had *anything* to do with you and me."

"I know. I know. I wish I knew that then, but I know it now. Please believe me that I'm so sorry. I would do anything to take it back, but I can't."

"This isn't just about the cheating, Melanie." His words shock me to silence.

"What do you mean?" I manage to croak.

"You don't trust me, Melanie. You never have, but what's even more difficult to get past is that you don't trust us. You don't trust that what we have is enough for me. My God, it was enough. But no matter how many times I told you that, you never believed me."

"No ... I do believe in us. Please, Bryan. Give me a chance to prove it to you. Please, please, please." I reach for his hand again and when he pulls away from me it's like I've been punched in the gut.

"I can't, Melanie. I can't move past this." He turns his face away from mine, but I grab his stubbled jaw and pull it back to me.

"Please. I'll do anything. Please don't leave me. Bryan, believe me. I'm sorry." I've never been sorrier for anything in my entire life.

Bryan reaches up and pulls my hand from his face. When he looks in my eyes, I can see tears shimmering in his, just beneath the anger and pain that hover at the surface. "I can't, Melanie. I need to be with a girl who loves herself as much as I do. I deserve to be with a girl who is secure enough with who she is that she doesn't need my constant reassurances." His hands clench into fists and his knuckles turn white under the pressure. "I can't be with someone who doesn't have enough faith in *us* and in *herself* to get through a rough patch. I'm sorry, Melanie, but I just can't."

And on his last words, he stands from the couch and picks my jacket up from the chair that he tossed it on when I walked in over an hour ago. As I turn to step into it, I realize that his small dining room table is romantically set for two. The take-out menu for Bella's restaurant is out next to the phone and there are unlit candles everywhere. Bryan tracks my stare and shrugs his shoulders and mumbles, "I was going to surprise you with an early Valentine's Day dinner."

Any last hope I had of leaving here without being completely and utterly broken, have now been annihilated.

I reach for the knob and feel an icy blast slap me in the face as I open the door. I hear the jangle of Bryan's car keys, but the thought of being next to him as he drives me home is more than I can bear.

I reach for the hand in which he's holding his keys and stare up into his eyes. "No. I'll walk." He nods and drops his keys onto the small side table.

Stepping over the threshold, I look at him one last time as the words, "I'm sorry" get stuck in my throat.

Bryan looks at me with pain in his eyes as he says, "Goodbye, Melanie."

I do nothing but stare numbly as he closes the door on me. My heart splinters into a million tiny fragments when I hear the lock click. He's gone from my life forever and I know that I've been irrevocably changed by what just happened.

They say that when one door closes, another one opens, but I think they're lying.

Part Two

Bandaged

Chapter 11

April 2013

"Melanie! Wake up, girl. You're going to miss your midterm. Come on." Peyton's not-so-gentle wake-up call includes yelling in my ear and shaking me somewhat violently. "Let's go, Melanie. If you don't get your ass out of bed right now, I'm going to get the ice water … again."

I lamely roll to my side and face her. Glaring at her from under my forearm,which is draped across my face, I give her the side-eye. "You wouldn't."

Her face lights up playfully. "Oh, but I would. Let's go."

Instead of getting out of bed, I roll back over and face the wall. Grumbling incoherent nonsense at Peyton's craziness, I don't even hear her leave the room.

But when the freezing cold water comes splashing down on me, I know that she's returned. "What the freak! I can't believe you just did that!" I screech as I jump out of my now drenched bed.

"Well, I did." She stands with her hands on her hips sticking her tongue out at me. "I've had enough of this moping around and not-doing-shit business. You haven't done much of anything these last six weeks and I can pretty much guarantee you that if *I* didn't wake *you* up, you'd be missing another midterm." She rolls her eyes at me as I stand before her wringing out my soaked pajama shirt.

"Fine. I'm up. Are you happy now?" I snap sarcastically.

"Thrilled, actually. Now get your ass out of here in the next ten minutes and I'll be ecstatic," she bites back as she starts tapping the face of her watch. When she stalks out of the room and closes the door behind her, I flip her off.

As I get ready for my last midterm before spring break, I think back over the last six weeks and realize that Peyton is not entirely wrong. I have been in a funk. Well, actually to call it a funk is quite an understatement. My grades have slipped. My attitude sucks. I'm angry most of the time, and when I'm not angry, I'm depressed. The real kicker is that the only person to be blamed for all of this is me.

Bryan's words about not being able to love myself and of not having enough faith in who I am as a person repeat on a continuous loop in my head. And, in these last six weeks, I have replayed the last eighteen years of my life through the lens of those words.

Did I not have many friends in middle school because the kids were mean? Or was it because I was just too insecure to meet new people? Was the reason I didn't date in high school because no one was interested? Or was it because I would never let anyone close enough because I was so afraid to show them the real me? Is my complete inability to receive a compliment a result of me not feeling that way about myself in the first place?

I've been so open and loving to all of the important people in my life – my mom, Maddy and even Reid in a weird brother-sister kind of way. I'm always there whenever anyone else needs me, but it's possible that I've left out one very important person – me.

Why can't I love myself the way I love my friends and family? Why can't I see myself the way that they see me?

Why can't I see me the way Bryan saw me?

Lost in my world of what-ifs, I don't realize that my ten minutes to get ready is coming to a close. When Peyton starts banging on the door, I call out, "Okay.

Okay. I'm coming."

I grab my bag and head out the door telling Peyton that I'll be back around noon. She's driving me home today for spring break. Since Elmira is on her way, she offered to bring me home. I didn't want my mom to have to deal with the inconvenience, so I took Peyton up on her generosity.

Maybe it wouldn't have been such an inconvenience to Mom, anyway. Maybe *I* just see myself as an inconvenience.

Maybe it is time to stop seeing myself as worthless. Maybe it is time to start seeing the value in myself.

Maybe.

My mini pep talk helps to lift my spirits a little, and as I settle into my desk for my mid-term, I catch a glimmer of hope dangling out in the horizon.

As I step out onto the quad after my exam, I breathe in the cool spring air and feel rejuvenated in a way. Walking back to the suite, I think over my mid-term and I feel okay about it. I don't think I aced it, but I doubt that I failed it. Laughing at myself, I realize that how I feel about my test is rather appropriate for how I feel about my life too.

I'm sort of stuck in this hazy, grey, no-man's-land. I'm not moving forward, not fixing anything. I simply exist. I haven't bothered talking to Bryan since we broke up. There'd be no point. I even resigned from the computer lab right after we broke up. Being around him almost every day was just going to be utter torture for both of us, so to be fair to him, I left.

As I walk past a tree under which Bryan and I often had lunch together last fall, I see new leaves springing to life. This winter was harsh in more ways than one. The snow and cold were unbearable at times as was the emptiness that grew in my chest. As April rolls in, the weather is warming slightly. As the sun is shining a bit more often, I wonder if it's time for me to change too.

Regardless of whether or not my future holds a chance with Bryan, like he said, I need to fix me for me. And if this newer and better version of Melanie has even a sliver of hope to get Bryan back, then that'll just be the icing on the cake.

This transformation isn't going to happen overnight; of that much I'm sure. Scary though it may be, it's a change that I know will be for the better.

"What's up with you?" Peyton chirps across the cabin of her small black sedan.

"Huh? What do you mean?" I twist toward her, genuinely confused by her question.

She huffs at me and leans her elbow on the door

as she turns to face me as well. "You've been a real lump lately. And now today, you're actually smiling. That's after I dowsed you with water, too. So, what's up with that?"

I shrug my shoulders and answer a non-committal, "I don't know."

I already told her about Bryan. There's only so much crying you can do in front of someone else before they call you out on it and make you talk. She was pretty great about it too. Nothing was sugarcoated in "everything will be okay and he'll take you back tomorrow" frosting. No, in true Peyton fashion, she told me that the whole situation sucked ass and that she hoped I could be happy again soon.

"Oh, cut the shit, come on. We've got an hour or so to kill on this car ride, so talk. What's going on in that pretty little head of yours?" She reaches across and pats my head with this big dopey grin on her face. I can't help but laugh at her.

I roll my eyes and give in. It'll be one hell of a long hour with her bugging me like this. "I was just thinking about something that Bryan said to me. He told me that I needed to learn how to love myself, that part of the reason he couldn't be with me was because I didn't have enough faith in who *I* am to be able to have faith in our relationship." I shrug my shoulders again and straighten in my seat. "I'm just thinking he might be right."

As she changes the station on the radio, she doesn't say anything, but she seems like she's lost in thought. When she settles on some 80s rock station, she stares out of the front window and avoids my eyes.

"I think he's right too," she says softly. "I know we're not super close or anything like that, but from what I see, I have to agree with Bryan. Hell, I've tried to get to know you better in the last few months, but you're always on guard, always concerned about what I'm going to think about you or say to you." Awkwardness stretches between us before she adds, "I think you're pretty cool, Melanie, but what I think doesn't matter. Your opinion of yourself is the most important one out there. And I can tell that you don't regard yourself all that highly." She faces me again and says, "Maybe if you stop worrying about the Melanie that you think everyone else sees, you'll grow to love the Melanie who is already there."

There it is again – *maybe*.

"You're right, Peyton," I sigh and inwardly yell at myself for wasting so much time hating who I am. "I've compared myself to other people for too long. But I'm not them; I'm me." Staring back out the window, watching the world pass me by, I mutter, "Now, I just have to figure out who *me* is."

Since it's late Friday afternoon, I don't expect anyone to be home. So when Peyton pulls into the packed driveway, I'm more than a little surprised.

"What and they didn't roll out the red carpet?" Peyton laughs and pokes me in the arm. "That's one hell of a welcome home party."

"Yeah, I guess so." I unplug my phone from the charger and grab my purse. "It's just my mom and her best friend Linda and Maddy. I don't know whose car that is." I tip my chin at the black SUV parked next to my mom's car. "Do you want to come in for a few minutes and meet everyone?" I want to make up for keeping her at a distance, but I also understand why she might not want to join me. I catch her eye the clock, and realize that if she comes in for a while, she'll have to drive through the night.

"Nah, it's okay. I should just drive straight through. I've got another five hours ahead of me." Peyton reaches for the gearshift and I feel like a huge dork for not even thinking about that.

"So stay the night. Please? It'll be fun." I clasp my hands together in front of me practically begging her to give in.

I feel like a kid in a candy store when she moves her hand from the shifter and kills the engine. "Alright, fine. I'm in." Peyton's nonchalance is bypassed by the smile that pulls at her lips.

Before we can even get our bags out of the car, Maddy comes barreling down the front stairs and races right into me. "Mel! I missed you so much," Maddy mumbles her words as she wraps her arms tightly around me. When I feel her growing baby-bump against my own belly, I pull away from her and hold her at arm's length. "Wow, Maddy. You look …" Words fail me as happiness washes over me.

Misunderstanding my pause, Maddy swats her hand in front of her and says, "Huge, right! I can't believe I'm only half way there. I'm only going to get bigger." Her hands automatically move to cover her belly.

"No, you look beautiful." I can't hold back the single tear that trickles down my cheek. I step to her side and introduce Peyton. After sharing an awkward "hi", we all walk inside where Maddy warns me that Mom, Linda - who I've missed almost as much as Mom, -and someone else who she knows I'll be very excited to meet, are all waiting for me. It's been a while since I've seen her, but that conspiratorial glint in her eye tells me that something is up.

Stepping through the door, an overwhelming sense of *home* engulfs me. I know it seems crazy, but even the air just feels different in here. When Mom catches sight of me, her arms are around my waist in an instant. "Oh Melly Belly! I missed you, baby." Feeling her tight embrace makes me regret every phone call I've avoided making in recent weeks; it makes me cringe thinking about all the times I didn't pick up her calls. "I missed you too, Mom." Before we can say anything else, Linda pulls me into her arms and carries on and on about how I need to come home more often. I realize that Peyton is still standing in the door way waiting for me.

"Oh, jeez. Sorry about that, Peyton." I step to the side and pull Peyton into the room a little more. "Mom, Linda, this is my new roommate, Peyton. She's going to stay the night and drive home in the morning." Peyton waves meekly at them and squeaks out a hello. She really is a tough nut to crack – all outspoken and quirky one minute and then shy and quiet the next. Peyton quickly excuses herself to the bathroom and Mom pulls me into the kitchen.

The man standing at the stove cooking something looks vaguely familiar, but I just can't place him right away. As we walk toward him, he wipes his hands on a dishtowel that's draped over his shoulder. His kind grey eyes shine at Mom as she approaches him. "Melanie,

I'd like you to meet Evan."

He extends his hand toward me and shakes mine firmly. "Hi, Melanie. It's good to see you again."

See me, again?

"Hi, Evan," I say, but it comes out sounding more like a question than a statement.

Mom notices the clumsiness of the conversation and chimes in to clarify. "Evan is Reid's stepdad's brother. You met him back in December, remember?" It feels like way more than just a few months has passed since then, but once she mentions it, I do remember him.

And then as Mom steps next to Evan and he gently pulls her to his side, another kind of awareness dawns on me. "Oh my God!" I point between the two of them rapidly. "Are you two …?" I feel like the world just tilted off its axis. My Mom, the woman who swore off dating for years, has finally found someone!

"Yes, we are, Melanie," Mom says sternly as she looks up to Evan for reassurance. I think she's mistaken my shock for anger, but that's the last thing I'm feeling. Sure, I don't know much about Evan, but I saw how he looked at her when she walked into the room. I see the way he's holding her close to his side. I'm not an idiot.

She's happy. That's all I need to know.

A warm feeling blooms in my heart and a smile

splits my face. "Well, it's about freaking time." I wrap my arms around her and squeeze her as tightly as I can. I feel her exhale deeply on a sigh as she relaxes. The three of us don't get much time to chat as Reid walking through the door interrupts our conversation.

Watching him hug Maddy, while gently rubbing her growing belly, makes my heart skip a beat. In the thirty minutes that I've been home, I feel like my heart has been recharged. Out of the corner of my eye, I see Peyton excuse herself from a conversation with Linda. When she stands next to me, she whispers, "So that must be the baby daddy, huh?" Elbowing me in the ribs, we share a giggle and make our way over to the happy couple for one last introduction.

Reid walks away from Maddy and pulls me into a tight embrace. "Hey, Mel. I've missed you."

"Me, too Reid. It's so good to see you." In the time that he's been with Maddy, Reid really has become like a brother to me. All of these years, I wished for siblings. Now, that I finally have them, even if not by blood, I feel like the luckiest person on earth.

"How about lunch sometime this week? I'd love to come and see you at work, maybe catch up with Dylan too." I miss my weekly lunch dates with Reid and I'm mad at myself for letting too much time go by since I've seen him.

"Nothing would make me happier, Mel." Reid

smiles down at me before we catch a suspicious glare from Maddy.

She snickers as she was over to us. "My God! You two are in the same room for less than two minutes and already you're scheming something." I could deny her accusation; I could tell her we're just planning a regular lunch, but where's the fun in that.

Reid and I exchange a conspiratorial wink and Maddy huffs at us.

Before long, Evan and Mom call everyone into the kitchen to grab some dinner. Apparently as a retired New York City Firefighter, Evan is a culinary whiz and knows how to make one hell of a baked ziti. Dinner is fantastic and not just because the food is great. Everyone is chatting lively and laughing at each other. Even Peyton joins in on the conversation.

I can't help but smile at Mom and Evan exchanging sweet looks at each other. If I'm not mistaken, I think they're holding hands under the table too. I am so going to have to get the run down on them later, but for now, I think I'll keep my mouth shut and not embarrass Mom.

Around eight o'clock, Linda starts to leave and Maddy and Reid follow her. Maddy shares a sly wink with me as she walks out the door. She let me in on her little plan to throw Reid a surprise party in a few weeks to celebrate his new job. I love that I finally get the chance to help her pull a fast one over on him.

Mom and Evan are still in the kitchen cleaning up when Peyton sits next to me on the couch. "So what gives?" she prods, but I don't know what she's getting at.

"What do you mean?" I ask as I absentmindedly flip through the channels.

"Well, with all that 'Melanie doesn't love herself' crap, I just figured you were from some kind of broken home or something like that." She pauses to survey the room before her eyes settle back on me. "But this place is pretty great and you clearly have a bunch of people who really love you." As she tucks both of her legs underneath her body, she adds, "So, I ask again, what gives?"

Dumbstruck, I can't think of a single logical explanation. So I simply say, "I don't know, Peyton. I just don't know."

An "ahem" from behind us, interrupts our non-conversation and Peyton stands from the couch. Mom and Evan must be done in the kitchen and they're now standing behind us. "I'm going to go grab a shower and get ready for bed. I want to hit the road early tomorrow." I nod as she walks past me. "It was nice meeting you guys. Thanks for having me."

"You're welcome here anytime, Peyton." Mom gives Peyton a small smile and Evan nods at her as she climbs the stairs.

Grabbing his coat from the rack in the entry way, Evan says, "Alright, Lucy. I think I'm going to head home too. I'll let you girls catch up." I get up to say goodbye and Evan tells me, "It was really great to see you, Melanie. Hopefully the three us can get together before you have to go back." Evan extends his hand to me once again and I politely shake it in return.

I excuse myself and allow them a little privacy for whatever they might have to say to each other. But, peering out of the kitchen, I can't help but catch a glimpse of Evan tucking Mom's hair behind her ear and kissing her tenderly on her cheek. When she places her hand on his chest as she leans up on her toes to reach his lips, I feel another piece of my heart come back together.

The door closes and I hear Mom walk into the kitchen. "Can I make you some tea, Mom?" She knows what I really mean to say is "Sit your butt down and fill me in on every single detail."

"I think I'll pass on the inquisition for tonight, Mel." She laughs as she gets a dishwasher tablet from under the sink. Loading one last dish and popping the tablet into its slot, she closes the door and hits the start button. Conversation would be pointless now over the loud humming and whirring of our ancient dishwasher.

When she smirks at me, I know that was her plan.

She's a smart one! Wrapping my arm around her waist as we walk out of the kitchen and up the stairs to our rooms, I tell her, "Fine. You're off the hook for tonight, but tomorrow I want to know everything."

She squeezes me back and kisses the top of my head when we get to the top landing. "You got it. Love you."

"I love you too, Mom." I stand there and watch her walk down the hallway toward her room and all I can think about is Peyton's question from earlier.

Surrounded by Mom's love daily, how is it that I never learned to love myself?

Chapter 12

Peyton is up around six the next morning and she leaves before Mom even gets up. Needless to say, Mom is disappointed. "I wanted to get to know her better." She shrugs her shoulders and adds, "Maybe next time, huh?" Reaching for the coffee pot as it beeps, she offers me a mug. We sit at the table sipping our coffee for a few minutes before I finally break down and start grilling her about Evan.

"He's cute." I drop that out there and wait to see what happens.

Before she asks, "Who?" her eyes shimmer with the tiniest flash of happiness.

Fine, I'll bend first. "Evan. Besides, Reid was the only other guy here last night and that would just be weird." I shiver and make a gross throw up sound in my throat. She giggles at me and I reach out to grasp her forearm. "I'm really happy for you, Mom."

When it seems like she finally believes me, she relaxes and her face takes on this dreamy, far-away look. "He is pretty cute, huh?" It's like she's a teenager all over again.

"Well, sure. If you like salt and pepper hair, a chiseled face and a muscular body, I'd say so!" I raise an eyebrow as I take a sip of my coffee. Swatting my arm, Mom's cheeks turn pink.

Over the next hour, we catch up on pretty much everything. It turns out that she's been seeing Evan since the end of December. He's never been married and doesn't have any kids of his own, so both he and Mom were good with taking things slow to start. As she tells me about him, I can see her face light up. I seriously hope that things work out for them.

"So then do you see a future with him or are you still in the 'taking it slow' mode?" I ask cautiously. I don't want to scare her from sharing.

She sighs and slumps in her chair a little. "Oh, I don't know. It just seems like such a fuss to change how things are. He's got his life and I've got mine. That's good enough for me." I can tell that her words belie her true feelings.

"But what if your life and his life came together somehow. Maybe it could be some kind of 'our' life." I use air quotes around the word "our" and she laughs at my silliness.

Pulling her mug up to her lips, she mumbles against the rim of the glass, "Ehh, who knows? Maybe, someday." Knowing all too well how it feels to be pushed into talking about something that you just do not want to talk about, I leave well enough alone.

I get up to pour us another cup of coffee. As I begin making some English muffins, I ask something that's been on my mind since last night. "How old is he anyway? He seems kind of young to be retired already." I push the button on the toaster and lean against the counter, waiting for her to answer.

"He retired early," she says curtly, but sadly.

"Oh, how come?" I question as I walk the two steps to the refrigerator to put back the bag of muffins and get out the butter.

"9/11." Her words come out at the same time that the toaster pops, but I sink into my seat rather than finish making our breakfast.

"Was he hurt?" I place my hand over hers as a sad look takes up residence on her face.

"Yes, but not how you're thinking." In true 'mom' fashion, she gets up from the table and finishes making me breakfast. Sliding our mugs back in front of us and sharing the plate with our English muffins, she tells me Evan's story.

"He wasn't even working that day, actually. He was out for a run that morning. You were only five at the time, so I'm sure you don't remember, but it was a beautiful fall day." She's right. I don't remember.

All I remember was being picked up from school early; I was in kindergarten. When I saw Mom walking down the hallway to me, I thought it was the best day ever. And it was in a lot of ways. We had ice cream for dinner and cuddled on the couch for hours. It seemed like she didn't want to let me go. When I asked her to read me another bedtime story, after she had already read four of them, she didn't argue. She just grabbed another princess book, held me on her lap and read to me until I fell asleep in her arms. Looking back on it, I now realize why those things occurred, but at the time, I just thought it was like getting an extra birthday or Christmas.

"Well, when he came home from his run, he saw the news and immediately left for work. By that point, all of the bridges and tunnels into Manhattan were closed for traffic, so he had to walk through the Lincoln Tunnel. By the time he got there, the buildings were already gone. So were thousands of people." A stray tear streaks down her cheek, which she quickly wipes away.

"Evan spent the next few weeks at The Pile. That's what the firemen and volunteers called it, even though the rest of us only knew it as Ground Zero." Mom tucks a piece of hair behind her ear and takes a bite out of our now cold breakfast. "Sorting through all of that rubble damaged his lungs. Finding the remains of his co-workers, the people who were his only family, well, that took a toll on his soul, too." Mom blinks back a few more tears, and with an emotion-filled, wobbly voice, she continues. "He was lucky enough to beat the lung cancer, but the stress of digging up body parts, that's what he couldn't handle. He eventually filed with the medical office and was cleared for early retirement." Unable to hold in her emotion any longer, the sobs take over her small body. I immediately move to hold her, unable to contain my own sadness.

After we've both calmed, I hand her a napkin so that she can blow her nose. "You've both been through so much." My words are barely a whisper, but I know she hears them.

"What do you mean? He's been through more than anyone should ever have to go through," she says as she wipes a final tear from her eye.

Taking a deep breath, I garner the courage to ask something that has plagued my thoughts since I was old enough to think them. "You lost Dad so long ago, though. And then all you had was me. Weren't you sad all that time? Weren't you always missing something?" Thick emotion chokes the last few words in my throat.

Mom wastes no time and pulls me into her arms. Brushing her fingers through my hair, she shushes me, but lets me cry until my eyes are dry. Pulling away from me, she looks into my eyes, which I'm sure are puffy and red from all the crying. "Of course I miss your father. I love him very much and he'll always have a piece of my heart, but I don't ever want you to think that my life wasn't complete because it was just the two of us." Pushing my curls behind my ear, she presses her lips to my forehead and smiles lovingly. "You are the best thing that has ever happened in my life. Being your mom has brought me so much joy and happiness that I can't ever imagine doing anything more important with my life." She kisses my forehead again as I wrap my arms around her and hug her with all my love.

We stay like that, comfortably wrapped in each other's arms, for a few more minutes until the sadness evaporates. Breaking the embrace, I tell her that I love her. "And I love you more than you'll ever know, Melanie." It's the look in her eyes as she says those words that mends another piece of my broken heart. Over the years, I really did feel like she was wasting her life on me. I felt like she deserved so much more happiness than the life we had together, like her life was on hold because of me.

It turns out that *I* was her life.

What about now, though? With that though in my

mind, I hit reverse on the conversation and loop back around to an earlier point.

"So don't you think you deserve all of that happiness that you missed out on with Dad? I mean, Evan is pretty great from what I can tell. And I know that he makes you happy. Why waste all of this time saying things like 'maybe someday'." I use the air quotes again and she laughs, again. But then she sighs in a rather resigned fashion.

"What if he doesn't feel the same way though?" Wait a damn second! Did my mom, the greatest woman ever made, actually just voice an insecurity?

She has got to be kidding.

"Mom," I say the word with added emphasis just to make sure that she's really listening to me. "I saw how he looked at you last night. Hell, he freaking made dinner for all of us and acted as if he's always been a part of this crazy-ass family. And don't think I didn't see you two hold hands under the table."

She opens her mouth to protest and I just waggle my finger in her face. "Oh, don't even think of denying it. I saw you." She moves her mug to her lips again knowing that anything she says will just be used against her anyway. "And I think he feels the same way about you that you do about him."

"But what about you, Melanie," she says hesitantly.

I hold my hands out to the side as I shrug my shoulders. "What about me, Mom? I'm good. I've got great roommates and a life of my own away at school. You don't have to worry about me; I promise." For added assurance, I make a crossing motion over my heart. Holding out my pinky to her, I say, "Pinky swear."

"Okay, fine," she laughs as she hooks her pinky around mine and we 'shake' on it. "So you're going to go for it with Evan?" Giddiness accompanies my words as I bounce in my chair.

"Yeah, I'll give it a shot," she mumbles, but I can see the excitement in her eyes.

Mom stands to wash out her coffee mug and she asks, "Speaking of boyfriends, how's Bryan? What's going on with you two?" Yep, I'm that jerk of a daughter who doesn't even keep her own mother up to date on what most would consider a fairly important piece of information.

"We broke up." I opt for the "rip the Band-Aid off in one fell swoop" approach and hope she doesn't prod too much. But this is my mom, after all.

Her face falls as she sinks back into her chair. "Oh no! What happened? When? Why didn't you tell me? Are you okay?"

So prodding it is, then.

I'm so not going to get into the whole cheating

thing. We're close and all, but I don't need to talk about *that* with my mom. Opting for short and evasive, I answer all of her questions at once. "Things just didn't work out. About six weeks ago. Life got crazy. And yes, I'm fine."

She's onto me and arches an eyebrow as she smirks. Holding her hands up in front of her chest, she surrenders. "Okay, fine. I won't push. I'm here for you though." She smiles and stands from the table. Kissing me on the top of my head, she asks if I want to join her and Linda in a fun filled day of yard sale shopping.

"Um, no thanks. I'll pass, but you two have fun." She hears the sarcasm in my words and rolls her eyes. "I think I'll call Maddy and see what she's up to."

"Okay, you two have fun, too," Mom says happily as she walks up the stairs.

I have to laugh because the only difference between Mom and Linda going to a few yard sales and Maddy and I strolling through the mall is about twenty-five years.

After about two hours of pointless shopping, we walk past a Starbucks and Maddy pulls me inside. "I need to sit. My ankles are swelling like crazy." I glance down at her feet, and even though they look fine to me, I choose not to argue with the pregnant lady.

After we each get a chocolate chip cookie and an iced tea, we sit in a small table off to the side, away from anyone else. That's when Maddy's plan comes into focus. She doesn't say anything; she knows better than that. I'll just answer what she asks. Instead, she gives me the death-ray stare, indicating that she wants to know *everything*.

I pop a piece of cookie into my mouth and stare back at her. She doesn't relent, so I roll my eyes and sigh. "Fine! I'll talk." Maddy leans forward across the table, well, as far as her protruding belly will allow her. "He broke up with me," I admit shamefully. Even though she reaches for my hand comfortingly, the look that passes across her face conveys that she'd figured as much.

"I'm sorry, sweetie." Her eyes crinkle in the corners as she squeezes my hand. "Why haven't you called? You know I'm here for you, right?"

I take a sip of my drink and chew nervously on the straw. "I don't know, Maddy. I was embarrassed and ashamed. Honestly, I was too sad to do much of anything." I take a deep breath before admitting the next part. "He told me that he loved me first, before I told him about the cheating. Before he broke up with me, I mean."

Maddy's face clearly conveys her shock and

concern. When she doesn't say anything, I nod and add, "I know. I told him that I loved him too, but after I told him about the text and the cheating, well, I guess love wasn't enough." Shrugging my shoulders, I take another sip of my drink as I try to swallow my tears too.

After a few minutes of tense silence, Maddy asks, "Do you think you guys will get back together? I mean, have you seen him or anything like that?"

"I doubt it. I really screwed up. I'm pretty sure he's done with me." I want to hold on to the small hope that maybe we can work things out. But, my grip on that idea is slipping.

With a knowing look in her eyes, Maddy breaks off a chunk of cookie and pops it into her mouth. "People screw up all the time," she says around her food. "Just because you make a mistake, it doesn't mean that it can't be fixed." She takes the last piece of cookie and a sip of her drink. I know she's talking about her and Reid. But how often do things work out like that in real life? That stuff is better left to romance novels and chick flicks. I doubt I'll ever be that lucky.

As we're clearing our garbage from the table, Maddy notices a guy in the line. "Mel," she whispers to me. "That guy is totally checking you out."

I peek over at him, trying to make it look like I'm reading the board hanging above the barista. He doesn't look familiar, but when he makes eye contact with me he smiles at me like he's just won the lottery.

Maddy sees it too. "Ohh, he's adorable. Go talk to him." She's nearly pushing me across the small café.

I actually have to pry her hands off my shoulders. "Shhh, I will not." My attempt at *not* drawing attention to us fails miserably and the cute guy actually starts laughing at us.

And, yes he is cute. Light blond hair, soft green eyes, and an athletic build – yeah, he's pretty easy on the eyes. But still, I'm not ready to strike up a conversation with some random guy. The only time I've ever done that was when I first met Bryan, and well, though this guy may be cute, he's not Bryan.

"Melanie, just go talk to him. Look, he's staring at you!" Maddy's voice is getting louder as we get closer to the door. He catches my name and as he steps away from the line, he walks toward us. "Melanie? I thought that was you." He jams his hands in his front pockets nervously and Maddy looks at me inquisitively.

I still have no freaking clue who the heck he is. I'm sure my face conveys those thoughts, because he laughs as he says, "You don't remember me, do you?" He tilts his head to the side and I really can't place him.

"No, I'm sorry." I try to walk past him, but he gently places his hand on my arm; there's no force in the move, but he clearly wants me to remember. "We met at Lindsey's party, back in December. I'm Tyler. Tyler Cole. You really don't remember me? We, umm …" As his words trail off, my stomach drops to the floor.

It's him.

Maddy sees the look of fear and sickness -that passes across my face. "Are you okay, Melanie? Do you want to get out of here?" She loops her arm through mine so that we're locked at the elbow.

I can't really get any words out of my mouth, but I know that I need to get away from here. I want to run. I need to move my feet, but they're super-glued to the floor. As my stomach returns to where it belongs and my brain starts to function again, my desire to run fades. Swiftly, I realize that I do want to talk with him. I have to know exactly what happened that night. I feel like it's the only way I'll ever be able to move past it.

Pulling my arm from hers, I finally get my mouth to work. "I'm good; I promise. I'll be out in a few minutes." She just nods and waddles out to a bench that is set up in between two kiosks.

"Can I get you anything?" Tyler asks as he walks me over to the table that Maddy and I just vacated.

I shake my head and opt for bluntness. "That night fucked-up my life pretty good, you know." Tyler recoils from my words and his brows knit together. My anger, though outwardly directed at him, is inwardly focused on my own stupidity and shame.

A puzzled and hurt look washes across his face before he says anything. "Okay," he draws out the word, clearly shocked by my anger. "I don't really know how, though." He folds his arms across his broad chest and leans back in his chair.

The nothingness of the last six weeks flashes before me and anger boils like lava in my veins. With a strangely even and calm voice, I manage to speak rather than yell. "You don't know how sleeping with you when I had a boyfriend screwed things up for me?"

"Whoa! Wait a second," he blurts out loudly enough to catch the attention of a few people standing on line. Realizing his little outburst, he leans across the table and adjusts his volume. "We did *not* sleep together."

No one could mistake the look in Tyler's eyes for anything but honesty and sincerity.

"What did you just say?" I demand, instantly needing him to clarify his statement.

His eyes scan my face, searching for any sign of me playing around with him. When all he finds is uncertainty, he takes a deep breath and rakes his hand through his platinum hair. "I said, 'we did not sleep together'. We met at the party and started talking. We were actually having a great time, until you got some text or call. Then you got plastered." Pieces of that night start to fall in place. He's right. We were legitimately just talking until Courtney texted me. I still can't place the rest of the night, so I silently prompt him to continue.

"Well, when you could no longer stand on your own, I helped you over to a couch and that's when you started talking about your ex-boyfriend," he admits sheepishly.

"I'm sorry, but did you just say, *ex*?" I'm sure that my face is twisted in confusion.

"Yeah, at least that's what you told me. Look, I wouldn't have kissed you if you said you had a boyfriend. I'm not a douche like that." Tyler holds his hands up in front of his chest in a sign of mock-surrender. His eyes convey his honesty yet again and I can't *not* believe him.

Holy shit! I can't believe this. Could this whole fuck-up with Bryan really have been avoided?

"So, you're telling me the truth? We never …" I motion my hand between the two of us as if that somehow clarifies what I mean to say.

Tyler laughs sympathetically and shakes his head. "No, we didn't. Believe me, I wanted to. We started fooling around and you were talking about finding another room, but you couldn't even stand up. You clearly weren't with it and like I said, I'm not a dick like that, so I wasn't going to take advantage of you."

I gasp and my hand flies to cover my mouth as I realize that he's right, we didn't sleep together.

"Do you believe me now?" he questions apprehensively.

Speaking through the fingers that are still covering my mouth, I nod and say, "Yes. Oh my God! I can't believe that I thought …"

Recalling visions of that night, the line of events becomes crystal clear. I was drunk. He was kind. We made out. Maybe we fooled around a little. I passed out. And then he drove me home. That's it. No sex. No cheating. Just me stumbling through my front door in the middle of the night and Reid helping me to bed before I woke anyone else up.

Holy mother of freaking shit!

Remembering one piece of information, I whisper, "But then how did I end up in a guy's shirt and bra-less?" Honestly, when I woke up the next morning in someone else's shirt and my bra was missing I just figured *everything* not *nothing* had happened.

"As I was driving you home, you pulled it off and threw it out the window." He laughs, and adds, "You were actually trying to take off your shirt too, but I managed to stop you before you got to that point. All of the moving around must have made you sick because you threw up. I had my gym bag in the back and I helped you change out of your shirt." Tyler smiles sympathetically at me and then quickly sobers when he realizes the sad look on my face. "Are you okay? You don't look so hot." Tyler's friendly tone brings me back to the here-and-now.

Quickly recovering, I stammer, "Yeah, I'm fine." Numbly standing from my chair, I vaguely catch a glimpse of Maddy through the window. "I just have to go now."

Tyler stands and walks me to the door. As Maddy walks over to us, he seems like he wants to say something more, but honestly, at this point, I just need him to go. So I dismiss him before he can say anything else. "I guess I'll see you around, Tyler."

Awkwardly shoving his hands in his pockets again, he says, "Um, yeah sure. See ya." And then he turns and walks away.

Maddy wastes no time in her interrogating. "What the hell was that about? What happened?"

Because no amount of explaining will clear the air, and because one small word can answer both of her questions, I simply say, "Nothing."

The rest of spring break goes by too quickly. And before I know it, I'm heading back to Ithaca for the final month of school. I was quick to take Mom and

Evan up on their offer to drive me back. Evan came over a few nights during the week and it was a little weird having a man in the house, but seeing how happy Mom is when he's around, it was pretty easy to get used to.

One night when Evan wasn't over, Mom confessed that she talked to him about their 'relationship'. She used air quotes that time. Much to her surprise, but not to mine, he felt the same way. She figured that since he had never been married, that he wouldn't be interested in a serious relationship. He stunned her into silence when his only answer was that he hadn't met the right woman yet.

About ten minutes into the drive, Evan turns down the radio and makes eye contact with me through the rear-view mirror. "So, Melanie, what's your major? Your mom never mentioned it."

I lean forward and rest my chin on Mom's shoulder. Poking her in the arm, I take the opportunity to joke around with her. "Why's that, Mom? Don't want to talk to your boyfriend about your boring daughter?" I draw out the word boyfriend to emphasize their newly and officially defined relationship.

She calmly places her hand over mine which rests atop her shoulder and pats it gently. "No, my dear." She quips with more than a little bit of sarcasm. "I didn't tell him because you never told me." She sticks her tongue out at me and smirks.

Her words sober me. I really have been out of touch. Having only recently decided on my major, it's something of which I'm very proud.

Beaming from ear to ear, I share my plan. "I actually just declared my major at the beginning of the semester. I'm going to study early childhood education with a focus on children with special needs. I start doing some field work next semester."

Mom twists in her seat and her face is beautifully lit up with pride. "That is a wonderful choice, Melanie."

"That's great," Evan chimes in. "What made you decide that?"

Neither one of them knows about Emmie, but she is the reason I made the decision. "I just figured helping kids who might not have all of the advantages as everyone else is a pretty good way to spend the next thirty years of my life."

"Oh, that's perfect for you, sweetie. You're so great with kids." Mom folds her hands across her lap, seemingly unable to contain her joy.

Evan places his hand atop Mom's and he laces their fingers together. It's a sweet gesture that makes my heart spill over with happiness. Meeting my eyes in the rearview mirror once again, Evan's face is decorated with a proud look not unlike Mom's.

"A buddy of mine from the fire department has a

kid with Autism. She goes to a summer camp right near Ithaca every year. If you'd like, I can call him and get some information for you. Maybe they need a counselor or something like that." Anyone else might mistake his offer as one meant to try and win me over, but I can see the honestly in his eyes reflected to me in the mirror. He's being genuinely kind.

"Wow, yeah, that would be great, Evan." I've really come to like Evan this past week based solely upon how he treats my mom, but seeing that he wants to do something nice for me as well, that he wants to develop a relationship with me too, makes me soften to him even more.

The rest of the drive is filled with laughter and fun conversation. And when we pull into the parking lot at my building, I'm happy to see Cammie, Lia and Peyton's cars are already in the lot. Evan carries my bags for me, and Mom and I walk up to the suite before him. I lean into her side and whisper into her ear, "I like him."

She smiles coyly in return and replies, "So do I."

Hearing our girlish giggles, Evan clears his throat. "What are you two laughing at up there?"

We say, "Oh, nothing," at the same time which only adds to our little giggling fit.

When we walk into the suite, the girls are busy doing a whole lot of nothing. Actually they're lounging on the couch sipping cosmos, watching my *Sex and the City* DVDs. When they realize that Mom and Evan are with me, they get a little nervous. That nervousness evaporates immediately when Mom claps her hands excitedly and runs to the couch. "Oooo, is this the one when Mr. Big and Aiden have that pissing match and wrestle in the mud?"

Lia and Cammie move to the sides of the couch and make room for Mom to slide in between them. It doesn't take long for the three of them to start arguing over who Carrie should be with. It's a pointless conversation, really. Because after all of the hardships and trials, Carrie ends up right where she belongs – in the arms of her true love.

Cammie, Lia and Peyton are all over twenty-one, but even if they weren't, Mom would never turn down a girl's night like this. I'm not going to say that my mom condones underage drinking, but she's not naive. I won't lay out all of the times I've been drunk, but she knows this is not my first drink and she seems fine with it.

I call out from the kitchen, "Mom, can I make you a drink?"

She peers over the back of the couch and looks at Evan. "Is it okay if we stay for a while, Ev?"

Evan's lips quirk up into a goofy smile. I doubt he likes the idea of spending a night with some cosmodrinking, *Sex and the City*-watching twenty-somethings, but, I see it in his eyes – he'd do anything to make Mom happy.

"Of course we can stay. I'll run out to Wegman's and grab something to make for dinner while you girls enjoy your sex show, or whatever the hell it is."

As I walk him to the door, I say, "Thank you" and plant a quick kiss to his cheek. I think the display of affection catches him off guard, but he smiles at me nonetheless.

After I hand Mom her drink, I make my way over to the large armchair where Peyton is sitting and she moves to the side, making room for me to wiggle in. She squeezes my knee and we share a knowing smile. I feel like this week has done me good and I think she sees that change in me.

When the episode wraps up, Lia situates herself so that she can make eye contact with all of us. "So, I've got good news." We all eye her cautiously. "Good news" with Lia can mean that she picked up a cute pair of shoes on sale.

When she doesn't say anything right away, Cammie holds her hands out in front of her. "Care to share it with us?" she prompts.

"I found us all an apartment for the summer and for next year! Off-campus housing, here we come!" Lia pumps her fists into the air, but my eyes immediately go to my mom. Can I really spend the whole summer away from her?

Mom looks directly at me and mouths the words, "It's okay," before saying aloud to the group, "That's fantastic, Lia. You girls will have so much fun! Where is it?"

"It's right behind the school on Coddington Road, right across the street from that cute little Italian place," Lia answers Mom's question and I know exactly what house she's talking about because the Italian place that she's talking about is Bella's.

All of us chat excitedly about the possibilities that this new beginning will bring. While we're making our second round of drinks, Evan comes in with some groceries and immediately begins cooking a quick meal of chicken fajitas and rice.

Before I even realize it, it's time to say goodnight to Mom and Evan. I really loved having them here and I silently vow to make a much more concerted effort to both visit home and have them here more often.

I giggle as I watch Evan help a slightly stumbling Mom into his SUV. Thinking back over this week and how much it has healed my heart, I'm sad to see her go, but so happy to know that she's got Evan now. Burying the last few weeks behind me, I'm suddenly looking forward to next few weeks and the hope that dangles out on the horizon.

Chapter 13

June 2013

By some miracle, and with a lot of Peyton's help, I manage to pull my grades out of the gutter and I finish my first year of college with a 3.4 average. Not my best work, but all things considered, I'm more than pleased with the results. I've actually surprised myself in recent weeks with the whole "you don't have to be perfect all the time" routine. A lot has changed since spring break, in fact. The most important change has been that I've actually grown to like myself much more than I used to. I've learned to forgive myself over what happened with Bryan. I still haven't worked up the nerve to talk to him, though. I walked past the lab the other day. I didn't expect him to be there so as I peered into the large window-lined wall of the lab as I walked past, I nearly tripped over my own two feet when his sad brown eyes met mine.

I wanted to go to him and ask him a million questions. How are things with his parents? How is Emmie doing? Is he excited about graduating? What are his plans for the summer?

Does he miss me?

But instead of doing that, I offered up a tight smile and a small wave. He nodded in return and then promptly busied himself with something on his computer. Part of me couldn't help but wonder if he was just touching random keys to avoid looking at me.

I miss him a lot. But it's not in that silly, pining, teenage girl way. I miss him in a way that actually hurts my bones. I didn't realize it back when we were together, but the way he made me feel about myself was more than just special. And, no, I'm not talking about the physical stuff. He helped me see the value in myself that I should have seen a long time ago. He loved me not because he had to, but because he wanted to. And, yeah, I hate myself for having ruined that love, but it served as an epiphany of sorts. I was loved despite the flaws I thought I had, and in the process of growing that love, I found out that what I saw as some of my worst flaws were actually some of my greatest assets. I just wish I could have one more chance; I wish I could get a do over with him – with us.

I've thought about telling him what I learned from

Tyler, but I just haven't been able to work up the courage. I'm not sure that it would make a difference anyway. I want to think it will change how he feels about me, like it will allow him to forgive me, but then his words about learning to love myself ring in my ears and I chicken out on talking to him again.

I've changed, but can I really say that I love everything about who I am?

Can anyone *ever* love everything about themselves?

Maybe the best you can hope for is learning how to appreciate who you are without paying much attention to who you aren't.

Maybe that's how I've changed the most. I've learned to love myself for who I am instead of hating myself for who I'm not.

And no, not all of my new-found self-appreciation has come from Bryan; that wouldn't really be true self-appreciation anyway. I've done a lot of soul-searching and I learned to no longer define myself by my flaws. Everyone has flaws. I refuse to be defined by mere imperfections.

I think a large part of being able to forgive and love myself has come from talking to Mom too. I no longer feel like I've been a burden to her all these years. Seeing her with Evan has lightened my heart. In a way, it's like I was holding back allowing myself to be happy until I knew she was happy.

I love that she's moving on, and in a way, it's given me permission to let go and move on as well. Well, move in actually. It's our last week in the suite and I am more than excited to move into our new apartment.

Cammie, on the other hand, is not so happy. It's her sad face that I see as I return to the suite from getting lunch with Peyton. She had to go work at the tutoring center and Lia is out shopping. I have no clue what else that girl could possibly need. When I asked her, she said "New clothes for the apartment, silly." Of course! Why hadn't I thought of that?

Rather glumly, Cammie is packing up some dishes and silverware in the kitchen. As I close the door behind me, I walk over to her and hop up onto the pale blue Formica counter. "Based on the look on your face, I guess he's sticking by his decision, huh?" I pull a tortilla chip from the half-eaten bag on the counter next to me and crunch on it as she contemplates her answer.

Leaning back against the counter, she grabs a chip and bites into it rather forcefully. Crossing her arms over her chest, she sighs. A resigned look flits across her pretty face. "Yeah, he is. I know it's what's best for him, but I hate the idea of being apart from him for a whole year."

I jump down from the counter and grab two

bottles of water out of the fridge. Handing her one, I say, "But you'll visit him and he'll visit you. Chicago isn't *that* far. Besides, when you graduate, you can move there with him."

Huffing a sigh again, she concedes. "I know. I know. I'm being a total girl over this. It's just that we've been together for five years now and we've never been more than a two hour drive away from each other." Sipping her water, she adds, "And now he's going to be starting a huge part of his life without me and it's scary."

Jack will be moving to Chicago in just a few weeks to start his two-year grad-school program for Physical Therapy. At the end of it, he'll be a real doctor and everything. It's weird to think of Solo-cup-filling Jack being called Dr. Parker.

I wrap my arm around her shoulder and give her a tight squeeze. "Cammie, you two are the strongest couple I have ever met. While it might take some getting used to, I know that you'll make it."

Lia takes this opportunity to barrel through the door carrying way too many bags for her own good. "Did you leave anything behind for anyone else?" I joke as I help her with the bags.

"Oh, shut it! I got lots of stuff for the apartment. I want it to be pretty," Lia declares as she starts pulling scented candles and colorful vases out of the bags.

There's no denying it; the girl has a serious sense of style. I am more than willing to let her decorate our place for us.

"This is all really pretty," I remark as I let a purple table runner glide through my fingers.

"I know! I'm good, right?" she says proudly.

"Did you ever think about doing anything with it? Your talent, I mean? Oh, you could go on one of those 'be the next big name designer' TV shows or something like that." Lia takes my wisecrack in jest and just laughs at me.

As she's wrapping a glass bowl in newspaper, she replies to my question. "Actually, I have thought about doing something about it. It turns out with just a few extra classes, in addition to my fashion design degree, I can also be a certified interior designer."

Cammie squeals with delight, her face beaming with pride for her cousin. "Omigod, Lia. That would be perfect for you!"

Not that I didn't think it wouldn't be, but I know that with Lia's touch our apartment is going to be much more than that. It is going to be a home and I can't wait to move in there. The three of us spend the rest of the afternoon packing up the suite getting lost in the memories and excited about the future.

Moving sucks. Jack and a few of his friends helped us with all of the boxes, and since the apartment is furnished, we didn't have too much heavy lifting, but still – this sucks. We've spent the last few days cleaning everything. Counters, floors, rugs, windows. I mean the place was sort of clean when we came to see it a few weeks ago, but then the shit must have hit the fan – or the old tenants threw one huge-ass party.

We've only been here for about a week or so, but already it feels like a home. It also helps that it is actually a home. We're renting a small single-level home. With four medium-sized bedrooms, a large living and dining room combo and a fairly new kitchen, it's nothing like the suite and everything like a real house. With a lot of elbow grease and Lia's decorative touch, the place is finally done. I fold up the final empty box and tie up the last garbage bag and take them down to the curb where the other garbage is piled high.

I'm a sweaty mess today. Wearing rolled up sweats and a beat up, hot pink tank top, I know I look like a hot mess. But, stepping out into the hot sun of the early summer, I feel new and alive. Scanning the small flowerbed to the side of the front stoop, I see that it's overgrown with weeds and decide that it too needs be fresh and new.

Hell, I'm filthy already. What's a little more dirt?

Crouching down on the lawn, I start ripping and tearing at the overgrown weed garden. After ten minutes, my nails are caked with dirt; sweat is dripping down my face and my shoulders burn both from the sun and the strain. But I've made progress and I'm excited to get a few flowers to plant.

After tossing the weeds into the pail, I wipe my dirt-covered hands on my sweats. Lifting my arm to wipe a drop of sweat from my face, I catch a whiff of myself and oh dear Lord do I stink. The girls will all be home in a little bit so I've got just enough time to shower in peace before the battle over the bathroom begins. One bathroom. Four girls. That's never fun.

Before turning to walk back inside, something across the street catches my attention. I should say someone, actually. I don't know how I missed it before, but that's Bryan's car parked in the small dirt lot. Just as my heart lodges in my throat and my stomach crashes down to the floor, Bryan catches sight of me.

Of all freaking days.

By some magnetic force, instead of walking back into the house, I am pulled to him. He must feel it too, because instead of getting in his car and driving away, he crosses the road walks right up the small walkway that leads to where I'm standing.

"Hey," he says tentatively as he rakes his hand through his hair. It's grown longer since I've seen him last and a few strands fall back into his eyes even after having pushed them away.

"Hi." My voice is shaky and uneasy. I hate that.

I raise my arm to my head to block the blinding sun that's beating down on us from behind Bryan, then I remember that I'm a smelly mess. Swiftly dropping my arm to my side, I hope he didn't just smell that.

"So you moved, huh?" Bryan scans the front of the house and nods in approval. It is a cute place, if I do say so myself.

"Yeah, just last week actually." Out of nervousness, I wipe my hands on my pants once more. His face is cast in the shadow created by the sun glaring from behind him so I'm forced to squint in order to see him.

"It's nice," Bryan states blandly.

"Uh huh." Oh God, this is going nowhere and fast. This conversation, if you can even call it that, is jilted and awkward. We haven't talked in three months, but it shouldn't be this difficult to talk to the person you once loved.

The person you still love, in my case at least.

Needing to fill the void of silence that is threatening to swallow us whole, I say, "So," as I shrug my shoulders lamely.

He shrugs his. "Well, I should get going." Just as he turns to move away, I grab for his arm. I forget about my dirty hands and my stinky pits. I need to talk to him. I want to talk to him. I know that I can't let him get away.

Staring down at my filthy hand wrapped around his tanned forearm, his face takes on a resigned look. I wonder if he feels *it* – that fiery crackle of heat that has existed between us since we first met.

I feel it.

Extending my arm to the small porch, I ask if we can sit and talk. He simply nods and we arrive at the steps in three short strides. Thinking back to just a few weeks ago when I saw him through the window at the lab, I remember wanting to ask him a million questions. But now, sitting here on my front steps, our legs almost touching, my fingers still vibrating from just having touched him, I can't remember a single one of them.

I opt for the topic that I think will make him the most happy. "How is Emmie? Is she excited about the summer?"

His lips tip up in the corners and his tense shoulders relax as her name comes out of my mouth. "Emmie's good. She loves the summer. Her birthday was just the other day and she went on and on about her party for days." Then his lips turn down and then tension is back. Hanging his head low into his hands, he sighs agitatedly.

"What's wrong, Bryan?" My fingers itch to be laced through his; my hands are almost shaking with the need to rub comforting circles on his back.

"It's the divorce. That's all." The abrupt curtness of his words tells me that things have not been going well.

"I'm here for you." He lifts his face from his hands and looks at me strangely. "I know we haven't talked in forever and I know that things didn't end well, but I can be your friend. We can talk. I hate seeing you like this, Bryan."

The strange look that was in his eyes morphs into something that looks a lot like longing. "No, we can't be friends, Melanie. I can't get over how you didn't trust me." He shakes his head and sighs loudly. "You know after we broke up, Courtney came after me again. I still didn't want anything to do with her. When I said something to her about texting you, she came clean – told me it was an old picture. I think she felt like if she told the truth, she would have a chance of getting back with me. But, I still can't wrap my head around how *you* couldn't trust me. I still can't … We can't be friends." He stands from the steps and turns to leave.

"Wait!" I call out when he's at the edge of the lawn.

Walking up to him, I only hope that he'll accept what I have to say. "I understand if you don't want to be friends. I just want you to know that I'm here for you if you need me." He nods and it makes the next words get caught up in my throat. "Just before you go, there's one thing I need you to know. I never meant to hurt you. I'm so sorry for immediately thinking the worst with the text." I start nervously fidgeting with the hem of my shirt and stare down at it like it's the most interesting thing in the world.

What looks like anger and sadness swirl together across his face. He simply says, "Yeah, I'm sorry too," before tipping his head to the approaching mailman. "Maybe I'll see you around."

"Yeah, maybe," I mumble but quickly realize that he's already too far to even hear me. All apologies about what I didn't do are lost to his retreating back.

"Here you go," the cheerful mailman says as he hands me a large padded envelope and a few flyers.

"Thanks." When I'm at the door, I turn back to look in Bella's parking lot and see Bryan in his car staring at me from across the street. When he sees me looking at him, he coolly slides on his sunglasses and pulls out of the lot.

And out of my life.

I didn't get the chance to tell him the things I wanted to say. He deserves to know about Tyler and what didn't happen. I want him to know about my new perspective on life. I think he'd be proud of me for all of my changes. As the dust of his departing car settles, I wonder if I'll ever have the chance to say those things to him.

After a much-needed shower, the girls pull up with some Chinese take-out and a box; yes I said a box, of wine. Jack left today, and based on the puffy redness to Cammie's eyes, I can tell she needs some girl time. When she puts down her bags, I pull her into a big hug.

"Oh come here, Cam. It's going to be just fine." I try to calm her down as I hand her a mug of wine.

Taking a big gulp of it, she says, "Yeah, I know. Just a little sad, I guess."

"Well, we're here to distract you for the night," Lia chimes in as she waves a DVD of *Magic Mike* in front of her.

Snatching the DVD from Lia's hands, Cammie's eyes roam all over the case. "Yeah, this'll do." A seductive grin plays on her face and we all share a laugh as we make up our plates for our little dinner date with a few shirtless hotties.

"He is so freaking hot," Peyton calls out as Matt Bomber struts his stuff across the screen.

Gulping down the last of her third, or maybe it's her fourth glass, Lia shakes her head wildly. "Oh no! Him. He's the one I'd do." Pointing at Channing Tatum, Lia looks like she needs to wipe the drool from her chin.

"What about you, Cammie? Who's your hottie tonight?" I elbow her in the ribs, literally prodding her to have some kind of reaction to the girls' night that we planned all for her.

She takes a sip of her wine and shrugs he shoulders. No response. "Come on, Cammie. Given the chance, who would you spend one hot night with?" Cammie flushes red at Lia's little quiz.

"None of them." Wow, she's in full-on pout mood. I suddenly realize what it must have been like to live with me back when Bryan and I broke up.

Determined to lighten her mood, I pause the movie as Alex Pettyfer's abs ripple on screen. "Not even him, Cammie. Look at him! His abs have abs. That man is a God. You're telling me you would kick him out of bed?"

With her lips up against the rim of her mug-o-wine, she mumbles, "Fine. No. I wouldn't kick him out of bed." When we all whistle cat calls and rip with laughter, Cammie rolls her eyes but eventually gives into the laughter as well.

After my third glass of wine and some quality time

with the girls, I decide to turn in and get some sleep. I walk past my desk and pick up the envelope I got in the mail today. It's from Mom, but even through the padding, I can tell that it's a spiral notebook.

Sitting on my bed, I tear through the paper and pull out the notebook. There's a letter taped to the front of it across which is my name scrolled in my mom's handwriting. I absentmindedly trace my fingertip along the curved lines of my name and instantly miss Mom. She'll be here this weekend, but after seeing Bryan today, I could use some comfort.

I open the envelope and pull out the letter.

> Dear Melanie,
>
> I was going through the attic the other day and came across this notebook. I know that he would have wanted you to have it. Please know that I love you more than the sky. He did too.
>
> Love,
>
> Mom (and Dad too).

With shaky hands, I drop the letter and run my fingers along the faded blue cardboard cover of the notebook. This belonged to my dad. He actually touched the same spot that I'm touching right now. Gently opening the tattered cover, I see his words scribbled on the lines of the paper and tears spring to my eyes. Thumbing through the pages, I see a few dozen entries and they all seem relatively short.

March 1995

Your mom told me about you today. I'll never forget how she looked and how happy her words made me. I just wanted to let you know that today was the first day you became a part of my life and I'm very excited for the day that I'll be able to hold you in my arms.

Tears stream down my cheeks, and no matter how quickly I try to brush them away, they're immediately replaced by new ones. My dad wrote this book to me. He didn't even know me, but he wrote these letters to me because he wanted to let me know how much he loved me.

I read through more of them, but one in particular catches my attention and makes me smile through the tears. By my quick calculation, my mom would have been just about half way through her pregnancy at this point.

May 15, 1995

I felt you kick today. It was kind of weird and creepy, but it was also the most exciting experience of my life to date. Your mom and I were just watching a movie in bed. She grabbed my hand and placed it on her stomach. It wasn't at all what expected – a small bubble of movement at best. But, from that one little kick, I caught a glimpse of your tiny fingers wrapped around one of mine, of your little feet poking out of a blanket. Today, you felt real to me and I just knew I had to share that with you.

The next letter that I stop at has sonogram picture taped to the top. It's a profile shot and I trace over the curve of my tiny nose.

June 1995

We found out that you're a girl today. A girl. Your mom started crying right away. I was … well, I was just scared. I want to protect you from everything. From scratched knees, to failed tests, to broken hearts. But what if I fail? What if you get hurt because I couldn't do my job? I just hope you know that no matter how many times we fight over curfew or sleepovers or whatever things dads and daughters fight about, just know that I'm fighting with you because I love you.

That last entry makes me laugh through the tears. Now I know where I got that pesky need for perfection from. I flip through the journal and read about how he set up my nursery and helped Linda surprise Mom with a baby shower. It's weird how I've never known him, but through his words, simple strokes on a piece of paper, I feel like he's right here in the room with me. When I get to the last entry, the tears return. He wrote it the night before he died.

September 29, 1995

Dear Melanie,

Your mom and I have been discussing names lately. So if one day down the line when you're reading this and your name is Jessica or something like that, just know that I lost the battle. But on some off chance that your mom decides in my favor, I hope that I've addressed this to the right person.

Since you're due to arrive any day now, I thought I would make this a longer entry. There are a few things I want to say and I feel like if I can get these simple lessons on paper, you'll be able to come back to them when you need them, when I might not be there to tell them to you. I'm a man of numbers and figures, lines and buildings so I apologize ahead of time for not being too poetic with all of this.

1. Be kind. A warm smile with kind words will go further than any ounce of belittling ever will. The world might not always be nice to you, but you'll find beauty in the world when you are kind to it.

2. Be patient. Anything worth doing in your life will take time. So be patient, but always persevere. When you get knocked down, and you will because it's an inevitable truth in life, get right back up and fight twice as hard for whatever it is that you're working toward.

3. Have fun. You've got your whole life to worry about bills and mortgages and all that grownup stuff. Never forget to laugh and enjoy the simple pleasures in your life. You never know when they'll be gone.

4. Love with everything you've got. I never knew love until I knew your mother. And then when she told me about you, I learned what true love really means. So when you find someone you love, don't hold back.

And remember that, if all of these pieces of advice fail you, your mom and I love you more than anyone ever could. You're the stars in our sky and the song in our hearts ... Don't laugh. I said I was no good at the poetry stuff.

I can't wait to meet you, baby girl (who I not-so-secretly hope to be named Melanie).

Love,

Dad

After closing the notebook, I clutch it to my chest tightly and whisper through the sobs, "I love you too, Dad."

Chapter 14

July 2013

I've been a counselor here at Camp Hope for the last two weeks and I love it. No, like seriously love it. I have never been around so much happiness and so many smiles as when I'm with these kids. At the end of the day, I'm covered in dirt and grime, and sometimes glitter depending on the arts and crafts activities, but I wouldn't change a thing.

I'm on sports detail today and we're playing soccer. It makes me think of Bryan. Actually, ever since I read my dad's journal, everything reminds me of Bryan. I want to give us another try. I just haven't figured out how. I haven't even seen him since we talked a few weeks ago. I drove past his apartment in some futile hope that he would still be living there, but since the building is technically part of Ithaca College's housing department, I knew he wouldn't be there. For all I know, he could have moved back home.

"Can I help, Melanie?" Ruthie, a ten year old camper with Downs Syndrome asks as she pulls on my shorts.

"Of course you can. Let's get this net out onto the field. You take that side."

"Okay, I got it. Let's go." Her enthusiasm has me tripping over my feet as we stumble out of the supplies closet.

When we get out onto the field, I'm swarmed by the group of kids. Then Will, the counselor who I've been assigned to work with for the summer, blows the whistle. The kids all line up in the sideline. They're so eager to please. Everyone is brightly smiling and jumping up and down as they not-so-patiently wait for our instructions.

Playing it up like he's some kind of drill sergeant, Will clicks his heels together and stands up straight as an arrow. "Okay, Cadets. Here are the rules." The kids laugh at his imitation. They know him too well to take him seriously. One of the boys at the end of the line gets a serious case of the giggles and Will calls out "Hey you! Stop that laughing now." The little boy chokes back his laughter and salutes Will. The second Will's back is turned, the boy starts laughing all over again.

Will winks at me and carries on with his little

routine. The kids count off into "odd" and "even" teams and they sprint onto the field. After about ten minutes, we call a time out so that everyone can grab some water. Will walks over to me and hands me a water bottle.

"You're doing great, Melanie. The kids really like you." Will's hazel eyes light up as he compliments me.

"Thanks, Will. I really like it here. I can totally see why you come back year after year." I take a sip of my water and sit under the shade of the tree.

"Yeah, this place is great." He sits beside me and dangles his bottle of water between his bent knees. We sit in companionable silence for a few minutes as we sip our water. Having worked with him every day for the last two weeks, we've built up a decent friendship. The conversation usually flows freely, but as I finish the last of my water, the stretched-out void feels awkward and uncomfortable.

Will chugs down the rest of his water and turns to face me. "So, are you busy tonight? Can I take you out to dinner?"

His question catches me off-guard and I stumble over my words. "I, uh, yeah, I mean, no." Taking a deep breath, I steady my shaking hands and nervous words. "Sorry, I can't. My mom and her boyfriend are actually coming in for the weekend. They should be at my place when I get home." I gulp down a large swig of water. Anything to keep me from having to speak again. I like Will, a lot, but just not like that. I knew that I would be assigned to work with a more experienced counselor for my first summer. But when I found out that I was being paired up with the tall, dark and handsome man with the blinding smile and witty charm, I was more nervous than excited.

Taking my rejection in stride, he stands and holds his hand out to help me up. "Well, then maybe next Friday, huh?"

"Sure. We'll see," I say as I brush the grass from my butt.

Just as we're about to walk back out onto the field where the kids are clamoring to get started again, our boss and camp owner, Holly walks up to us. There's a girl standing meekly at her side and I recognize her immediately.

"Hey, Melanie, Will. I'd like you to meet our newest camper. This is Emmie. She just registered today." When she hears my name, Emmie glances up at my face. Recognizing who I am, she runs into my arms and squeezes me tightly.

"Melanie!" She squeals with delight. The power of her hug has us spinning in circles. When Bryan and I were together, I spoke to her on the phone constantly. I think she liked having another girl, besides her mom, to talk to. I'm not surprised that she remembered me, but her recognition warms my heart like the glowing sun.

Pulling away from her, we exchange smiles. A look of confusion passes between Will and Holly before Will asks, "How do you know each other?"

Tucking Emmie into my side and draping an arm around her shoulder, I tell him, "Emmie here is my BFF. We go back a long time." Emmie's big brown eyes twinkle with pride and admiration. "We're just about to get back to our soccer game. Did you want to be on my team, Emmie?"

"Yes. I love soccer!" She jumps up and down and claps her hands excitedly.

Holly squats in front of Emmie to make sure that they're at eye level. We're all very conscious of never talking down to the kids. "Okay, well you have fun then, Emmie. If you need anything, let Will or Melanie know. I'll be back before lunch, okay?" Holly ruffles Emmie's hair as she nods.

Squeezing my hand tightly, Emmie pulls me out onto the field. She's pretty much my shadow for the rest of the day which works out perfectly for me. It means that I don't have to explain how I really know her to Will. And he knows better than to get too involved in a conversation around the kids. They're little sponges who absorb everything you say so we're very careful to hold off on the personal talk until after work.

At the end of the day, I walk Emmie out to the parking lot. It's not a sleep-away camp so we all wait with the kids until their parents pick them up. Waiting there with Emmie, I ask her the question that's been on the tip of my tongue all day.

"So Emmie, who's picking you up today?"

In true thirteen-year-old-girl fashion, she shoots me an eye-rolling look. "Bryan is, silly. Who else would?"

I want to say that I wasn't sure where he was. That I haven't seen him in weeks and that I didn't even know he was still living in the area, but I know that wouldn't be fair to Emmie. Besides, I don't even know what she knows about us.

"There he is." Emmie grabs my hand and pulls me toward Bryan as he steps out of his car.

He looks about as surprised to see me as I was when I saw Holly walk onto the soccer field with Emmie in tow.

"Bryan, look! It's Melanie. She works here."

"Hey, kiddo. Yeah, I see that." Bryan takes in my counselor attire letting his gaze rest on my bare legs just a beat too long.

Emmie is twirling around so that her pigtails swing in the air. "Aren't you supposed to kiss your girlfriend, Bryan?" she teases.

Suddenly nervous, Bryan shoves his hands in his back pockets and rocks on his heels. "Uh, well …" As his words trail off, I mouth "It's okay," so that only Bryan sees me.

"That's sweet, Emmie, but I'm still at work. He's going to have to wait to kiss me until later." I wink at her and she lets go of the subject. Bryan mouths "thank you" to me.

"Come on. Let's get you back home for dinner, okay?" Bryan takes Emmie's backpack from her shoulder and plants a sweet kiss to the top of her head.

Before she runs over to his car, she gives me one last hug. "Will you be here Monday, Melanie?"

"Yep, I'll see you then, Emmie." I smile and wave at her as she opens the passenger door and pulls the seat belt across her shoulder. Gently closing the door behind her, Bryan faces me and a look of anguish and confusion knits his brows.

"Thanks for that save back there."

"No problem, Bryan." I nervously pick at a non-existent piece of fuzz on my shorts.

"Okay, then I guess I'll see you Monday." His words are rushed and I can tell he's just trying to avoid the conversation, but I can't let him get away that easily. Not this time.

"Wait, Bryan. We need to talk." He opens his mouth to speak, but I hold up my hand to stop him.

"Please, just let me finish." He nods and I try to gather my thoughts.

"There's so much that I need to say to you, so much that I need to explain." I pause as my emotions start to get the best of me. "I miss you," I add quietly.

I'm afraid to look at him. I'm afraid to find what his eyes will reveal about his feelings, so instead of looking at his reaction, I let my stare fall to the ground.

Needless to say, I'm startled when I feel his hand cup my cheek. I lean into his touch and peek up at him. "I miss you too." His whisper can barely be heard over Emmie knocking on the window to get his attention.

He turns to her and holds up one finger, letting her know that he'll just be another minute.

Looking back at me, he surprises me when he says, "You're right. We do need to talk. Can I call you tomorrow night?"

All weekend plans with Mom and Evan fade into the background. "Of course you can."

His face lights up briefly, but he quickly recovers. "If you still have the same number, I'll call you after Emmie goes to bed. I don't want her to get all confused. Okay?" When he clarifies the purpose behind our call, my heart hurts more than a little.

I quickly regain my composure, though. "Yeah, that sounds perfect. I'll talk to you tomorrow."

Reminding myself that I need to take baby steps

and that I need to be patient, helps me grasp onto the fleeting sense of hope that I had when he brushed his thumb lightly across my cheek.

I watch him get into his car and pull out of the parking lot. With a new-found sense of hope, I walk back to the main building of camp and gather my things to go home.

As the evening sun paints the sky a beautiful mix of orange and red, I recall the words that my dad wrote for me nineteen years ago. We've loved each other with everything we had. Now, all I need to do is be patient to see if we can get there again.

Chapter 15

As promised, Mom and Evan are at the house waiting for me when I get home. I made sure they got an extra copy of the key when I moved in. You know, just in case.

There's a car in the driveway that I don't recognize. It's a white Subaru and from the looks of it, it can't be more than a few years old. I've never seen it here before, so when I walk in the door, I call out, "Mom? Evan? Who's with you guys?" As I round the corner of the hallway that leads into the living room, I quickly shield my eyes as Mom readjusts her shirt and Evan his khaki cargo shorts.

"Oh my God! You two were totally making out!" I peer at them through my fingers.

"Stop it! We were not, Melanie!" Mom's defensive

tone does nothing but make her sound guiltier.

"So that means I can look now?" I spread my fingers into wider slits over my eyes as if I'm watching a scary movie.

That's essentially what I just walked in on.

"Yes, you can look. Stop it already!" I drop my hand at Mom's last words, but as she walks toward me something looks off. Recognizing what it is, I laugh.

"Um, Mom? If you weren't doing anything, can you explain how," I point at the buttons on her shirt as I count, "three of your buttons are still undone? Or did you just forget to do those this morning?" I put my hand on my hip and pop it to the side.

She quickly turns around to fix the uneven buttons and Evan chuckles softly at being caught red-handed. "It's good to see you, Melanie. How's camp working out?"

"It's great, Evan. I really can't thank you enough for telling your friend about me. I love it there." I drop my backpack to the floor and flop on the couch. "The only real pain in the butt is having to walk there and back. It's not bad, but two miles each way, especially after playing soccer all day with the kids is killer." I toe my sneakers off and stretch out my legs in front of me. After flexing my toes back and forth a few times, my legs feel a little better.

"So whose car is that out front?" A rather

conspiratorial look passes between the two of them, but neither of them says anything right away. "What gives, guys? Spill it already."

"Well, now that you're off-campus, we thought it would be nice for you to have your own car," Mom explains with excitement tingeing her words.

"We?" Another confused look passes between the three of us before Evan speaks up.

"Well, I was the one who actually suggested it. I didn't like the idea of you walking to and from campus." Evan scruffs his hand over his face. He seems like he's searching for the right words. "I would ... I mean, your mom would be too worried. So I made the suggestion and we found you a car."

Once I wrap my head around it, I jump up and clap my hands excitedly. Throwing my arms around Evan's neck, which I have to get on my tippy-toes to do, I plant a loud kiss on his cheek. "Thank you, thank you, thank you! This is so cool."

Mom joins us in our little group hug and hands me the keys. "Let's take it for a spin."

The three of us spend the next fifteen minutes driving around town and through the campus. Mom's been here a few times so she kind of knows the lay of the land, but Evan's never seen more than the parking lot for my old suite. Of course, he's most interested in the athletic fields.

As we pull back into the driveway, Mom suggests that we eat dinner at "the cute little Italian place across the street." I've avoided going to Bella's in the month or so since we've moved in because it holds too many memories for me. I know Bella will remember me, and I just don't know if I can deal with having to explain to her what happened. I haven't seen Bryan's car parked there since that day he saw me weeding the front flowerbed. I can't imagine that he gave her the run-down on everything so I'm pretty sure she'll grill me the second she sees me.

I'm formulating my response to say we should go somewhere else, when Evan chimes in as he rubs a hand over his stomach. "I could definitely go for home-cooked meal with my two favorite girls." Wrapping his strong arms around me and Mom, he kisses the top of her head. Okay, fine. I guess I'll have to give in. There's no denying someone who's that sweet.

Later that night, we're sitting at a table that Bryan and I sat at once. This time around, the candles don't have that same warm glow. The music seems off and the food, while still delicious, doesn't have the same yum factor that it did when I was eating it from Bryan's fork. It makes me sad to realize that the magic held within Bella's came mostly from the magic I felt with Bryan. It just makes me miss him even more.

After we've all devoured our lasagna, Bella walks over to our table. I guess I was lucky to have avoided her all night.

Standing to my side, she places her hand on my shoulder and squeezes gently. "Melanie? I thought that was you. Bellisima." She leans down and kisses my cheek. "You look beautiful. How are you?" Bella rambles on while Mom and Evan smile kindly at her.

I cup my hand over hers at my shoulder. "Mom, Evan, this is Bella, the owner." The both shake her hand as they tell her how wonderful everything was.

"Oh, thank you, thank you. We've been a little short staffed, so I'm sorry if you had to wait." Bella's hands twist nervously at the thought that her service was sub-par.

"No, everything was wonderful. It's a beautiful restaurant." Bella's face shines with pride at Evan's compliment.

"Perfect. Well, dessert is on me tonight. It'll be right out." Bella then leans down to whisper in my ear. "Don't leave without coming to see Bella, okay?" I pat her hand gently and nod in agreement. I have a feeling that I know what she wants to talk about, but I can't tell her no.

As Bella walks away, Mom excuses herself to go to the ladies room. Evan starts nervously fidgeting with his hands. Clearing his throat, he pitches his voice low as he speaks. "Melanie, I need to talk to you."

I lean forward so that I can hear him better. "Sure, what's up?" When he doesn't say anything immediately, as if he's trying to figure out exactly what to say, I start to piece things together. I gasp and cover my mouth. "Are you …?" My question trails off as Evan shushes me. I didn't realize I was being that loud, but when the couple at the next table peers over at us, I check my excitement and pipe down.

"Shhh. No. Not that." His face twists in discomfort. Evan's a big sweetie, but he's definitely a man's man through and through. I decide to cut him some slack and just sit intently and listen to him. "I know your mom and I haven't been together too long, but, well … I … I really like her."

That last line makes me choke on my water. "Not for nothing, Evan, but I doubt we'd be having such a hushed conversation if you just 'liked' Mom. Besides, you guys aren't sixteen." I raise an eyebrow at him. So much for cutting him some slack.

He sighs and leans across the small table. "Okay, fine. You win. I love her." His words are confident and proud, not at all shy or ashamed.

I make a "carry on" gesture. I knew he loved her; I just wanted to hear him say it.

"Anyway, I was thinking of asking her to move in with me."

"But …" I drag out the word, hoping that he'll fill in the blank. He better spit it out before Mom comes back.

"Well, I wanted to check that it was okay with you before I asked her. My place is tiny and I know how much your mom loves your house. I don't want to talk about moving in there with her before I know that it would be alright with you." He grabs for my hand and, as he gently squeezes it, a tear trickles down my cheek.

Swiping it away quickly, I catch Mom walking toward the table. "I think it would be amazing for you two to move in. As long as Mom wants it, then I want it. And my answer to the question I *thought* you were going to answer is yes too, just so you know." I wink at him as Mom slips into her chair. Evan becomes awkwardly silent and it doesn't take Mom long to pick up on it.

"What were you two chatting about?" She points between Evan and me and gives us "The Look."

Evan looks like he's about to choke on his tongue so I cover for him. "Evan was just going over some things about the car."

Picking up on my little, white lie, Evan adds, "Yeah, I noticed that the gear shift sticks sometimes." He takes a sip of his water and even though he doesn't say anything, his eyes tell me "thank you."

After we finish our dessert and take care of the

bill, Bella pulls me to the side. Mom and Evan walk back to the house; it's only right across the street. I let them know that I shouldn't be long.

"I need another waitress," Bella says bluntly.

Wow, that wasn't what I was expecting.

"Oh, Bella. I don't know if I can. It's just that …" She shushes me and waves her hands in front of us, literally trying to clear the air.

"I know what you're thinking. But Bryan doesn't come here anymore. He's too busy with grad school – at least that's what he said. He moved closer to Cornell and got his own place and everything. He set me up with one of his friends about a month ago and now he does all of the computer stuff." As Bella is explaining this, I have to admit that I do recall seeing someone who looked an awful lot like Simon from the computer lab walking out of here the other day.

And did she just say a month ago? So he left Bella high and dry just because I live across the street now. I feel bad for Bella. Bryan was so much more than a tech guy for her. She genuinely liked him. My heart softens for this kind grandma-like woman standing before me.

Without much thought, I tell her yes. "But I have a job at a camp during the week until the end of the summer. I can only do weekends." We're momentarily distracted by a waitress walking past us. The over-loaded tray that she's carrying wobbles precariously on her shoulder before it crashes to the floor.

"Oh dear!" Bella calls out as she grabs the broom and some dishtowels to clean up the mess. Of course I help her and the waitress apologizes profusely for screwing up. Bella tells her that it's okay, and instructs her to go place another order.

Over a pile of spilled ravioli, Bella clasps my sauce-covered hands and says, "Thank you!"

Before I leave, we figure out a few details of when I'll start. She reassures me a few more times that Bryan won't be around. I'm surprised and a little hurt that he talked to her about us. But, I guess it's for the best. We're not together, and as much as I might be hoping for that to happen again, I'm not so sure that it will.

The next night, I anxiously wait for Bryan to call.

But he never does.

I kind of feel like a fool for thinking that he would call. I ghost my fingers over my cheek and wonder if I'll ever get to experience his touch again. He's moved on; I know it. I hate it, but I know it.

Rather than dwell on it though, I spend the night with the girls and Mom watching a few movies. Evan goes to bed early, though I don't think he is all that tired. There's no spare room so I've let Mom and Evan take my room while I camp out on the couch. He must be watching a baseball game or something because every now and then we hear him yelling at the television.

I'm sad to see them go on Sunday morning, but at the same time, I know that very happy things are on the horizon for everyone. Mom and I solidified plans for Maddy's baby shower at the end of the month and we've also made plans to go wedding dress shopping for Maddy when I come home in August. And hopefully, helping Evan move will be part of my future too.

Waving at Evan's car as it pulls out onto the main road, my heart feels happy. Despite Bryan blowing me off, I know that I have people who love me. And it's weird how since I've let them love me, I've been able to love myself too.

I don't want to be mad at Bryan for not calling. He doesn't really owe me anything, but later that night, as I'm getting my things ready for camp in the morning, I realize that we do owe it to Emmie. I don't want her to keep thinking that we're together. That's not fair to her.

Going out on a limb, I hope that he still has the same number. I never deleted his contact information. Somehow, that seemed too permanent.

I dial and nervously wait for him to pick up.

He doesn't.

I understand that he's hurt, but if he would just give me a chance to explain. Who knows that he would even believe me about Tyler? But the fact of the matter is, that he at least deserves to know and I deserve …

Nothing, really.

But I do need to tell him and I want to talk to him about Emmie.

I try him once more, but again, he doesn't pick up. A deep breath and a punch to the pillow later, I've calmed myself down a bit. I decide that I just need to give him some space. He probably never expected to see me again; I know I didn't expect to see him.

As I'm finishing getting my things in order for the morning, part of the perfectionism that will never leave I guess, Peyton comes into my room.

She's leaning up against the door frame, smiling like an idiot. "Why are you so cheery? That's very unlike you." I stick my tongue out at her as she feigns a sarcastic laugh.

"I just came to tell you that you have a visitor." She smirks again as she crosses her arms over her chest.

"Who the hell would be visiting me at," I glance over at the glowing red numbers of my alarm clock, "ten on a Sunday night?"

There's that silly smirk again. "Well, I guess you'll

just have to find out." And with that she walks out of my room.

Pulling back the curtain on the front window, I take a look at the front porch to see who's paying me a visit. When I see Bryan not-so-calmly pacing back and forth, one hand in his pocket, the other combing through his hair, the air is sucked out of my lungs.

I take a deep, calming breath, but it does nothing to ease my racing heart.

I open the door and step out into the humid summer air. Bryan stops his pacing and just stares at me with a lost look on his face.

Softly clicking the door behind me, I suddenly can't find any words.

"Sorry for coming by so late." He rakes his hands through his hair again and then folds them behind his head.

"It's okay." I motion to the front step and we take a seat. Perched on opposite sides of a somewhat wide step, we both gaze out into the night sky. As I get lost in the blackness that is speckled with thousands of points of light, the lines of Grace Potter & The Nocturnals' "Stars" play through my head.

After a few beats of silence, we both say "So." at the same time. "You go first." I concede, mostly because I want to hear why he came here.

Propping his elbow up on his bent knee, he turns

to face me. "I didn't expect to see you ... at the camp, I mean. Or living across from Bella's, for that matter."

"You can imagine how surprised I was to see Emmie, then. How come she's here, Bryan?" His leg starts bouncing wildly at my question. Even though I'm shaking, I reach over and place my hand on his knee. When he calms down, I remove my hand, though it's the last thing I want to do.

"It's my parents. The divorce is a fucking shit storm." He stares up into the night sky and with an unsteady voice, he continues. "My mom is not dealing well at all." He pauses and sighs loudly. "She got really depressed and she started drinking." After another brief pause, he adds, "A lot – a-whole-fucking-lot actually. It got so bad that my dad was going to file for sole custody for Emmie. The asshole who walked out on us actually wanted to take Emmie away." An angry, flippant snarl escapes his mouth.

I don't know what to say, so I don't say anything. I just give him some room to breathe and think.

He pinches the bridge of his nose and looks over at me. "By some stroke of luck, the judge decided that he would give my mom one last chance if she went to rehab and got herself cleaned up. I drove down there to get her this past weekend." He sighs loudly trying to gain his composure. "So while she's away, Emmie is living with me. Hopefully it's just for the summer."

"Bryan, I'm so …"

"Don't you dare say you're sorry. I don't want anyone's pity." His harsh words cut through me worse than any knife would.

Twisting my fingers together nervously, I recover my thoughts and try for something a bit more hopeful. "Emmie seems to be doing well, though. I mean she was really happy at camp." I offer up a smile, but it goes unnoticed. "Where is she now?"

"She's asleep. My neighbor is watching her," he answers tersely. After a deep breath, he adds, "She's doing better now that she's not at home. But then seeing you …" The pained look on his face breaks my heart.

I want to believe that it's not his intention to hurt me, but that belief is fading – quickly. "That's why I tried to call. I just wanted to see what you told Emmie so that I don't say anything to upset her."

With his penetrating stare searing through my soul, I feel vulnerable, but for the first time in a long time, I feel alive. I feel renewed, like maybe there's a chance that he's seeing this new Melanie. Maybe he's seeing how different I am. He always saw the version of me that I wanted to see myself as, so maybe, just maybe, he's seeing the new me. But, when he looks away, I lose hope in that theory.

"I told her that we're just friends now. She asked if

we were divorced like Mom and Dad." Well, damn. There goes *that* hope. I want to ask if he meant what he said when he told me that he missed me. I want to wrap my arms around him and take away his pain. I want to curl up against his side and fall asleep in his arms.

But this isn't about what I want.

"So if she asks about us, just tell her that we're friends. And if she says anything about my parents, tell her that they are trying to be friends too. She understands that. It'll just make it easier on her." His voice is resolved and guarded.

"I can do that. I do want to be friends, Bryan. I know I hurt you, but ..."

He cuts me off again. "I don't know if I can be just friends with you."

Does that mean he wants to be more?

In a moment of bravery, I decide to share my feelings. Twisting toward him and grabbing his hand, he shoots me a shocked look at the contact. "Look, Bryan. I don't *want* to be friends. I meant what I said on Friday when I told you that I miss you. I *want* to be like we used to be ... no, wait ... what I mean is that I want to be *more* than we used to. I'm different, now. I never ..."

Just as the words "I never cheated." are on the tip of my tongue, he stands abruptly and bellows a frustrated scream out into the darkness.

He turns toward me once more, his voice a smidge lower than a yell. "I loved you! I loved you more than I've ever loved anyone. And it meant nothing to you. *We* meant nothing to you." On a growl, he turns away from me once again and stares up at the twinkling stars. "Fuck, Melanie. I needed you. These last few months …" His words get stuck behind the emotion he's working so hard to stifle.

Unable to see him in this much anguish any longer, I stand next to him, but don't touch him. "I can be here for you now. If you'll let me, I can be your friend and then maybe …"

The rest of my sentence is swallowed whole by his kiss. His lips are on mine hot and fast. With one hand tangling in my hair, and another gripping hard at my waist, he pulls our bodies together. The feel of his hard muscles pressed up against my soft curves is more than perfect, more than heavenly. It's a hard and passionate kiss, one that is sure to leave my lips swollen. His tongue licks and dips into the corners of my mouth, tasting me – no, devouring me. I inhale his sweet cinnamon breath – breathe it into my lungs, make it part of my existence.

Sucking hard on my lower lip, he pulls it into his mouth. He absorbs the groan of pleasure that I make when he bites on my captured lip. My arms wrap around his neck and tangle into his soft hair. Just as I'm about to pull him closer to me, he pulls away, leaving me breathless.

With our foreheads pressed together, he whispers, "Maybe what, Melanie?"

"Maybe we could …" I get distracted by his nose running up the length of mine.

"Yeah, maybe," he states calmly with a hooded and lustful look on his face.

And then he walks away from me, confidently strutting toward his car - leaving me speechless, hopeful and completely confused at the same time.

Since I don't have to walk to camp anymore, I can sleep in another thirty minutes. Which of course means that I oversleep. Jumping from bed, I call Will right away and let him know that I'll be a few minutes late. He laughs at my harried and frantic voice, but tells me that it's okay.

"Do you want me to come pick you up?" I'm sure that his offer has more to do with getting to talk to me alone than it does with getting me to work quickly.

"No, it's okay really. My mom bought me a car this weekend. I'll be there in like ten minutes." I hang up quickly and thank the OCD lords that I've laid out my clothes and packed my lunch the night before.

I would have liked to get to camp early today too. I never got the chance to tell Bryan about Tyler and what *did not* happen between us. Oh well, I'll just have to tell him today when he picks up Emmie.

I pull into the parking lot and race over to the arts and crafts room. The kids start out every Monday morning drawing pictures of what they did over the weekend. I find Emmie immediately and when I catch a glimpse of her picture, I am blown away.

"Wow, Emmie! Did you draw that?" I lean over her shoulder and instantly recognize what she's drawn. It's a picture of the gorge that Bryan and I went hiking through on our first date. I'll never forget the beauty of that place for as long as I live.

"I did," she says proudly. Emmie smiles at me and it's as beautiful as the stars I saw in the sky last night. "Bryan took me there this weekend." Emmie returns her attention to her picture where she carefully writes a title in bold capital letters across the top. "Happy Times Waterfall." She then adds "To: Melanie" at the top and "Love: Emmie" at the bottom before handing me her work of art.

"Thank you so much, sweetie. Are you sure I can have it?" Emmie nods excitedly, and I know that not accepting it is not an option. Holding it before me, I examine it once more; it really is a beautiful drawing. I can tell that art is her thing. "That's a really cute title, Emmie. How'd you come up with that?"

"That's what it's called, silly," she quips with as much sarcasm as any thirteen-year-old girl is supposed to have.

I poke her in the arm. "No, *silly*. It's called Hemlock Gorge."

"You can call it whatever you want. But when I asked Bryan, he said something about happy times. I like Happy Times better than Hemlock or whatever you called it."

Clutching the paper to my chest, this crayon scribbled picture from a teenage girl has now become one of my most precious possessions.

I feel like I'm walking on clouds the rest of the day. Knowing that Bryan took Emmie where he was happy with me makes me even more hopeful. The day passes by in a blur and my stomach is in knots as I wait in the parking lot for Bryan to pick up Emmie. She's running around in the small field to the side of the parking lot with a few of her friends and another counselor. I'm lost in my daydreams of the maybes that Bryan and I spoke about last night, so when Will sits down next to me, I'm momentarily startled.

"Hey, how was your weekend?" He sees me jump slightly and laughs.

"Good. It was great to see my mom." I might be

speaking to him, but I'm preoccupied with scanning the lot for Bryan's car.

"And you got a car out of it too, huh? That's a pretty sweet deal." He grins at me as he points to my car parked next to his.

"Yeah, it was a total surprise. I love it though."

Standing before me, he holds out his hand. "Come show me." He doesn't ask so I can't really say no.

"I can't. These kids are …"

Will waves over to Samantha, the other counselor and she waves back at us. "The kids are what? They're fine. Samantha is out there. I want to see your new ride." I give in, but stand on my own – without taking his hand.

When we're over to my car, I stand by the driver's door as he peers into the window. "Well, here it is. Not much to it. Four doors, a few tires and a steering wheel." I think he can tell that I'm trying to avoid him. I've been doing it all day.

Without saying anything, he leans up against the car and smiles at me seductively. "So, about Friday. Are you free?" That was his ploy the whole time. He wasn't really interested in my car. He just wanted to get me far enough away from the kids so that he could talk to me privately.

Nervousness sets in. Bryan should be here any minute and this is the last thing he needs to see – me pressed up against a car while Will is trying to get me to go out with him. "Look, Will. I like you, but only as a friend."

"Okay, so we'll go out as *friends*." He's not getting it. The truth is that if it wasn't for Bryan, I would be more tempted to give in. Will's attractive and funny. At only twenty-two years old, he's still well within my acceptable dating age.

"Thanks, Will, but I'm still going to have to say no." Without missing a beat, he reaches for the strand of hair that just fell from behind me ear. After he sweeps it back in place, he lightly traces his thumb down my cheekbone. "Are you sure about that?" he asks softly.

"I'm flattered, Will. Really, I am. I just can't." I pull his hand away from my face and he takes that opportunity to bring my knuckles to his lips.

Grazing over them lightly, he mumbles against my skin, "Can't or won't?" His eyes are pleading with me to give in.

I close my eyes and take a deep breath. Searching for some kind of strength, I huff out a frustrated sigh. "No, Will. I won't. Thank you but really, we're just friends." Before I can even push his hand away from mine, I hear the gravel crunch under someone's approaching footsteps.

"Just friends, huh?" Bryan's angry voice quietly

rumbles from behind Will's back. Throwing his hands up in the air, Bryan mumbles, "Fuck this!" as he stalks away.

Running after him, I call out, "No! Wait, Bryan! Wait!" He turns on his heel so quickly that I nearly collide into his hard chest. "What, Melanie?" There's pain in his eyes and I can see the fight leave his body as his shoulders sag.

"I can explain." The lame words die in the air between us.

"There's nothing to fucking explain. You're apparently *just friends* with him too," he seethes, but doesn't yell as he recalls our talk from the night before. Scrubbing his hands over his face and through his hair in restrained anger, he leans down so that only I can hear him. "Just when I thought I could trust you … when I thought I could possibly let you in again … you go and fuck me over … make me look like a fool. I-I'm done, Melanie. I just can't …" There's so much pain and anguish in his voice. The last of his words are muffled almost painfully as he walks away from me. He sounds as if he's about to cry and part of me wishes that he would. I deserve his anger – his yelling and cursing. But instead, I get restrained anger and seething pain.

Standing there numbly and near tears, I watch as Emmie runs over to Bryan. He helps her get into the car and he pulls away from me.

But this time, I feel like it's really for the last time.

Part Three

Healed

Chapter 16

November 2013

It hasn't been easy, but I've finally let go of the idea that Bryan and I will ever get back together. No matter how many times I tried to talk to him over the summer, whether it was calling him or waiting for him to get Emmie at camp, he always avoided me. He wasn't rude or mean. Keeping up the appearance of being friends for Emmie's sake, he was usually cordial. As nice as his attempts at civility might have been, I could always sense his anger and hurt bubbling just beneath the surface.

I was sad to see Emmie leave at the end of the summer. I cried as I hugged her goodbye because I would genuinely miss her, but also because I knew that when she walked out of my life, so would Bryan. He waited by his car on that final day, giving Emmie and I our space. She drew me another picture that day – one of her and me holding hands. There were tears in her eyes too as she pulled away from me and walked toward Bryan.

I wanted to run to him. I wanted to yell and scream and explain myself until I ran out of words to tell him, but the resolute nod that he directed at me across the parking lot was my cue that whatever maybes existed on that night that he kissed me, were dead and buried.

Absolutely refusing to go back to that dark place where I resided after Bryan and I broke up, and completely loathing the girl I was before that, I made a promise to myself to hold my head high. I waved at them as they pulled away and whispered "I love you," to him even though he would never hear it.

I'd like to say that with everything else that happened over the end of the summer, I didn't think about Bryan much, but I'd be lying. When Maddy and Reid's baby was born, I cried more tears of joy than I thought possible. And when Evan moved into the house, it instantly felt like more of a home than it had ever been. Mom is the happiest I've ever known her to be and that makes me feel freer than ever.

Even now, as the cool fall air breezes through my open window, I feel at home. That's what this place has become for me. What started out as a dusty and dirty place to live, quickly transformed into home filled with laughter and tons of happy memories. I know that when Cammie and Lia graduate at the end of the year I'll be sad. More than sad actually.

But I also know that I'll survive. Hey, maybe even Peyton will stay in Ithaca after her grad-program ends, but who knows. What I do know is that I've found happiness in the moments of quiet, and for the first time in my entire life, I am really and truly happy with who I am. I've made peace with my mistake and with the insecure girl I used to be. Those feelings of guilt and unworthiness have been replaced by ones of pride and love.

As I step out onto the front porch, I fix the Jack-o-Lantern that we carved the other night. It's lumpy and bumpy, not perfectly round, so it never stays upright for long. Maybe that's why I picked it. It reminded me of myself in some ways. Picking up a few stray candy wrappers from last night's eager trick-or-treaters, I walk across the street to Bella's and get ready for my Friday night shift.

Bella was right when she hired me. I haven't run into Bryan once since starting here back in July. The thought saddens me more than a little. But it also reminds me that he's moved on as well. I hope for his sake, and for Emmie's too, that things have worked out with his mom. I imagine that the divorce is finalized and things are hopefully back to normal.

Whatever the hell "normal" means, anyways.

As I'm setting up the wait station, Laurie, the hostess, comes up and hands me a ticket for a table she just seated in my section. "He's really cute too." She winks before walking away. Cute, huh? Okay, I could go for some cute in my life. I haven't had much of any cuteness since Will took me out on our one-and-only date. It was at the end of the summer after I knew Bryan and I were definitely done. I couldn't help it. Will was sweet and persistent as hell. It was an *okay* night; I can't deny that. But when he walked me to my door and gently pressed his lips up against mine, there was no spark, no desire, no rapid fluttering of butterflies in my belly.

Dismissing thoughts of how pathetic my love life has been since Bryan, I focus my attention back to the hottie who Laurie just seated at one of my tables. Knowing my luck, he's probably with his girlfriend. The cute ones don't come here with their grandmothers.

I peek out from behind the wall that separates the wait station from the dining room and when I see Bryan sitting at the table I was just assigned, I laugh inwardly at Laurie's "cute" description. He's not cute.

He's freaking gorgeous.

And he's with a girl – a girl who is most definitely

not his grandmother.

From where I'm standing, or spying, depending on how you want to look at it, I can see them, but they can't see me. Bryan's wearing a pale blue, fitted, polo that pulls oh-so-nicely across his muscled chest. If he were standing up, I'd be able to comment on how fine his ass looks in the charcoal grey dress pants he's wearing, but since he's not, I'll just have to use my imagination. His hair looks longer than usual, but it still has that styled-yet-unstyled look to it. My fingers twitch at the thought of running through the silky strands.

And of course the girl he's with is gorgeous too. Petite with shiny brown hair that sways gently at her shoulders when she laughs, she looks like a model. When she brings her glass up to her plump red lips, I ghost the pad of my thumb over mine and try to recall what it felt like to have Bryan's lips pressed there.

The feeling is fleeting though.

He hasn't been mine for months, and watching the two of them share a laugh across the candle lit table, it's clear that he'll never be mine.

Deep breath. Head high. Big-girl panties on.

I step out into the dining room and immediately trip over the leg of a chair that hasn't been pushed in all the way. Quickly recovering, I hope that no one has seen me, but of course I can't be that lucky. When the "oh shit," slips out of my mouth, Bryan looks up at me from his table. I wave shyly from behind his girlfriend and the most adorable and sexy grin splits his face.

I take that as my cue to approach them even though my heart is hammering in my chest at the thought of speaking to him again. Add in the minor complication that he's on a freaking date and well, you can just imagine my current pulse rate.

Swallowing back my nervousness, and my pride for that matter, I stand before them. "Hi, Bryan. It's so good to see you again." Wow, that sounded cheesy even to my own ears.

"Hey, Melanie. Yeah, you too." A spell of awkward silence falls in our little bubble as we just stare at each other for a moment. The silence is broken by a throat being cleared.

"Hi, I'm Abbey." Of course she has a cute as a button southern drawl. I don't want to be rude, well I do, but I won't. Extending my hand to her, we shake politely.

"So how do you guys know each other?" She gestures her hand in between me and Bryan. Quickly gauging his inability to speak, I answer for him.

"We used to work together when he was at Ithaca." She nods at my answer as Bryan busies himself with taking a sip of water. In desperate need to get away from the awkwardness, I pull out my notepad and pen. "So what can I get you tonight?"

They place their orders and I try my best to maintain the composure I thought I had. But, watching them talk and laugh with each other, wears on me. Every now and then, I catch Bryan looking over at the wait station, or his eyes track me as I serve the other tables. By the end of their meal, I feel trampled on. It's one thing to feel like you've moved on, but to see the other person actually moving on right in front of you, well, it forces you to take a few steps back.

Their conversation draws on well past the "finished with dessert" portion of their date, so when I drop the check on their table, I let them know that there's no rush before abruptly turning away. My words and my eyes do not conceal my pain though. It's crazy how I thought I was doing well, how I thought I had moved on.

So much for that.

Collecting their bill, and rather generous tip, about twenty minutes later, I say "thank you" with as much politeness as I can muster. But the other table that has been busting my non-existent balls all night has frayed my nerves. Add that to my crushed-to-a-million pieces heart from Bryan's table, and I'm just glad that I'm the first to be cut tonight. It's slow anyway so it's not like I'll be losing out on that much money.

Sometime around ten, I step out into the autumn night. The air is cool and crisp, and if I had to walk further than just across the street, I would need much more than my thin white button up waitress shirt. Taking a few minutes to regain my composure, I lean against the back of the building and pinch the bridge of my nose. On a deep inhale and a shaky sigh, I push off of the beat-up wood siding and nearly scream when Bryan appears before me.

Out of pure instinct, I punch him lamely on the arm in self-defense. "Holy fucking shit! You scared the crap out of me." I am practically panting as the fear recedes.

Feigning injury as he rubs the spot on his arm that I just punched, Bryan's face contorts into a knot of faux pain. Calling his bluff, I smirk at him – once I realize it's him – and laugh at his antics. "Oh, stop it. I barely even got you."

"I don't know. There might be some bruising," he jokes as he lifts the short sleeve of his polo shirt up over his bicep. When I see the small, red welt that I've caused, I reach out to soothe it and then realize that touching his muscled and goose bump-covered flesh would not be a good idea.

So instead of doing what my fingers feel compelled to do, I shove my hands into my pockets and rock on my heels. "Sorry 'bout that." While both of us sober from our momentary burst of playfulness born from my inner scaredy-cat, Bella steps out of the back door with an over-stuffed bag of trash in tow.

"Here. Let me get that, Bella." Always the gentleman, my swoon-radar goes into full swing. I doubt there will ever be a time when what Bryan says or does will not have an effect on me.

With a wink and a nod, Bella retreats into her restaurant while saying, "You two have a good night."

But a "good night" is the last thing I'll have. Bryan was here on a date. With snarky accusations resting on the tip of my tongue, I stare up into the night sky and try to gather as much strength from the beauty that I see there as possible.

Turns out that it isn't much.

Before the silence can descend upon us, I step to the side and offer up a lame smile. "I should get going." I point in the direction of my small, but cozy home.

When I'm no more than a step past him, I hear the gravel crush under his feet as he turns toward my retreating back. "Melanie." My name sounds more like a question as it tumbles off his soft lips. When he adds, "please," right after my name, I stop dead in my tracks.

Unable to ignore the pained tone of his words, I turn to face him. Still unable to look in his eyes, I keep mine glued to the rocks and pebbles beneath me.

They're suddenly *very* interesting.

Bryan's shiny black dress shoes inch into view. For

each step that I take backward, he takes another one forward. My head is a scrambled mess, and after seeing him here with another girl tonight, I just don't know if I can be in such close proximity with him again.

His long fingers grasp my wrist as he pulls me into his space. With his other hand, he tips my chin up so that our eyes meet.

As his thumb gently traces the line of my jaw, I want to lean into it. I want to inhale the woodsy, clean scent of his cologne, but I know if I do, I'll melt into a puddle of nothingness at his feet.

He doesn't say anything at first. We just stand there – gazes locked, skin aflame, hearts pounding. As Bryan leans in to kiss me, his lips are so close that I can smell the cinnamon on his breath. My stomach flops both out of desire and of disgust.

Drawing on every ounce of strength I have come to find in myself over the last few months, I force myself to take a step back. "Bryan, I can't. I mean you were just ... we shouldn't." I sound like I'm chewing on my tongue – the words just don't come out as easily as I want them to.

Stepping toward me once more, he extends his hand to my face and cups my cheek. "It wasn't a date, Melanie." For the second time tonight, my world spins slightly off its axis.

"But you two were ... it looked like ... I don't get

it." So much for inner strength – or eloquence for that matter.

Lacing his fingers together with mine, he brings my knuckles up to his soft lips. "I know what it *looked* like, but it wasn't." He brushes our joined fingers across his stubble-roughened jawline and leans into my them as they move across his skin.

"But, Bryan …" My breathless words are lost in the cool autumn air.

Pulling our hands from his face and back to his lips once more, he plants one last gentle kiss on the palm of my hand before releasing it all together. "There are no *buts*. It wasn't a date. Abbey is a new student in my grad-school program. She wanted me to show her around, and when she saw Bella's, she insisted that we eat here. I had no idea that you worked here, but I should have known better when Bella laughed and wagged an eyebrow at me when I walked in."

He tucks a rebellious strand of hair that is blowing wildly in the breeze behind my ear and lets his fingers tangle in the hair at my nape for more than a quick beat. Angling my head up to his, he cups my cheek with his other hand and whispers, "I miss you," when he's less than a centimeter from my lips.

When his mouth touches mine, time stops. He moves so slowly that I can almost feel every line and crevice on his plump lips. The heat of his kiss brands me; it sears through my soul and sets flight to a swarm of butterflies in my belly. His tongue lightly traces the crease of my sealed lips seeking permission to enter, but when I open my mouth to speak, to tell him that we need to talk, he takes it as an open invitation to make love to my mouth.

His tongue presses up against mine and tangles and weaves it magic; I'm lost to any kind of logical thought. Out of pure lust, I wrap my arms around his waist and pull his body flush against mine. With the cool chill in the air and the sweltering heat radiating between us, my nipples harden instantly. Feeling them rub up against his chest, even if it is through the layers of clothing that we're wearing, forces a flood of moisture to pool in my panties.

With his lips still dancing erotically over mine, Bryan mumbles, "I want you. Please, let me have you."

"I'm yours, Bryan. Only yours." As our lips fuse together once more, all thoughts of the things I need to say, of the things he needs to know, simply vanish.

I don't think either of us know how it happens, but in what feels like seconds we're crashing through my front door, pulling and tearing at each other's clothes. The girls may very well have been in the living room. I think I heard Cammie call out our names while Lia whistled loudly, but when I hear the soft click and turn of my bedroom lock, all other noise fades into the background. Our collective and ragged breaths are the only sound that remains.

Opening my mouth in an attempt to start explaining myself, to tell Bryan what *didn't* happen with Tyler, proves to be a fruitless effort. Bryan inhales my exhale and his lips are sealed to mine.

Passion and desire take over rational thought as my body melts into his. We stumble backwards until my legs hit the bed. Needing to feel more of his skin against mine, I pull at his shirt until it's freed from the waistband of his pants – in which his ass does look fantastic, by the way.

His abs ripple as he pulls his shirt over his head the rest of the way. As if his chest has some kind of magnetic pull, my fingertips are drawn to his skin. Tracing through the dusting of light brown hair that's scattered across his chest, I trace the line of hair that descends down his stomach and under his belt. His breath hitches and my name tumbles out of his mouth on a garbled moan.

At a painstakingly slow pace, Bryan unbuttons my top. Instead of taking it off all the way, he surprises me when he leaves it and pulls at the button on my pants. I kick off my ugly black waitress shoes and shimmy out of my pants. Standing before him in my white lace bra and matching panties with the flaps of my white top billowing around me, I feel anything but virginal.

I feel renewed – like a fresh start might be within my grasp.

Embracing my new-found confidence and my wanton desire for the man standing before me, I slowly pull the shirt from my body. I release the clasp of my bra and drop it rather unceremoniously to the floor. An unsteady breath hisses through Bryan's teeth. "Oh God, Melanie. You're … beautiful."

As Bryan starts raining down kisses on my lips, across my jaw, down my neck and to the upper swell of my breasts, my breathing becomes labored. Need spikes through my veins and threatens to consume me whole. All thoughts of talking disappear. We can do that after.

Wrapping one arm around my waist, Bryan lifts me slightly and places me on the bed. I prop myself up on my elbows so that I can watch him undress the rest of the way. When he steps out of his tight-fitting navy blue boxers, my mouth goes dry. All moisture is being sent south as my body pulses with need for his naked body.

A quick second later, Bryan has my panties off and on the floor with the rest of our clothes. We stare, wide-eyed and lust-filled, at each other for a moment, lost in the beauty of one another. As he lowers his body onto mine, I revel in the feel of his weight pushing me into the mattress. The need to lick and taste him overwhelms me and, as I devour his neck, I murmur, "I missed you so much. Please … I need …" My words evaporate into thin air as my hips begin to roll and gyrate on their own accord.

His large palm grips my waist to calm me. "Shh … we'll get there. I just need to kiss every inch of you first." When his kisses across my neck and chest turn into hot, wet, sucks and licks, my nipples pucker as if they're reaching out to take part in the torture he's unleashing on my skin. And what a beautiful torture it is. The flicking of his tongue on one diamond-hard tip partnered with rolling the other with his fingers, stokes the fire he's already set low in my belly. I tangle my fingers in his silky, brown hair and hold him to my breast before pushing him further down my body.

When he stops at my belly button to plant a kiss there, I surprise myself by not trying to cover myself up. I know he finds me beautiful. It's a knowledge I wish I had months ago, but at that point, I didn't believe it about myself. Bryan gazes up at me both awestruck and proud of my newfound confidence.

I believe it now.

Pushing my thighs open, he takes in the sight of me bared before him. His fingers lightly trace over my wet lower lips with such sweet reverence. Almost without warning, he dips his finger inside. "Ahhhh … Bryan …" It's a bite of pleasure mixed with pain.

"Are you okay, Melanie? Talk to me, please. I don't want to hurt you." His eyes are wide like saucers and filled with concern.

"No, you are definitely not hurting me. It's just … been a while, that's all." While my brain scrambles to find the next set of words that should logically follow those, my tongue gets tied in my mouth.

When Bryan says, "Yeah, for me too." I'm shocked into silence.

I sit upright and kiss him with everything I've got. He may not have been mine these last months, but maybe in some way he was. So I claim him with my lips and tongue and only hope that he's doing the same. Still sitting up, still lip-locked, Bryan slides two fingers through my folds and works them deep inside of me.

"Yes, Bryan. Yes! Please don't stop!" His fingers thrust deep inside of me, hitting a spot that literally forces me to grind down harder on his hand. When his thumb begins gently rubbing small circles on my clit, the grinding becomes frantic and my impending orgasm causes my insides to flutter wildly.

My need to touch him is spurred on by my need to come. Kneeling before me, his cock is jutting out at me, beckoning me to stroke it.

So, I do.

The feel of him pushing his hips up and gliding his length through my unskilled palm makes me feel powerful. The smell of sex is all around us, and when he calls out my name on a stifled groan, it becomes a heady mix.

Somehow he maintains his stroking while I maintain mine. My clit is on fire within minutes and my legs shake as my orgasm builds. "Bry, I'm gonna ... oh God, Bryan ... Bryan ... Bryan ..." His name falling from my lips matches the rhythm of his thrusts and on one last push to the sweet spot deep within, I'm coming ... hard.

Bryan wraps his arm around my back to hold me in place and his fingers continue their relentless, yet delicious torment. Pulling a nipple deep into his hot mouth, his sucking mimics the motion of his fingers, and before I realize it, a second wave of pleasure crashes straight on the heels of the first. "Bryan ..." His name disappears in our kiss - heated and hard, full of passion and angst, gone missing for far too long.

I flop back on the bed, no longer able to hold myself upright, even with Bryan's arm banded around my waist. A sheen of sweat covers my skin and goose bumps dot my flesh, which is now chilled in the absence of Bryan's warm body. He kneels between my legs, his cock in hand just staring down at me with something that looks a lot like love shimmering in his eyes.

But now is not the time for words.

I pull a condom out of my nightstand and hand it to him. I reach up and wrap my hand around his. Together we stroke the length of his cock, from root to tip a few times. He pulls out of my grasp and rolls the condom down his length. When he's covered and ready to go, I pull him down on top of me. He wastes no time gently nudging at my entrance. Rolling my hips up to meet his, we're both tempting each other, dancing together in a dangerous temptation.

"Please, Bryan. Please make love to me." I know that my plea is a risky one, one that could push him away, but this is what I want right now. I'm finally not afraid to voice what I want and I don't know how many more chances I'll get with him.

When he finally enters me, inch-by-agonizing-inch, it's a risk I am so glad I took. Jaw clenched, veins bulging and muscles straining, Bryan looks like he is holding onto his control by a thread. "Ahhh, Melanie ... so fucking tight ..." His movements are slow and shallow at first, but I open to him immediately. A startled scream fills the room when he fills me completely – a noise mixed of our joined pleasure.

"Please move, Bryan, please ... I need more." Lightly grazing my nails down his muscled chest leaves angry red streaks in their wake, but it spurs him on to give me exactly what I asked for. Hooking my legs into the crooks of his arms, he holds them there as he drives into me hard and fast. "Fuck ... Melanie ... I'm gonna come ... Melanie ..."

He pulls out and removes the condom and tosses it on the floor. Stroking his cock in his tightened fist, he comes in thick white ropes on my stomach. It's the hottest thing I've ever seen. My clit pulses with the need to be touched one more time. So I reach down and rub slow, lazy circles on it while Bryan continues milking the last of his orgasm. "Yeah, Melanie ... touch yourself ... my God, you're so beautiful when you come. Come for me, baby," he calls out as he moves to my side to toy with my breast.

The second his lips wrap around the pink bud of my nipple, I come in a hot rush of pleasure unlike the previous two. My body splinters into a million pieces, and just when I think I can't take any more, Bryan nuzzles into the crook of my neck and whispers, "Simply breathtaking, baby."

Did he just call me baby?

But before I can say anything, the bed shifts and he gets up. Grabbing a clean washcloth from the pile of folded laundry sitting atop my dresser, he cleans my belly before pulling the comforter over us.

With my arm wrapped around his waist and my leg draped across his, I rest my cheek on his chest and revel in the feel of being next to him. It's a place I never thought I'd be again. He kisses the crown of my head and exhales a deep breath.

After a few minutes of relative silence punctuated only by the sound of his heart beating beneath my ear, I finally gather the courage to say what I've needed to say since I found out about it myself. "Bryan, we need to talk."

"Yeah, we do."

As his fingers tangle in my auburn locks, sleep claims me before any words can be spoken.

Chapter 17

When Bryan's arm bands around my waist from behind, pulling me closer to his body, I'm startled awake. I gasp and he chuckles at me. The deep rumbling in his chest vibrates against my back.

"What's so funny back there?" I smirk even though I know he can't see it.

"You are." He squeezes me more tightly and plants a sweet kiss on my shoulder. "Guess you're not used to waking up with anyone, huh?"

I wiggle my ass into his growing erection. "No, I'm definitely not used to waking up to this." One more wiggle emphasizes exactly what I mean by *this*.

I'm surprised by how easy it is to joke with him, but then again, that's how it's always been with Bryan.

Easy.

We both share a light laugh before the stilted silence descends upon us. I turn over to face him and prop my head up on my hand. Tucking his arms under his head, he stares up at the nothingness that the ceiling provides.

"Bryan, I need to say some things." On my words he abruptly turns to his side and faces me. "So do I, Melanie." His voice is laced with pain and I can only imagine what put it there.

Me.

We sit up and rest against the headboard. With the sheet pulled tightly across my chest and draped loosely around his waist, I inhale a cleansing breath and offer up a small prayer that things turn out well.

His hand falling on top of mine and squeezing gently gives me the last push of strength I need to start talking. "I never slept with that other guy," I blurt the words and feel instantly lighter they are out of my mouth.

He shifts abruptly and stares at me with a knot of confusion marring his beautiful face. My stomach twists with guilt at having not told him this piece of information months ago.

Pinching the bridge of his nose, he closes his eyes tightly. "I'm sorry, but what did you just say?" The stupefied look that's plastered to his face does nothing to hide his emotions.

"I know I should have told you a long time ago, but every time I tried to, something happened." I can see the look of confusion recede slightly as he recalls our few and angry encounters over the summer. Feeling the need to clarify the course of events, I add, "There really was never a good time to tell you. When you first told me about knowing that the text from Courtney was an old picture, the words just got jumbled up in my brain. I wanted to tell you, but you just walked away from me. I even tried to last night, but you were so adamant about ... other things ... that I just, well, call me selfish, but I wanted you too and I just didn't want to talk about *that* and ruin the chance to be with you again."

On a loud exhale, he rubs his hands over his face as if he's trying to wake up from this nightmare. "I know. I didn't want any words to get in the way last night either," he says softly as he brushes my hair out of my face. I take his nod as a cue to continue my long overdue explanation.

"You already know that I was in a shitty place before we both went home for vacation." He nods again and it gives me a little strength to carry on. "Well, my mood had a lot to do with us, but it also had a lot to do with other things. I wasn't happy with who I was. I wasn't happy about the twists and turns that my life was taking." I inhale what I hope to be a calming breath, but it gets caught in the thick emotions clogging my throat. "Maddy almost died, and then I found out she was having a baby and leaving me alone. Mom was alone and sad again. Then the stuff with you not calling and thinking you had moved on from me ..." My rambling trails off and mixes with the tears that streak down my cheeks. The pad of his thumb wiping away my tears lifts my downcast gaze.

He pulls my lips to his as both palms now gently cup my cheeks. "Tell me the rest. Please." His eyes are begging for the rest of the story.

"I was partying a lot, too, when I was home. I think Maddy knew, but she never really confronted me. It got bad real quick. It was a way to numb everything, to not have to feel all the things that were making me sad. I didn't even want to hang out with Maddy all that much. It was like her happiness just made me sadder." On a deep shuddery breath, he sweeps my hair back once more. "The night I got that text from Courtney, I had already convinced myself that you no longer wanted me. I was drunk. Well, actually shitfaced is more like it. I was talking with a guy. We were drinking, a lot. And after the text, I drank some more, a lot more. We kissed – fooled around a little - but that was it. I promise."

We sit in silence for a few moments. He doesn't say anything and I want to give him the space to absorb what I've just told him. He finally looks at me. "But I don't understand, Melanie." He sighs as he scratches his head. "You said … I mean … how did you … what made you think that you slept with him." The last few words catch in his throat.

I've actually thought about this a lot. I blamed myself for ruining our relationship for so long; I had a lot of time on my own to try and figure it all out. "Bryan, I'm so sorry. I never meant to put us through this, but I think part of it was that I always thought the worst of myself. I remember talking to him. I remember the kiss and the call and then the rest is a blurry mess." I sniffle and wipe my nose with the back of my hand in a rather unladylike fashion. "I woke up the next morning with in someone else's shirt, my jeans were unsnapped, my bra was missing and I guess through my hangover fog, I assumed the worst. When I happened to run in to Tyler over spring break, that night came into focus. I wanted to tell you right away, you have to believe me, but you wanted nothing to do with me." Bryan looks utterly disgusted with me. Hell, so was I when I first found out. But, sitting up a bit straighter, I feel lightened by the truth I've just unveiled.

Scrubbing a hand through the light stubble that decorates his jaw, he huffs and closes his eyes. I can tell he's struggling with what I just told him, but the reality is that he wanted me last night *before* he even knew about any of this. Emboldened by that thought, I scoot an inch closer to him and cup his cheek. Turning his face to mine, I call him out on last night. "But you didn't know this last night, Bryan. You didn't know any of it, but you still wanted me. I saw it in your eyes and felt it in your touch too. Last night was not just a one night thing for you." I lace our fingers together in my lap and squeeze gently.

At least, I hope it wasn't.

"You're right. It wasn't just about last night." His words sober me immediately; they're words I never thought I would hear. "When I saw you at Bella's, I could tell what you thought about me and Abbey. I saw how much it hurt you and I knew. I just knew that you still had feelings for me. When I saw the hurt in your eyes as we were leaving, I decided to finally own my feelings for you, too."

A lone tear trickles down my face. Bryan kisses it away and smiles at me. "I don't think I ever stopped loving you." He opens his heart to me and I shoot him a wry look. "Okay, okay." He holds his hands up in surrender. "Right after you told me what you *thought* happened, my feelings *may* have changed, but even still, there was always a part of my heart that belonged to you."

"So, what changed between then and last night?" I

ask timidly.

Bryan stares absentmindedly out of my bedroom window as the sunlight dances through the thin purple curtains. Closing his eyes, as if he'll find the answers hidden behind his lids, he finally starts talking. "I spent the last few months struggling with my family. Watching the people you love the most fall apart right before your eyes is pure torture. But when Emmie was staying with me for the summer, I felt alive again. I know it's cheesy, but she gave me hope again. And then when I saw you again, I knew I had to take a chance." He pulls my face to his and lightly grazes his lips across mine. "I just didn't know how. And then when I saw you with that guy at camp, I lost my shit. Everything I thought about what happened between us, came crashing down around me." Through tensely clenched jaw, he mutters, "I let my anger about everything – about you, about my dad, about my mom – I let it consume me. It changed me. "

I softly press my lips to his cheek and whisper against his skin, "It's okay. You're still you." He leans into my lips and my heart swells. I missed him so much.

"But I wasn't for a long time and I didn't like who I was. I spent a lot of time thinking about how unfair I was to you when we broke up. I told you that you weren't good enough, that you had to change." His face twists in guilt. "How fucked up is that? We could have worked on things. Maybe we could have figured them out, but I told you to go fix yourself and here I was becoming the exact same kind of person I told you not to be."

That's pretty harsh to hear and it kills me to think that we could have figured things out a long time ago. Opting to take the high road, I bite back what could be a very pissed-off outburst. The truth is that he was right. Back then, I wasn't a whole person; I was a shadow of the woman I've become.

"But Bryan, don't you realize that I wouldn't be who I am now, if you didn't do that." I take a deep breath and hope that my words make sense. "Most of what you said back then was right. I didn't have faith in myself. I didn't love myself. If we hadn't broken up, I might have never found the strength to figure out who I am. I'm not going to lie; it wasn't a pretty time for me. But I did a lot of soul searching and I spent a lot of time with my family. I learned so much about who I really am and I found out that I'm pretty awesome." I flip my hair playfully to emphasize the dorkiness of what I've just said. His goofy grin and small laugh reassure me so I continue. "Maybe that's just how things were supposed to be. We were meant to spend some time apart to figure things out, to pick up the pieces so that we could both be whole when we found each other again."

Before I can even offer up my lame smile, his lips are on mine. His hands are in my hair and he's pulling me so close to his body that I feel like we're going to melt together as one. Pulling back from the branding kiss, he leans his forehead against mine. "I'm still scared." His admission knocks me for a loop because it's as if he's just read my mind.

"Me too, Bry. I'm scared I won't be enough for you, for us."

"Shh … Melanie, I see how different you are, but you're the same too. Sweet, kind, funny. You're everything I fell in love with in the first place and so much more. I'm just afraid we'll screw it up again." His thumbs brush my cheeks tenderly. "What if we're *too* different?" His vulnerability cuts through me.

I don't want to verbalize the fear I feel. There's some truth to what he's saying, but in my heart, in my gut, I have a feeling that the different people we've become are the people who were meant to be together.

Recalling the words he said to me so long ago, I laugh softly. "Do you remember what you said to me when we first met? That you would *show me* rather than *tell me* all of the ways we would be perfect together?"

He pulls his face away from mine. Tapping his finger on his kiss-swollen lower lip, he acts as if he's trying to recall some long-lost secret. "Yeah, I think I remember saying something like that." I swat him teasingly on his arm.

I shoot him a look of seriousness and get lost in his melted-chocolate eyes for a minute. "Let me *show* you just how good we can be. Let me wear *you* down and prove to you that even though we've both changed, we're better off for it."

"I think I can do that, Melanie. But just what did you have in mind?" He arches an eyebrow at me on his last words.

I drop the sheet from around my breasts and straddle his hips. "A little of this," I say as I wiggle on top of him. On another wiggle, I add "And a little of that."

His fingers dig into the soft flesh of my waist as he nudges his hips up into mine. "I think I like your plan," he mutters lustily. I lean down onto his body and mumble against his lips, "Oh, no. You're going to *love* my plan."

We spend the rest of the day *showing* each other just how good we are for together, coming up for air and food only when necessary. As dusk settles in and the sun descends behind the mountains, the sky is set ablaze in a fiery hotness that mirrors the day we just spent together.

Sprawling out in my bed, Bryan is wearing only his boxers and I've opted to cover up with an extra-long

T-shirt and panties. Cuddled at his side, I let my fingers trace random patterns across his chest.

"So where does this leave us?" Damn me and my stupid need for definition.

Bryan clears his throat as he tucks his hand behind his head. "I don't know, Melanie. I don't know."

"Yeah, me either." And that's the honest truth. Sure, the last day has been great and we've talked a lot – among other things – but, there's still so much to figure out. "How about we just take it slowly, one day at a time? We'll see how things go, day-by-day. Sound good?" My suggestion actually doesn't seem half bad.

Kissing the top of my head, Bryan nods his agreement. "It's perfect, Melanie."

"It might be a little cold tomorrow, but we could start back at the beginning." I point to Emmie's picture of Happy Times Waterfall that hangs on the wall above my computer.

"Just be sure to wear your sneakers." I poke him in the side and stick my tongue out at him. He just pulls me closer to his side and inhales the sweet citrus scent of my hair. "Cold or not, I can't think of a better way to spend the day. As long as I'm with you, it'll be perfect."

I roll my eyes. "Will you stop saying that?"

"What?" He looks down at me, clearly confused by my words.

"Perfect. Things are never going to be perfect. It's impossible." I pull him closer to me and kiss his lips tenderly. "We're not perfect, neither one of us. And we never will be, but we can be imperfect together."

His lips dance across mine and happiness shimmers in his warm, brown eyes. "Then here's to one imperfect day after another."

Chapter 18

December 2013

It's lame to say, but very true – Bryan and I have spent the last month together basking in the glow of our not-so-perfect love. We've fought and made up and then fought again, but through it all we've learned to be honest – both with ourselves and with each other. When we first got back together, there were a few times that I thought we wouldn't make it. Like when he gets stressed out and angry about home. Or when I feel like I don't deserve his love and affection after all I put us through. That's usually when he reminds me that it wasn't entirely my fault.

As mended as we may both be, there's obviously still a lot of healing that needs to happen. I'm not disillusioned enough to think it'd all be rainbows and glitter, so at least I was a little prepared for the struggles. I wasn't as prepared for just how amazing the good times would be, though.

Just this past weekend we volunteered at the local Special Olympics and it was, by far, the most rewarding experience of my life. We were paired with Joey, a twenty-year-old with Downs Syndrome. When he won his first of three medals, he actually cried. Which of course made me cry and even though Bryan will still deny it, I know that I saw a tear or two fill his eyes.

The last event for the day was an indoor group soccer game. It wasn't at the level at which Bryan was used to playing, but he was in his glory. It was clear that he missed the game, but based on the way he was running with the other players and coaching them along the way, he missed his sister even more. I think it was a defining day for us, not just as a couple, but as individuals as well. Bryan has always been a helper – be it for Professor O'Neil, Bella, Emmie or even his mom, Bryan has always had a kind heart and a caring soul. I think he got a piece of that back as he ran his final lap around the soccer field with Joey.

I know I got a piece of myself back that day too. For so long I thought I didn't deserve to be loved, that the people who did love me only did so out of obligation. But after reading the letters from my dad, and seeing my mom find love again, I know that I am surrounded by loads of unconditional love. That's why

I love working with kids with special needs. At the end of the day, when Joey, Bryan and I walked off the field, he asked us if we would be back next year. Without missing a beat, at the same time, Bryan and I said, "We wouldn't miss it for the world."

That day was proof positive of how much we've changed, but it was also a testament to how closely we've grown together.

So here we are, one year away from the week that forced us apart and the same nervousness about our distance is seeping into my soul all over again. We're at Bella's on our last date before we have to spend the holiday break apart again. Bryan can feel my leg shaking under the table. "What's wrong, babe?" His hand stretches out across the table and I willingly place mine into it.

"Forget it. It's silly." I swat my other hand in front of me and reach for my water.

Squeezing my hand tightly, he locks me in his persistent stare. "Stop it. Something is bothering you. What is it? Please tell me."

Remembering out promise to be honest with each other, I take a deep breath and divulge my foolish concerns. "I'm just nervous about being away from you."

Bryan releases my hand and starts lightly tickling my forearm. Leaning in closer to me, I close my eyes and enjoy the feel of his fingertips on my skin. Just like that, I'm calmed. His touch has that kind of power over me. "Okay, now that you're relaxed, listen to me." I nod and stifle my rising emotions.

"I don't want to be away from you either. I kind of like waking up with you, but I have to go home. It's Mom's first Christmas alone and she's been doing well, going to AA meetings and all that, but I just … I need to be there with her and Emmie." He pulls my hand up to his lips and sweetly kisses my knuckles.

"I know, baby. I understand, but it doesn't mean I'll miss you any less." His thumb gently stroking over my knuckles calms me a bit more. I take a deep breath and throw out my last Hail Mary. "Are you sure you won't be able to make it to the wedding next week?"

"You know I want to be there. We've talked about this. It's just too close to Christmas. I can't …"

"I know, Bryan. I just thought I would ask one more time. Let's drop it and enjoy our last night together."

An impish grin spreads across his face. "We definitely will "

After dinner, we settle the bill and Bella hugs us as we walk out into the blustery air. We hurry across the street back to my empty apartment. Cammie flew out to Chicago this morning to spend the week with Jack. They'll both fly into Elmira for Maddy and Reid's wedding next week. I've honestly never seen Cammie happier than when she knew she would be with Jack again. Lia is out with her current boy-toy, at least that's what I'm assuming. She never does bring them around here. Peyton is actually staying in Ithaca through the break. She got a job at the local bookstore and coffee shop combo to make some more money on top of the meager salary she earns at the tutoring center. That's where she is tonight, so we have the place to ourselves.

Barging through the door, I'm shaking from the frigid winter air. After brushing off the few snowflakes that landed on my shoulders, I take off my coat and hand it to Bryan. He hangs both of our coats up on the rack near the front door and reaches out for my hand. "Come with me."

Dumfounded, I stare at him. "Where else would I go?" I waggle an eyebrow at him, but he just tugs me down the hallway to my room. The sight before me stops me in my tracks and forces my words to get stuck in my throat. There are candles everywhere and flower petals dot the floor.

"What's this for?" I ask on a whisper. Bryan comes up behind me and wraps his arms around my waist. With his front pressed to my back, he nuzzles into my neck and presses his lips there.

"Well, this was the plan I had in mind for the first time I told you 'I love you', but that didn't go as planned." He gently nips at my earlobe but quickly soothes the bite with his tongue. "So this time," those words cause my breath to hitch and force me to turn around in the circle of his arms.

"Yes, this time. This time when I tell you 'I love you', I wanted it to be just right." I stretch up on my toes and kiss him with the love I think he just professed to me.

Leaning his forehead against mine, he takes a deep breath. "I know we said we would take it day-by-day, but I need to tell you that I love you. I thought I loved you before, and I did, but it was different. The person you are now, I love her even more."

"Bryan, I love you too. Thank you for tonight. It's …"

He laughs as he mumbles the word "perfect" against my lips.

Pulling him further into the room by the waistband of his pants, I laugh and deepen the kiss. "Get in here so I can show you just how much I love you," I say against his lips. His only response is a low groan of appreciation as he grips my ass tightly.

In a fevered rush of passion, we're naked in a matter of seconds. Clothes fly to the floor and moans rumble through the air. We stumble toward the bed and I push him down on the mattress. His body is hot and hard beneath me. Settling in between his legs, I take his cock into my mouth. His breath hisses through his teeth as he pulls my hair into a loose knot in his hand. "Fuck … Melanie … ahhhh" He pushes up to my mouth and I lick, suck and taste every single inch of him. Looking up at him, I can tell he's close. The veins in his neck, and elsewhere, are bulging and pulsing with barely contained desire.

I grab a condom from the nightstand and roll it over him. Straddling his hips, I sink down onto him, slowly. Before I take him all the way, I pull back until he's almost completely out of me. Inch-by-agonizing-inch, I torture us both. Never sinking fully down onto him and never completely lifting off of him. "Melanie, you're fucking killing me. Please …" His fingers dig into my hips as he pulls me down onto him. No longer able to maintain the torturously slow pace, I slam my hips down onto his as he pushes up into me.

He angles his hips to his that sweet spot deep inside of me. Heat flashes across my skin as I teeter on the edge of my control. A handful of long, hard and deep thrusts push me to and over the edge. "Bryan … I'm coming. Oh God, Bryan!"

He stills himself inside of me as he loses the battle with his own orgasm. My legs shake and I flop down on top of him, no longer able to hold myself up. Bryan wraps his arms around my back and lazily tickles my skin.

Our lovemaking has just washed away whatever worries I had earlier about spending a few weeks apart. I now realize how silly it is to be worried about it. His heart beating against my chest is all the reassurance I need that we'll make it work somehow.

"I can't believe you're married!" I squeal at the top of my lungs as Maddy and Reid walk into the private room at the quaint reception hall.

Hugging me with all of her might, she says, "I know. It's crazy, right?"

"Yeah, kinda. But Reid is your forever," I reassure her as we exchange a sisterly smile.

She stayed at my house last night and we shared the same bed like we did when she first moved in. It feels like a lifetime ago and in many ways it is. She shared her fears with me, but no matter how cold her feet got, she knew that the feeling was fleeting. Her and Reid were meant to be and today is a celebration of their hard-won happily ever after.

I've only been home for a few days and in all the wedding craziness, I haven't had much of a chance to update Maddy on all things Bryan related. We talked about it and she's elated that we're back together, but it just hasn't been the main topic of conversation.

After our little pep-talk upstairs in the suite, we line up outside of the ballroom, ready to make out entrance. Hooking my arm through Dylan's, the best man, he pats the top of my hand. "Ready, Melanie."

I bounce on my toes to the beat of the music playing loudly inside. "You betcha, Dylan. Let's do this." The DJ calls our names and we join the crowd waiting for Maddy and Reid to be announced.

The DJ's voice booms through the music. "Now, let's hear it for the new Mr. and Mrs. Reid Connely!" Everyone claps, cheers and whistles as my eyes fill with happy tears. I glance over at Mom standing next to me. She has tears in her eyes, too. Evan notices them and hands her a tissue. He wraps a strong arm around her shoulder and peeks at me over her head. Winking at me with a smirk on his face, I know that after Christmas another wedding will be in our near future.

Of course, Mom doesn't know yet. That would ruin the surprise.

Later in the night, I catch a quiet moment alone at my table. Mom waves at me from the dance floor as Evan twirls her around to the lyrics of Eric Clapton's "Wonderful Tonight". Wistfully, I think about dancing with Bryan. I can't wait to get back to school and to continue on our day-by-day journey.

Lost in happy thoughts, Maddy sits down next to me. "Hey, sweetie." Maddy smiles cheerfully at me.

"Are you okay, Mel?" she asks when I don't answer her right away. Honestly, she just caught me off guard as I was recalling images of the last time Bryan and I made love before I came home. That was a good night, indeed.

I sigh softly, wishing Bryan were here with me. "Of course I am. But let's not talk about me. You look beautiful today, you know?" I don't want to bring her down. So even though I know she thinks that I'm just trying to change the subject, I sway the attention back to her.

"Thanks, girl. You look pretty good yourself, Ms. Maid of Honor slash Godmother." Maddy elbows me in the side, and I finally find the genuine smile she's been looking for since she pulled her chair up next to mine.

"Thanks, Maddy. Why don't you go out there and dance. I don't want to bring you down. I just miss Bryan, that's all." Averting eye contact, I start picking at the corners of a napkin on the table. I don't want to get into all of this on her night. She should be enjoying herself.

Smiling at me as she stands, Maddy says, "I know, Mel. I wish he could be here too. It'll all work out." I think it'll work out too. I'm actually certain of it, but tonight I just feel off. Being surrounded by all of these couples and all of this love makes me long to be in his arms.

As if on cue, one of the only other single people here comes up behind Maddy. "Would you care to dance with me?" Dylan asks as he stretches out his hand.

Dylan used to date Reid's brother, Shane, before he died. He hasn't found the courage to love again. I can't say that I understand his pain; it's a totally different breed than mine. I just hope he can find the other half to his heart.

Standing from my chair, I place my hand in his. "I would love to, Best Man slash Godfather." I wink at Maddy as Dylan escorts me out to the dance floor.

As Clapton's words mix into the next slow song, Dylan and I move in circles on the floor next to Cammie and Jack who are staring dreamily into each other's eyes. A deep male voice sings out about finding love again and Dylan laughs flippantly. "What? You don't think you'll find love again?" My prodding is laced with concern. Dylan deserves love, but apparently he doesn't think so.

Shaking his head, he says in a cool, unaffected voice, "Nah, I don't think love is in the cards for me."

"I don't know, Dylan. Don't cut yourself short.

You're young, hot and pretty sweet. I know there's someone out there for you." I pat him on the shoulder as the song comes to an end.

He kisses my cheek sweetly. "I guess we'll just have to wait and see, Melanie."

As I watch him stalk off the dance floor, my heart breaks for him. I know what it feels like to think you don't deserve love. I know that black and gnawing void of emptiness that is capable of chewing you up and spitting you out.

I just hope that Dylan can avoid it.

Just as the night is about to wrap up, I make my way over to the bar and get a diet Coke. When an arm snakes around my waist from behind, I jump out of shock.

"Hey, babe."

Turning quickly, I'm stunned to see Bryan standing behind me. "What the hell! I thought you couldn't make it!" I jump into his arms, squeeze him tightly and kiss him through my huge smile.

"I couldn't, at first. But when I got home and talked to Mom about it, she insisted that I come up for at least the wedding." He places a chaste kiss to my cheek and smiles at me proudly. He may have just won the coveted "Boyfriend of the Year" award. "She's doing really well, better than I thought."

"Bryan, that's awesome. I'm so happy for her. But

what about Emmie, how is she?" I'm bouncing on the tips of my toes with excitement to hear about his sister.

"Are you kidding? Once she heard I was missing a wedding, with 'pretty princess dresses'," he air quotes those words to make sure that I know they're Emmie's words and not his, "she practically shoved me out the door."

"But all the traveling and it's almost the holidays, and it's just … it seems like more trouble than it's worth. What about Christmas and then New Years? You wanted to be with your family." The pace at which my words race out of my mouth is dizzying and I can barely catch my breath.

Bryan pulls me close to him and presses his lips up to my ear. "Yes, but I wanted to be with you, too." Rubbing his nose up the length of mine and popping a soft kiss to my forehead, he adds, "You are never trouble and you are always worth it." Those words cause me to melt into him and exhale a sigh of relief that he's here with me.

"Dance with me?" he asks as the DJ announces the final song of the night.

"Always." Lacing our fingers together, we slowly sway and move together on the dance floor.

He steps on my toes a few times and me on his. We share more than a few laughs as we both sing the wrong lyrics to each other, horribly off-key, I should add. It's fitting, though.

Ours has always been a clumsy dance to a sweet tune. With lots of bumps and mishaps along the way, we've arrived at where we are not because we did everything perfectly, but because we learned to love each other despite our imperfections.

We've decided to love each other through the mistakes that we've made, and in the end, we've become stronger for it.

Who knows what tomorrow brings, but promising each other honesty and love, I have a feeling that Bryan and I will be together for many tomorrows to come.

Epilogue

June 2014

"I can't believe that tomorrow is our last day here." There's a nostalgic quality to Lia's words as she carefully folds up the soft, navy-colored throw blanket that has decorated our small, beat up couch for the last year.

Flopping down onto the couch next to her, I rest my head on her shoulder. "I know. This was the best first apartment ever. I'm going to miss it." Blinking back the tears that are threatening to stream down my cheeks, I add, "I'm going to miss you guys more, though."

So much for blinking them back. Cue the waterworks.

Cammie sits next to me and hugs both Lia and I as tightly as she can. Through her quiet sobs, she manages to croak out, "Hey, I thought we promised no tears today."

"I know, Cam. It's just crazy to think I won't be seeing you girls every day." We've promised to email, call and visit whenever possible, but the honest reality is that we're all going in our own directions now.

Remembering that we should all be celebrating our new beginnings helps to shake me from my little pity party. "You're right. No tears." I wipe at my cheeks. "So what time is your flight to Chicago?"

"It's at nine. Lia's going to drive me on her way down." Cammie shares a sad smile with her cousin. I know it's going to be even more difficult for them to be a part. I don't think they've ever been more than arm's length away from each other.

"I still can't believe you're going to be working in Manhattan, Lia. That's so freaking cool." I sound like a giddy fan-girl or something like that, but there's something really impressive about working in the city.

"I know. I am pretty awesome, huh?" Lia remarks as she flips her hair over her shoulder in a rather dramatic fashion. With the tension and sadness now broken, we break into a fit of giggles.

"I wouldn't laugh so hard over there, Miss Melanie. You're going to have to live with a boy." Lia sticks her tongue out at me after dragging out the word "boy".

Yep, that's right. Bryan and I are moving in together and I couldn't be happier. It was a no-brainer, really. It's not every day that you get a second chance with your first love and we're both determined to hold on with all of our might.

Rather than give her mocking any credence, I turn the tables back to Cammie. "So is she, you know." In an equally playful manner, I also stick out my tongue and point my finger.

"Yeah, but Cammie and Jack are pretty much married already, so it doesn't count." Lia's words are cut off as Cammie tosses the only remaining throw pillow at her face.

"We are not married." She pauses before adding, "Yet".

We all share a few more laughs before the reality of tomorrow morning settles in one last time. Even though we're all heading off into different directions and it's exciting in so many ways, I'd be lying if I said it wasn't scary as hell, too.

Staring blankly out of the window, I watch the bright, afternoon sun as it shimmers and dances across the rippling lake. We're all shaken from our sad goodbyes when the front door slams shut, jarring the door frame. If there were any pictures left on the walls, they surely would have crashed to the floor.

"Peyton? Is that you?" My question is met only

with a harsh groan from the kitchen.

As she walks into the living room, she nearly trips over a box at which she grits out a loud, "Fuck!" Twisting the cap on her water bottle, she flops down onto the smaller of the two couches while we stare at her, willing her to speak.

When she doesn't say anything right away, Cammie, Lia and I exchange wary glances, wondering who should break the strangled silence. Before we can say anything, Peyton covers her face with her hand and starts crying. In the year and a half that I've known Peyton, she's never cried. Ever.

Moving quickly, I sink down to the floor next to her and squeeze her knee gently. "What's wrong, Peyton?" I ask softly, afraid that I might scare her away.

She's not much of a sharer either.

When her breathing calms, she wipes away her tears. Straightening in her chair, she takes one final deep breath. "It's nothing. Really, I'm fine." The white-knuckled, death grip that she has on her water bottle says she's anything but fine.

"You're not fine. Please, talk to us." Cammie's kind words work their magic as usual.

"Something got fucked up down at the registrar's office. Apparently, when I started here, one of my classes didn't transfer, but no one thought to tell me." Pulling her long hair back into a loose bun, she gives us a resolute nod. "So, it looks like I'll be here for at least another semester. So much for moving back home, I guess

"Oh, Peyton. That sucks, sweetie," Cammie offers her best condolences, but I'm fairly certain that it's going to take more than a few apologies to make Peyton feel better right now.

In true Peyton fashion, she just shrugs her shoulders and rolls with the punches. "It's okay. I mean I'll survive. Just have to figure things out."

"Do you want me to see if I can-" Peyton holds her hand up to stop me from speaking.

"Don't you dare finish that sentence. You are moving in with your man tomorrow and that's that." She takes a deep, calming breath as she gathers her thoughts. "One of my friends at the coffee shop has an extra room. I can stay with her until I find my own place for the fall." Her words are final; her decision is made. I'm not even going to bother arguing with her. The last thing I want to do is change my plans with Bryan.

We spend the rest of the night eating pizza, drinking wine and reminiscing about our time together. Somewhere around our third glass, I have a brilliant idea.

"Let's make a promise to have a girls' weekend every three months. No matter what we're doing, or what's going on in our lives, we will get together every three months for one whole weekend." I hold my white-wine-filled coffee mug up to the group. "I'll even make Maddy join in. It'll be so fun."

Lia clangs her glass against mine first. "That's a motherfucking-awesome idea!" Okay, the wine always hits Lia the hardest, but she's a freaking riot when she's tipsy.

"That could totally work," Cammie adds with the same enthusiasm minus the cursing. "We could rotate between locations, too. This way we'd all get to see where everyone is living and how they're doing." At the mention of that idea, I notice Peyton shift somewhat uncomfortably in her seat, but she quickly recovers and says, "Cheers to that!" as she extends her mug.

In the blink of an eye, the night is over and we're all stepping out onto the front porch trying to block the early morning sun. Somehow, we manage to croak out a few simple words of goodbye through our tears. Watching Lia and Cammie drive off physically hurts my heart, but at the same time, I couldn't be happier for them.

I walk Peyton over to her car, helping her with the last of her bags and give her a tight squeeze. "Don't get all emotional on me, Melanie. I'll be back soon enough." She smiles cheerfully at me, but I can see the tears shining in her eyes.

"Just please call me when you get home. Okay?" I say as I take a step back from our hug. She gets into her car and drives down the road waving her hand as she pulls away.

I get the last of my bags from the front steps and load them into my car. Bryan helped me move everything else over the last few days, so all I have left is a bag of my toiletries and suitcase filled with some clothes.

I stop on the bottom step and scan my flowerbed one last time. It used to be overgrown with weeds, the soil not rich enough to sustain any life. But, in the last year, I've made it my little pet project. I've nursed it back to health, kept it weed free, planted some of my favorite flowers and watched it grow into a thing of beauty.

Pulling the delicate, hot pink petals of a freshly bloomed stargazer lily up to my nose, I inhale its sweet scent. I consider snipping it from the stalk and bringing it with me, but I decide to leave it and let it bask in the warm summer sun.

It's only a ten minute drive to my new apartment and Bryan is already up and waiting for me. Lugging my suitcase through the front door, the heavenly smell of freshly brewed coffee mingles in the air.

"Hey, baby. Coffee?" Bryan hands me a bright purple mug as he plants a sweet kiss to my cheek.

"You're a lifesaver," I mumble against the rim of the mug. After one too many glasses of wine last night and shedding more tears than I have in a long time, my brain is in serious need of some caffeine.

After a few sips, I put my mug down on the counter. Bryan grabs my bag in one hand and laces our fingers together with the other. "I want to show you something."

He pulls me down the short hallway to what will be our bedroom. I'm less than enthused about it. It's definitely a boy's room, but I guess I'll just have to call Lia for some decorating help.

Bouncing excitedly in front of the closed door, Bryan tells me to close my eyes. It's too early for me to argue with him, especially when it's clear that he's got something up his sleeve, so I just roll my eyes and then close them.

When Bryan opens the door for me, my nose is inundated with the sweetest scent I've ever known. Unable to keep my eyes closed any longer, especially now that I know what the surprise is, I stare wide-eyed into the lily-filled room. "Bryan, this ... wow ... this is so sweet." There must be dozens of lilies in a few vases scattered about the room. The fragrance is bold and distinct, but not at all overpowering. The petals are strong and vibrantly colored, resilient in their own way. Holding a bloom up to my nose, I inhale deeply as

Bryan wraps his arms around my waist from behind. "I know they're your favorite and I want my place to be *our* place. Besides, I know how you love your flowers so I wanted to have them waiting for you when you got here today."

I turn to face him and plant a soft kiss on his lips. "They're beautiful, Bryan. Thank you."

"Anything for you, Melanie. I love you." His lips dance along my neck and shivers race across my skin.

Leaning into his kisses, I mumble, "hmmm." We stand there with our arms wrapped tightly around one another swaying to music that's not even playing. Nuzzling into his warm chest, I inhale the combination of woodsy cologne and pure Bryan that makes my heart skip a beat.

"I love you too, Bryan. So much." I stretch up on my toes and kiss him fiercely. When I begin to feel the effects of my kiss pressing into my lower belly, I pull back and arch an eyebrow at him.

Bryan winks and smirks at me, saying "What? He loves you too."

"Oh my God! I can't believe you just said that." I laugh at him while hugging him tightly. "You're such a dork."

Staring down at me with a look that's a mixture of seriousness and playfulness, he says, "Yeah, but I'm your dork."

"Yes, you are. All mine." With that statement, he effortlessly lifts me up and carries me over to the bed – which is covered in a very old and ratty 'boy' comforter. This place is in some desperate need of purple.

Dropping me rather unceremoniously on the mattress, his lips curl into a seductive grin. "Wanna christen the bed?"

Propping myself up on my elbows, I watch as he pulls his shirt over his head. His abs and chest make me incapable of speaking, so I just nod dumbly and prepare myself for delicious torment of our lovemaking.

As he presses his body down onto mine, in between sweet kisses, he mutters, "I can't believe this is really real. I can't believe I'm lucky enough to have you in my life every single day."

Focusing my stare directly into his caramel-colored irises, I let a lusty breath fill my lungs. "Bryan, I'm the lucky one. You loved me when I thought that love was the last thing I deserved. You loved me when I didn't even love me. I can't say that I'm prefect; God knows I'm far from it, but I'm finally okay with that. I'm so lucky to have you in my life because you taught me how to love myself." I pull his face down to mine and kiss him with all of the love I feel. With a look that's a mixture of light-heartedness and desire, I mutter against his soft lips, "So after we christen the bed, can we christen the couch?"

The rumbles of his deep laughter vibrate against our pressed-together chests. Smiling sexily, he says, "Oh, we'll get the couch. And then the kitchen table, and then the laundry room. And don't forget the shower, too."

As his lips and tongue work their magic across my skin, I know that today will be a great day.

And tomorrow, well, tomorrow will kick today's ass.

The End

Acknowledgements

When I wrote *Let Love In* and *Let Love Stay*, I had no idea that there would be other books for the other characters. But, when readers fell in love with the supporting cast, I knew I had to write about them – and I knew Melanie's story had to be next. What I didn't know is what the heck I would write! When I was in the early stages of thinking about what to write, I came across a blog post from Monica at *If These Boobs Could Talk*. Monica had a simple request in her post (which can be read here – http://siliconealley.blogspot.com/2013/07/hi.html): to read about an average size, not-so-stick-thin heroine. It was after that post that Melanie truly came to life for me. Never having been a size two in my life, I always struggled with my body image and feeling beautiful. Ashamed of what I looked like, or what I thought people saw when they looked at me, I felt undeserving of love for so long. So sadly, Melanie's story is my story in a lot of ways and I have a feeling that hers is the story of all too many women. No matter your size, I hope you have one take-away from *Let Love Heal* – you deserve love.

I owe a huge debt of gratitude to so many people that it would be impossible to list them all. The community of indie authors is warm and inviting and so utterly helpful. Whether you answered a question for me or helped me develop a scene, I want to say thank you from the bottom of my heart.

Carey Heywood, who has earned the affectionate title of my Book Wifey - I will forever be thankful for our friendship. Our late night and early morning chats about all things book related – and lots of things not-so-book related help to keep me grounded and focused. And they make me laugh, a lot!

I have a truly amazing group of beta readers who have helped so much. Thank you Susan Griffiths, Laurna Hamilton, Malinda Burchett, Jennifer Diaz, Jennifer Short (my ninja fairy God mother), Kristy Bruno, Chelsea Camaron (thank you so much for loving my characters as much as I do) and Pamela Schaeffer (I'm so sorry for making you cry – but I'm not, really). Without your feedback, I know that *Let Love Heal* wouldn't be what it is today.

I know that I wouldn't have nearly as many

readers as I do if it weren't for the fantastic bloggers out there who have reviewed and promoted for me. There are too many to name, but please know that, whether it was sharing a post, doing a cover reveal, taking part in a tour or running a spotlight on me, I am so grateful for each and every single one of you. Debra, at Book Enthusiast Promotions, you are a God send. Thank you for everything. I don't know how you do it, but I'm so glad that you do.

Angela McLaurin at Fictional Formats is my knight in shining armor. I'll never forget how you came to my rescue at the last minute right before I published *Let Love Stay*. You're finishing touches truly bring my words to life on both their virtual and paper pages.

Before a good book can become an exceptional one, it needs a great editor. I am so thrilled that I've found one in Becky Johnson at Hot Tree Editing. Thank you for working over my manuscripts with scrutiny and precision. I don't know how I found you, but I'm so glad I did.

I really don't know where to begin with thanking my family. I have to admit that when my mom told me that she read *Let Love In* and she asked for a copy of *Let Love Stay*, I blushed quite a bit. But, just knowing that she has taken an interest in my writing has helped me feel more confident in sharing it with everyone else. So, thank you Mom for reading and supporting my work.

Thank you for being the first person who ever made me feel like I deserved to be loved.

I might very well be the luckiest woman on the planet to have a husband who loves and supports her as much as mine does. So many of the words that Bryan tells Melanie are echoes of the words that he has told me more than once before. Forever my cheerleader and my number one tech-guy, I love you with all of my heart. Thank you so much for helping me see just how beautiful I am.

To my sons, I apologize in advance for any torment that my romance novels cause you when you're teenagers. I have a good feeling that you might never read these words, but on the off chance that you do (sometime way down the road in the distant future) please know that every time you've held one of my books and said it was pretty, or pointed to the computer screen and said "That's your book, Mommy.", you've made my heart swell with pride.

About the Author

I've always been an avid reader. Majoring in English Literature was a no brainer. Becoming a teacher and instilling my love for reading into my students was also a no brainer. I've spent the last ten years teaching and I've loved (mostly) every minute of it. When I was home on maternity leave for my third son, I discovered a new genre that sparked my creativity. My passion for writing sprang from my love of reading and once I knew I had a story to tell, I couldn't wait to get it out there. I only hope that my readers enjoy reading my story as much as I enjoyed writing it.

Future Projects:

Need some more Maddy and Reid? Looking for a follow up to Melanie and Bryan? Let Love Shine, a Love Series novella, will be out in January 2014. Then in the spring of 2014 book four in the Love Series will be released. Let Love Be will follow Lucy (Momma) on her journey to finding love when she thought it was the one thing she would have to do without.

Social Media Links:

Web and Newsletter Sign-up
www.melissacollinsauthor.com

Facebook
http://www.facebook.com/MelissaCollins.Author

Twitter
@mcollinsauthor

Pinterest
www.pinterest.com/mcollinsauthor

Turn the page for a preview of
HER
by Carey Heywood
Coming October 26, 2013

New York Times Bestselling Author

HER

He'll never forget...

Carey Heywood

a novel

You know her side of the story, now learn his.

"It was useless. I felt branded beneath my skin by a girl who left without even saying goodbye."

When Will Price was assigned a partner for a sixth grade class project he had no idea she would become his best friend. After years of friendship, she eventually became so much more. Then, one day she left with no explanation.

Will's life shattered right before his eyes and he was left alone to pick up the pieces. Floundering, Will must figure out a way to carry on, to find a way to exist without her.

Seven years later, a chance encounter leaves him desperate to get her back. He has one week to make her his again. Not everyone gets a second chance with the love of their life and Will is determined to never lose her again.